Smith's
MONTHLY

Every Month Original
Novels, Stories, and Articles

USA Today Bestselling Writer
Dean Wesley Smith

TABLE OF CONTENTS

Smith's Monthly Issue #36

Dean Wesley Smith

Introduction
MY FIRST NOVEL

Almost thirty years ago, in Eugene Oregon, I got a letter from a major book editor from Bantam Books. The editor had read one of my short stories in *Night Cry Magazine*, a sister magazine for *The Twilight Zone Magazine*. She liked my writing and my style and wanted to know if I had a novel.

I did not, but I wrote her back and said I did and what would she like to see.

While that letter was winging its way across the country, I started writing a novel.

I had written two other novels before, but both were lost in a house fire. So I knew I could write a novel. I just didn't know if I could do it well enough for a publisher to buy, even though I was selling short fiction regularly.

And I didn't know if I could write it fast enough to make her happy.

She got back to me in a week and asked for a couple chapters and an outline of the rest of the book.

In another week or so I managed to do a few chapters and an outline and send it all to her.

Then I kept writing.

She got back to me at what seemed like light speed, before I had finished the entire novel, and loved the first part and wanted to see the rest of the book.

So in the winter of 1987 I finished it and sent it to her.

She tried to buy the novel for her company, but turned out it wasn't right for her book line and she ended up in March 1988 sending it back to me with regrets.

But sitting in a bar that same month at a science fiction convention, I had talked to another editor from Warner Questar books and he liked the idea of the book. So when Bantam rejected the novel I sent it to him.

And he bought it in May of 1988 and it came out in the spring of 1989.

My first published novel, *Laying the Music to Rest*.

As with most traditional books from that day, after a few years it was out of

Thanks for the Support

Dean Wesley Smith

print and I got the rights reverted in the middle 1990s.

The book stayed out there in used bookstores as my first published novel and I signed a few fading copies of it at times over the decades. But I never looked at the book again.

When the indie revolution came along and Kris and I started up WMG Publishing, I thought about republishing that book, but decided to write a bunch of new novels instead.

But this last summer someone brought a copy for me to sign and I looked at it and thought it would be fun to give that first novel a new life.

So I started to serialize it here in this magazine as a wonderful woman working for WMG Publishing typed the entire novel into a computer file. (I wrote it on a typewriter originally.)

Then comes this special issue.

This is the 36th issue of *Smith's Monthly*.

Three straight years every month without missing a month.

I would have never thought that possible when I started this journey. But here I am. And I started to wonder what I could do to mark this special issue.

And then someone said something about it being almost thirty years since my first novel was published and I realized that putting my first novel here, untouched, not changed at all from that original version, would be the perfect thing to do for this special issue.

The readers of this magazine have been reading my new novels and stories—might be fun to show them my first major published work as well.

So thank you all for the support of this crazy magazine project and I hope you enjoy my very first published novel complete and unchanged from the Questar edition here in these pages.

Now onward into year four. No telling what the future will bring.

Enjoy.

—Dean Wesley Smith
Lincoln City, Oregon
September 18, 2016

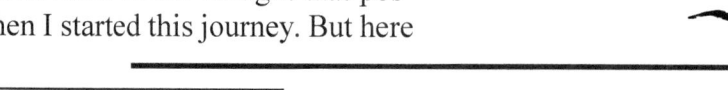

Coming Next Issue in *Smith's Monthly*

STARBURST

A Seeders Universe Novel

NUMBER THIRTY-SEVEN
OCTOBER, 2016

*Original Stories,
Novels, and Articles*

Smith's MONTHLY

DEAN WESLEY SMITH

STARBURST

A Seeders Universe Novel

USA Today Bestselling Writer

DEAN WESLEY SMITH

*Sometimes
a Second Chance
Seems Better Than a First*

MEETING THE SUNSET KID

A Ghost of a Chance Story

You never plan on dying.

Well, at least when young you never plan on it.

But Gail Kelly died. And then things got really, really strange.

Another wild and whacky story in the popular Ghost of a Chance series, where ghosts work as superheroes and anything seems possible.

MEETING THE SUNSET KID
A Ghost of a Chance Story

ONE

YOU NEVER PLAN on dying.

Well, at least when you are young you never plan on it.

Gail Kelly sure hadn't. She was twenty-eight, still slim and single, and still very happy in her job as a prosecuting attorney in a small Oregon coastal county. And she was really good at it as well.

Dying was a long ways from her thinking. In fact, marriage and kids were still a long ways from her thinking. She didn't even have a steady boyfriend.

So when that chip truck came across the center line on a curve on Highway 101 and hit her before she could even blink, she didn't have time to think about dying then either.

It just happened so fast.

One minute she was driving her wonderful BMW convertible, headed north to meet some friends for some drinks and dinner, the next she was sitting on the soft hillside next to the highway.

A very friendly woman about Gail's age was kneeling next to her, smiling. And a handsome man stood on the highway watching, with a short guy dressed in a purple jogging suit who looked completely out of place on the rough Oregon coast.

Both the man and the woman looked comfortable, dressed in jeans and expensive shirts and running shoes.

"Go slow," the woman next to her said.

"So what happened?" Gail asked, trying to look around but only seeing the three people and the edge of the highway. The forest around her and the ocean below seemed to be a blur.

"You were in an accident," the woman said.

Gail looked down at herself, her legs, her arms. She had on a silk blouse with a jogging bra under it, jeans, and her best running shoes. There didn't seem to be a mark or scratch anywhere. The road was a good ten feet below her. Why she would have climbed up here was beyond her.

And she felt fine.

Gail stood and the woman helped her up with a gentle touch on her arm. The two of them went down the soft hillside and through a slight ditch to where the handsome man and the guy in purple stood on the pavement.

"I'm Jewel," the woman said. "This is my partner, Tommy."

The good-looking man nodded and smiled slightly at Gail. He had a short military-cut brown hair and broad shoulders. Gail could see in his eyes that he was worried about her.

"This is K.J.," Jewel said, indicating the short man with the purple jogging suit. Now that Gail was closer, she could also see that the man's hair was purple and his shoes were purple and he wore purple fingernail polish. Wow, she hoped

he wasn't going into any bars along this coast. He didn't fit. In fact, she had a hunch this K.J. person didn't fit anywhere outside of San Francisco.

K.J. just nodded and smiled, showing purple caps on his teeth.

Gail looked around, trying to focus but actually not seeing anything but the hill and some trees and the blue of the ocean beyond.

"I must have bumped my head," Gail said. "I'm having trouble focusing."

"That will pass," Jewel said.

"How do you know?" Gail asked staring into the woman's green eyes. "Are you a doctor?"

"Actually, she is," the guy in purple said. "But that's not why it will pass."

"Then why?" Gail asked, slowly starting to get angry.

"Because you're dead, that's why," a voice said from behind her.

She turned to look into the dark brown eyes of the most handsome man she had ever seen. He looked like he had come right out of court and had just taken off his tie. He had perfectly styled brown hair and large brown eyes. His dark suit was made of silk, as clearly was his shirt, and he had on expensive shoes Gail was convinced were not sold anywhere in Oregon.

"I'm Dan Carson, but a lot of my friends call me The Sunset Kid."

Gail was convinced those brown eyes of his were seeing right through her. Because of that, it took her a moment to realize what he had said.

"Dead?"

"Oh, nice timing, Kid," the guy in purple said, clearly disgusted.

The guy nodded to Gail, ignoring the man in purple. "Afraid so. But trust me, you're going to love it."

He smiled at her as he took her elbow and turned her up the road. Suddenly everything came into clear focus around her.

The evening still had some light as the sun had just set over the ocean. The forest was on her left, the sea down a steep cliff on her right. She could see what was left of her wonderful convertible under the front of a large truck right in the middle of the two-lane highway.

Someone was hosing the entire thing down with a fire extinguisher and a number of others were standing to one side, most with their hands over their mouths.

She could see part of her body twisted in an unnatural way against the grill of the truck. And the truck driver had come about halfway through the window of his truck and was still just hanging there. He looked dead or almost dead.

The sight was so horrific, it took her a moment to realize that was her against the front of the truck.

Holy shit, Dan was right.

She was dead.

How could that even be possible?

She turned to face him and her knees started to give out.

Dan and Jewel caught her and eased her to the ground.

"So, Kid, what are you doing here?" K.J asked.

Jewel held Gail's arm and Tommy, her partner, had stepped back.

"Here to train Gail," Dan said.

Gail had her head down and was focusing on just breathing. She knew this feeling from having too many drinks and she knew just solid breaths of air would help.

And no way was she calling someone as handsome as that a kid, so she was going to call him by his real name.

"Jewel and Tommy train the new recruits," K.J. said.

"Not this time," Dan said.

"Train me to do what?" Gail asked, finally letting the anger come out as she stood. She didn't need any training.

Jewel patted Gail's shoulder and stepped back.

"To be dead and worthwhile," Dan said, smiling at her.

"How about I be *not* dead?" Gail said.

"Not really possible," Dan said, pointing in the direction of the wreck. "It was your time. See the truck driver? It's almost his time as well. Watch."

Dan turned her toward the wreck again as suddenly the truck driver sort of moved away from the cab of his truck while his body still remained sticking out of the window.

For a moment he seemed perfectly healthy even though his body in the window clearly wasn't.

Then the driver looked upward and sort of floated in the air and after a moment was gone.

"So how come I don't float out of here?" Gail asked. "And get away from you nut-jobs."

She was angry and scared, but mostly angry, and when angry, she pulled no punches.

"The powers-that-be think you would be a good help in saving people," Jewel said, her voice gentle.

"I don't save people," Gail said, her voice stern. "I put people in jail."

"Sometimes that's saving people," Dan said, smiling at her and clearly ignoring her anger. "You hungry?"

That question surprised her. "I thought you said I was dead."

"Oh, you are," Dan said. "And from here on out, the food tastes better."

"You are just confusing Gail," Jewel said, stepping up and putting herself between Dan and Gail.

"I did just fine when I died," Dan said.

"That's not what I heard," K.J. said.

Gail glanced over. The little guy in purple clearly had some issues with Dan.

Dan was about to say something when Jewel raised her hand. "Not here, not now. You can help in Gail's training, if she wants help, but not until I say so."

Dan looked at Jewel who clearly wasn't backing down.

Finally Dan nodded to Jewel and smiled at Gail. "See you soon I hope."

Gail was so confused, all she could do was nod.

Then Dan just vanished right in front of her eyes.

"I'm having the weirdest damn dream," Gail said, deciding to sit down once again on the pavement.

Jewel helped her down and then looked at K.J. "Find out what that was all about. We'll be at the Golden Nugget having dinner."

K.J. nodded and then the little guy in purple also just vanished.

"I haven't even had a drink yet," Gail said, shaking her head.

Then she looked up at her twisted body against the front of the truck and wondered if she would ever drink again.

TWO

DAN APPEARED ON his favorite stool at the Sushi bar in Fong's Restaurant just off Broadway in Portland. He was angry at himself. He had screwed up something awful with that introduction and he knew better than to go up against Jewel and Tommy and K.J.

Dan had been a Ghost of a Chance agent as long as K.J. Actually, slightly longer since Dan died in 1901 and K.J. didn't show up until a few years later.

And Jewel and Tommy were already forces in the agency, even though they were fairly new. They had worked with Poker Boy and others, which was far more than Dan had ever done. Up until just a few years ago, he hadn't even known the superhero part of all this existed.

Dan always liked to work alone and he had done just fine that way for over a hundred years. But now, the powers-that-be had told him he was getting a partner even though he had no desire for one.

He hadn't expected his new partner to be so beautiful. That had caught him by surprise, but was still no excuse for him being a jerk. He had figured she could just stand the blunt truth.

He knew she was smart. He had researched her life a little and knew she was still single, a prosecuting attorney with almost a perfect record, and she liked her drinks.

Dan liked his drinks as well, which is how he had gotten his name, the Sunset Kid. He loved to drink tequila sunsets, which was basically like a tequila sunrise with tequila and orange juice, only instead of the sweet red grenadine syrup that sunk to the bottom of the orange juice, a red soda water was put on the top, holding the red to the top of glass.

And it was a lot less sweet than a sunrise. He had started drinking them back when he worked the New York area after the Second World War. No bar out west served them regularly, so he made them in his Portland condo for himself. He never seemed to tire of them.

He grabbed a plate of California rolls as a waitress carried it past and started to work on them. He loved how, as a ghost, he could eat the ghost part of any meal and no one knew he was doing it.

And the ghost part of a meal tasted so much better than a regular meal ever had when he was alive.

He sat eating and thinking about Gail and how they were going to have to work together and how, now after seeing her, he actually wanted to try to work with her.

Damn, he wished he hadn't screwed up the introduction.

He needed to do something about his mistake and do it now.

He pushed what was left of the sushi roll aside and stood.

"Come on, Dan. You can do humility. Honestly you can."

With that he jumped to the Golden Nugget Buffet in Las Vegas. He was going to apologize and see if he could help in her training, see if he and Gail really could be a team.

He didn't do apologies that often. As a ghost agent, working alone, he had never really needed to. But he had a hunch with Gail, it would be worth taking his pride down a few notches.

THREE

ONE MINUTE GAIL had been on the main coastal highway in Oregon looking at an ugly wreck that she had supposedly been in, then she found herself standing near a wooden table in a well-lit buffet.

The food smelled wonderful and a low level of talking filled the air.

The buffet was all in brown wood tones and bright polished brass. It was a huge place and the table they were beside was in one corner and a distance away from any other people.

The place was comfortable, even though impossible. Gail knew for a fact she couldn't be here.

Yet it seemed she was.

It sure felt and smelled and sounded like she was.

Jewel and Tommy were both standing beside her.

"How did we get here and where is here?" Gail asked after looking around.

"The Golden Nugget Buffet in downtown Las Vegas," Jewel said, indicating that Gail should take a seat. Jewel pulled the chair out slightly for her. "We jumped you here from Oregon."

"I'll get us some water," Tommy said and turned away.

Gail sat down facing the buffet area and Jewel sat beside her at the four person square table.

"This is the strangest dream I have ever had," Gail said, shaking her head. None of this was making any sense to her. Not a bit of it. She hadn't even had dinner yet, so it couldn't be something she ate. And she really didn't know anyone or had even been to Las Vegas before, so a place her dream would take her shouldn't be here.

"We all think this is a dream at first," Jewel said. "I know I did."

"So did I," Tommy said, handing Gail a glass of water and then giving Jewel one as well.

Gail made herself take a long drink. The water tasted pure and fresh and wonderful. Best glass of plain water she had ever had.

Now she knew she was dreaming when water tasted good.

Jewel must have been reading her expression. "You think that was good, wait until you taste the food."

"So the Dan guy was right?" Gail asked.

"He was," Jewel said.

"Who is he?" Gail asked as Dan's handsome face and perfect body came clearly back to her mind.

"He's another ghost agent like we are," Jewel said. "Like you'll be if you decide to stay after you learn everything."

Gail just shook her head. "You know how silly that sounds?"

Jewel nodded and smiled. "Very silly. But very serious at the same time."

"Okay," Gail said, ignoring that her stomach was rumbling just twenty minutes after she had supposedly died, "until I wake up, I'll play along. What do ghost agents do?"

"We save people," Jewel said.

Beside her Tommy just nodded.

"Yet we are ghosts?" Gail asked.

Jewel and Tommy both nodded.

Gail shook her head. All this silliness was impossible to believe. She must have caught a horrid bug and was feverish and in a hospital somewhere. Fever dreams were the only thing that could make any of this make sense.

And if she was having a bad fever dream she would think of dying. That made sense.

"Let me see if I can show you a few things," Tommy said.

He stood, then walked right through the table in front of Gail as if it wasn't there.

Then he walked over to a couple starting to leave and let them walk through him.

Then he came back and sat down. He was frowning and Jewel noticed it as well.

Jewel reached over and put her hand on Tommy's arm.

"That older couple that went through me just had their last meal," Tommy said. "They have used the last of their money. They have a gun in their car."

Gail felt stunned. "How do you know that?"

"When you touch a living person, you can read their thoughts," Jewel said, not looking away from Tommy.

"I'm going to follow them," Tommy said, standing. "See if I can figure out something to do."

"What can he do?" Gail asked.

"So many things," Jewel said. "And so few at the same time."

At that moment Dan arrived, standing to one side of the table. His silk suit was perfect, his shirt open under the suit jacket, and he had a slight look of worry in his eyes.

Gail felt a jolt go through her as she looked up at him. She had never had that reaction to a man before, ever. More than likely part of her fever dream.

And he looked slightly startled as well, then nodded to her and turned to Jewel. "If I apologize for my boorish behavior on the coast, and promise to behave myself and help where I can, may I join you?"

Jewel nodded and smiled, indicating he should take a seat next to Gail.

Then Jewel stood. "Tommy's going to need my help with that couple. I'll be back when I can."

And she vanished.

"What couple?" Dan asked.

"An elderly couple that walked through Tommy when he was trying to convince me I'm not dreaming," Gail said. "Tommy said the couple had just had their last meal and were out of money and he wasn't sure what they were going to do next."

"Oh, no," Dan said softly.

"Is that what you ghosts do? Save old folks from themselves?"

Dan nodded, clearly serious. "Sometimes that, sometimes more. Jewel and Tommy and K.J., along with a superhero and his team and a few of the gods helped save the world just three months ago."

"Saved the world?" Gail asked, ignoring the gods and the superhero part.

Dan nodded and looked at her for the first time since she sat down. "Jewel will tell you all about it at some point. But I want to apologize for my first meeting. I hope you will give me a second chance to get off on the right foot."

Gail smiled and offered her hand.

"I'm Gail," she said.

He took her hand and instantly she felt a surge of pleasurable electrical force going through her.

"I'm Dan," he said, clearly noticing the connection.

They sat there for a moment like that, holding the handshake, then he pulled his hand away and looked down.

She felt instant disappointment.

They sat in silence for a long moment, then she finally said, "How do I wake up from this?"

He looked at her, was about to say something, then clearly changed his mind.

"We need food," he said, offering his hand to her as he stood. "Let me show you how ghosts get our food."

"Ghosts are hungry?" she asked, glad he was again holding her hand. If this was a dream, she might as well enjoy it.

"We get hungry, we sleep, and we have to use the bathroom," he said. "Nothing changes on any of that except that no one can see us except other ghost agents."

"And we can read people's thoughts?" she asked.

"That," he said, leading her toward the buffet, "and so much more. You'll see. Jewel will train you."

"You're not going to help?" she asked.

Can't Get Enough of Poker Boy?
These stories and more are available at your favorite booksellers.

"I'll help as much as you would like me to," he said.

"I would like you to," she said.

He nodded and smiled.

"I'll do my best."

And with that, once again they returned to silence. But he was still holding her hand as they made their way toward the buffet.

And that felt right.

FOUR

DAN WAS EXCITED that maybe he had made up for some of his behavior out on the highway. And he was stunned at the connection he and Gail had. Her touch had sent shivers through him like no other ever had in a hundred years.

That was exciting all by itself. He couldn't believe how attracted he was to her.

As they got near the buffet, he said to her, "Be careful not to touch anyone else."

"Read their thoughts?" she asked.

"Just give it some time before you do that. Let Jewel be here to help you through some of those issues."

"Have you ever trained anyone?" she asked. Then she laughed. "I'm acting as if this dream is all real."

"Pretending for the moment it is real," Dan said, "the answer is no."

They stopped in front of the plates. There was one plate sitting to one side of a stack of others.

"Pick that one up," he said, pointing to the single plate.

She did, holding a plate in her hand.

He pointed at the plate also still sitting there.

"How?" Gail said, looking at the plate in her hand and then the one on the counter.

"You are holding the ghost version of that plate," Dan said. "Everything has a ghost version as I call it."

She stared at the plate in her hand. "It feels real."

"It is, except no one can see it. And if you put it down, after a half day or so it will vanish."

She just nodded and he moved them along to where there were some pizza slices that looked pretty good. He took one slice and she just stared at where the slice still remained on the serving tray.

And yet there was the same exact slice on his plate.

It was at that moment, when neither of them had been paying any attention, that a solid, middle-aged woman who smelled faintly of cigarettes came right up behind them and at the pizza.

The woman plowed right through Dan and Gail.

Dan quickly pulled Gail aside, but not before they both knew the woman's full history, about her affair with an office worker, her divorce, about her inability to stop eating and smoking and gaining weight since the divorce, and how her two children really hated her for causing the divorce.

One romp in the hay had cost the woman everything she treasured and she had no idea how to even start to get it back.

Dan put the plates they had been carrying down and took Gail's hand and led her back to the table.

Gail seemed to be in shock.

When they sat down, Dan pushed the glass of water toward her. "Take a drink, it will help."

She did, then nodded.

Then she looked into Dan's eyes. "I'm not sure I want to see inside people's heads, into their lives, into their secrets."

Dan nodded. "I understand that. Thankfully, what we saw will fade quickly from our minds."

"This isn't really a dream, is it?" Gail asked after a moment of staring at the woman they knew so much about.

"No, it's not," he said.

"I'm really dead?" Gail asked. "That accident on the highway really happened?"

"It did," Dan said, his tone gentle and understanding. "But you now get a very rare chance of living an even better life, a very long life if you want, and to help others at the same time."

She nodded.

And Dan couldn't think of one other thing to say. He really sucked at this training stuff.

FIVE

ONCE GAIL ACCEPTED that she was dead, she wanted to know more about this crazy new world she found herself in. Dan struggled a few times, in a very cute way, to try to explain a few things, and then looked massively relieved when Jewel and Tommy returned.

Gail was impressed that they had gotten the elderly couple to toss away the gun and call their children and tell them what was happening.

It seemed their children were very well off and had been worried about the couple. But the couple was too proud to say anything about not having any money left at all.

Gail was stunned at how Jewel and Tommy had literally saved lives. But Tommy had been a cop, Jewel a doctor. How did Gail being a prosecuting attorney help?

When she asked that question, Dan had said that only time would tell. He had been an attorney as well and he had been doing fine.

So Gail had agreed to training with Jewel and Tommy, with Dan helping every day, but taking only a supporting role.

Over the next month, Gail stayed in Jewel and Tommy's home in Las Vegas in their guest room and they trained in the casinos, helping people where they could.

Finally, after a month, as the four of them were eating breakfast back in the Golden Nugget Buffet, Jewel turned to Gail and said simply, "You ready to find your own place?"

Gail had known that was coming, but it worried her because she didn't know what she should do. She wanted to go back to Oregon, but she was fairly certain she didn't want to return to the coast. Portland was the only town she liked, but Dan lived there and she didn't want to be too forward. They were both very attracted to each other, but so far during her training had kept arms distance.

And she was going to have to work with him, so having an affair with a partner might not be such a hot idea, even though she wanted to. She had a hunch they would decide that later.

Gail pushed her waffle away and sat back.

Jewel just smiled and Tommy kept eating.

"I own this wonderful penthouse condo in Portland that is just sitting empty," Dan said. "You can have it if you would like."

"You own it?" Gail asked. "How do you do that?"

"Actually a corporation I formed owns it," Dan said. "I'll explain how all that is possible someday down the road on a really long and boring day."

"And you are willing to give the condo to me?" Gail asked.

"No problem," Dan said, shrugging. "Money is never much of an issue for us ghosts, you know."

Dan turned to Jewel. "Could you get some of your superhero friends to move some real furniture into the place. Furniture Gail picks out if she wants to take it?"

"Glad to," Jewel said, smiling.

Gail smiled at Jewel. "Thanks."

Then Gail looked back at Dan, her future partner, who was smiling. "That's very kind of you and I accept. Thank you."

Dan nodded.

Gail turned back to Jewel. "Does this mean I'm done with my training?"

"Dan can take it from here," Jewel said. "But we'll always be here if you need us for anything. We all work together you know."

Gail nodded.

"One condition to all this," Dan said, smiling at her. "Once you are all moved in, you throw a party. I'll make the tequila sunsets."

"You're damn lucky I love that drink," Gail said, laughing.

"Yeah," Dan said, "I think I am."

Gail pulled her waffle back toward her and took another bite, savoring the rich maple syrup flavor.

Around her the wonderful sounds of the morning in the Golden Nugget Buffet.

People talking, people laughing, people being alive.

She hadn't planned to die on that highway on her way to dinner a month ago.

No one expects to die.

But now, sitting here with other ghost agents in a restaurant full of the living that she knew she might be able to help if they needed it, dying didn't seem so bad.

And sitting beside Dan just made it all the better.

She had to die to meet The Sunset Kid. She had a hunch it was going to be worth it.

Now Available
from all your favorite booksellers
in trade paper and electronic editions.

USA TODAY BESTSELLING AUTHOR

DEAN WESLEY SMITH

AN EASY SHOT

A GOLF THRILLER

USA *Today* Bestselling Writer

DEAN WESLEY SMITH

REVENGE SERVED
WITH A SCREWDRIVER

THE REMODELING
OF A LIFE

A Mary Jo
Assassin Story

Mary Jo's last client tried to have her killed and then shorted her on her money.

Mary Jo needs to remodel the client's life. And get her money.

In the process, she also remodels her own life while enjoying the occasional vodka and orange juice.

A cold, calculating modern assassin story of revenge served with a screwdriver.

THE REMODELING OF A LIFE
A Mary Jo Assassin Story

ONE

MARY JO NEVER understood why someone with money seemed to automatically think they could get away with anything, including murder. Granted, enough money bought a murder.

And even more money bought her skills at the murder.

But it never bought a double cross.

Over the thousands of years that she had been an assassin in the Order of Assassins, she had had clients who had not paid her after she finished a job. That client always paid dearly with his or her life and the life of those that were treasured by the person doing the double crossing.

To Mary Jo, a deal was a deal. Yet often people with money thought otherwise.

The man she watched now, Newport Summerfield, a tall, thin man with two body-guards, owed her two million dollars for killing a chief of police. Mary Jo had lived with that target for almost a year as his wife, enjoying the time with him, before finally killing the chief.

The fact that she had liked her last target and now good old Newport thought he was too good to pay her just made her even angrier.

Mary Jo watched as Newport helped a young woman out of his limo and past the doorman of his condo, laughing as he went. The woman was barely old enough to be legal in Manhattan and had long blonde hair, just as all of Newport's flings had. If nothing else, the man was predictable in his affairs with younger women. It would not have surprised Mary Jo in the slightest if Newport's wife knew about this secret condo as well and just looked the other way because of the kids and the money and their beautiful apartment overlooking Central Park.

Mary Jo had seen that a great deal over the years as well.

She closed the window on her apartment across from Newport's private condo. She still had the house back in upper New York State where she played the part of the chief's widow, but she had kind of liked this little apartment.

But she had given notice on it and when she walked out the door shortly she would be done with it.

In four or five months or so, she hoped to buy Newport's condo across the street in a fire sale. She would, of course, buy it under a brand new name than she had used in the apartment renting. She could afford to live anywhere, but she thought it might be fun to take over Newport's love nest after he was long gone.

Besides, at two bedrooms, a wonderful penthouse view, and a kitchen that would make a magazine for top kitchens, living there for a time sure wouldn't be an issue or a hardship on her.

Besides, she liked the city. Almost more than anywhere else in the world. And she had lived almost everywhere.

Since she had killed her husband, the chief, she had stayed low, playing the grieving widow of the chief, and letting Newport think he got away with not paying her.

Of course, he had no idea that it had been the chief's widow who had done the job. No member of the Order of Assassins ever showed themselves to any client.

Ever.

And since she was barely five-five, with short brown hair that made her look like a pixie, no one would ever mistake her for a professional assassin either. Her looks had been one of her most powerful tools over the centuries.

While Newport was getting lax in not worrying about anyone coming for him, she had been exploring every detail of his life, his wife's life, his two kid's lives, his parents' lives, and his businesses and bank accounts.

Her two million fee might have stung for a few days, but he could have easily paid it. He was just a greedy bastard, the very same reason her former husband had been building a case against him.

Now Newport was going to pay a much, much higher price than two million.

And Mary Jo was going to be far, far richer.

Over the last year, to start with, she had been slowly buying up stock in his two publicly held corporations under various hidden names. He was the president of both of them and major stockholder.

In the last week she had started selling puts on the stocks she owned, betting that the stocks would fall through the floor. Because of what she was about to do, she had no doubt those two company stocks would quickly vanish from the stock market. And she would get rich as it happened.

And with her skills at using computers, she had managed to get all Newport's passwords and bank account numbers, including his two off-the-books accounts.

All told, transferring all his money from those accounts to hidden offshore accounts and then moving it around like scrambling up cards would get her another six hundred million.

And she had all the corporations' bank account numbers and passwords as well. That would get her another five or six hundred million.

Granted, before this, she had more than enough money for anything she ever needed. But now she would have even more. All because Newport was greedy and didn't pay her after he had hired her.

This afternoon, all her planning would be set into motion.

She went to the fridge of the apartment and pulled out a pitcher of orange juice and some chilled vodka and filled a tall glass with ice.

Then she sat on her couch, watching her favorite soap opera and sipping on her screwdriver.

This would be the last drink until the job was done later tonight, so she was going to savor it.

TWO

NEWPORT'S PARENTS WERE the country club types. They had a huge mansion in the Hamptons and loved being retired there. Newport paid for it all.

And the two of them were creatures of extreme habit, just as their son. Last night, late, Mary Jo had set a very, very powerful bomb in the Mercedes they always drove to the country club for their afternoon tennis lessons.

Mary Jo wondered if Newport knew that his parents then paid the tennis pro a very large bonus to have sex with Newport's mother while his father watched, sucking his thumb.

More than likely not.

Mary Jo finished her screwdriver at the exact same moment her soap opera ended. She sighed, washed out her glass and set it in the dishwasher for someone to run later. She was also leaving the pitcher of orange juice and bottle of vodka for the next tenant.

She had rented this place under a fake name that was now dead to any tracing. And nothing here would ever trace back to anything that was going to happen to Newport and his family.

She locked up and put her keys in the landlord's mailbox with a thank-you note, then with just a backpack, she left the building. She had moved all her clothes out of the apartment yesterday and given them away to a charity.

Two blocks up the street, she hailed a cab and was dropped off along the edge of Central Park within a few blocks of Newport's large apartment looking out over the park.

There, sitting on a park bench so she could see the large apartment balcony, she had her laptop open like any writer out working on a story on a nice afternoon.

She glanced at the time and then she started the ball rolling.

It was exactly three-fifteen in the afternoon.

First, she drained every dollar of both corporation accounts, making the transaction look as if Newport had taken the money in all respects.

She made the transaction look like it started from his personal laptop computer and then she started the international programs that would make the money completely vanish after dozens of transfers through holding and shell accounts around the world, ending up eventually in one of her many accounts.

Then she did the same with every one of Newport's bank accounts, making it look like he had transferred all his money offshore. She cashed out everything he had.

She had also purchased in his name and some phony woman's name, ten different plane tickets for this evening from three different New York area airports to countries that did not extradite.

To anyone, it looked like he had cleaned out everything and was fleeing the country.

Then, at twenty-nine minutes after the hour, she clicked on a camera link she had hacked into on a camera on a pole in the Hamptons.

The Hamptons had great security cameras. But far too easy to hack into to

be worthwhile. It was how she had gotten in and out undetected to plant the bomb.

As she watched, Newport's parents, all dressed up in their tennis outfits, came out of the back door of the house as the garage door opened.

They climbed into their Mercedes.

A few seconds later the camera flashed and when it cleared, it showed most of the house completely destroyed and in flames. Debris was flying through the air.

"Boom," Mary Jo said.

Then she destroyed that link and clicked into a second link.

Newport's wife was also a creature of extreme habit. The kids did not get home until four in the afternoon, so at three-thirty, she always took a shower.

Mary Jo watched the feed of the bathroom door of Newport's wife's bedroom in their penthouse apartment. After a shower that lasted exactly five minutes, Newport's wife, a brunette with dyed blonde hair came out of the bathroom with a towel on her head and headed for her closet.

At that moment, the link flashed and went dead.

Mary Jo looked up to see the explosion shattering the entire top of the building, making people on the sidewalk below flee in panic from all the falling debris.

"Boom," Mary Jo said a fraction of a second before the sound of the real explosion reached her.

Newport had now lost his wife, his parents, and every penny he had. And he would be quickly arrested, since she had tipped off a number of police, the FBI, and the Security and Exchange commission about Newport and his plans to skip town.

His children would be without money and would end up living with his wife's parents, two nice people outside of Chicago.

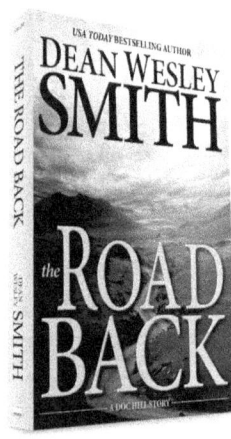

He should have paid Mary Jo her two million.

She closed her laptop, put it in her backpack, and headed for the closest subway stop.

Four hours of riding the train later, she was back in her home in upper New York State.

She called Jean, the widow of her neighbor, to tell her she was back. Since both were widowed on the same day, the two of them had become friends, first in the grief, then in drinking screwdrivers.

Mary Jo just might hang around in this home, in this small town even longer. It wasn't often she had a drinking friend.

"I hear there was an explosion in the city?" Jean said. "You weren't near it were you?"

"Really?" Mary Jo asked. "I hadn't heard. I've been on the train for the last four hours. Was it bad?"

"The press is saying some rich businessman blew up his wife so he could escape with his bimbo."

"Did they catch him?" Mary Jo asked.

"They got him coming out of a love nest."

"Perfect," Mary Jo said.

"Oh, you poor dear," Jean said. "You sound exhausted. You want to come over? We can soak in the hot tub and I'll make us both screwdrivers."

"I thought you would never ask," Mary Jo said, laughing.

"I'll make some fresh orange juice," Jean said, clearly happy.

"I'll change clothes and be right over."

Then, Mary Jo put her laptop in a large black plastic bag and took it out behind her house where she kept the metal garbage cans. She poured bleach and then a special chemical in with the bleach that would melt the plastic and then quickly harden it.

The laptop and the black garbage bag would be fused together in a nasty pile of plastic in the morning.

She dropped it all into the garbage can and closed the lid.

Then she went back inside to change and put on her bathrobe and slippers to walk the three houses down the street.

After an hour in the hot tub and three screwdrivers each, Jean and Mary Jo made love for the first time that night.

Mary Jo enjoyed that a lot. A perfect way to celebrate a job well done.

THREE

FOUR MONTHS LATER, Mary Jo, while in Manhattan again to put a bid in on Newport's love nest, used a burner phone that she had never touched with anything but gloves and put in a call to Newport where he was being held on suicide watch.

She had sent money through channels to make sure one of the guards gave Newport a burner phone as well at exactly the right time.

"Yes," Newport said.

"You should have paid the two million," she said.

Then she clicked off the phone and dropped it into a bag of bagels she had just bought. Then ten steps later she dropped the entire bag into a garbage can. She had rigged the phone to melt into a pool in two minutes after she used it.

Three months later, she and Jean were looking over the empty condo Mary Jo had just bought, planning furniture and acting like excited school girls on a mission, especially when they saw the wonderful roof-top hot tub.

Jean was going to live there with her.

Mary Jo loved the city.

It seemed Jean did as well and had only been living upstate because of her husband. Both of their homes were now on the market and they were headed for the city, two single women enjoying a wonderful friendship, among other things.

And Mary Jo was starting to realize that she loved the city and screwdrivers even more when she had someone to enjoy them with.

At least for a few years.

Now Available
from all your favorite booksellers in trade paper and electronic editions.

USA TODAY BESTSELLING AUTHOR

DEAN WESLEY SMITH

STAR FALL

A SEEDERS UNIVERSE NOVEL

USA *Today* Bestselling Writer

DEAN WESLEY SMITH

HE NEVER
WASTED HIS TIME

SOMETHING
WASTED ON

Professor Johnson Hubbs, professor of psychology, knew exactly when he came up with the idea of his new study of human nature and patterns.

In his new study, he wants to know how many times people say, "I wasted my time on (blank)."

He overhears a woman say that to another woman about her husband and then expand in great detail while Hubbs attempts to eat a wonderful chopped beef smothered in marinara sauce. Ruins his lunch, but gets him a new study.

A story of a simple professor asking a simple question.

SOMETHING WASTED ON

PROFESSOR JOHNSON HUBBS started counting the number of times someone said, "I wasted my time on (blank)."

The blank, it seemed, didn't seem to matter.

Johnson, who taught psychology undergrad courses at the local university, always dressed in a silk suit with perfectly coordinated ties for every day of the week. It was Tuesday, so his tie was light blue and his shirt was light eggshell color under the gray silk of the suit and vest.

He stayed fit by walking to every meal and around campus. He felt proud that he had not moved his car from its garage under his apartment building in five months.

He was barely in his thirties and had never been married or even much shared a fleeting relationship. Relationships seemed too much trouble to his orderly mind, actually.

He knew it was a Tuesday when he came up with the idea of counting the number of times "I wasted my time on…" phrase was used. It seemed to be a perfect assignment for his second level Human Studies class.

Johnson wasn't sure exactly when on Tuesday he had decided that would be a good assignment. It might have been over a lunch down at Bettie's Steak and Pasta. That lunch had a memorable moment in it.

The afternoon was perfect for the late spring in the Midwest. He had been enjoying his wonderful chopped beef smothered in marinara sauce with a side of mushrooms twisted among fine thin spaghetti. Nothing better in his mind for a Tuesday afternoon reprieve from the grind of young students and their questions, especially as finals drew nigh.

He had a napkin tucked perfectly into his collar to protect his tie and suit from any over-exuberant splashes he might make in the eating.

One of two middle-aged women at the next table wore too much makeup by factors of hundreds, most of it purple and red. He had no idea where she found such colors that did not occur naturally anywhere in nature and most certainly not on a woman's face.

She smelled like a department store perfume counter after kids got a hold of the spray bottles when the clerk wasn't looking, and she had on a green pants suit that clashed with both her perfume and her makeup.

A horrid mess of a human, in his fine opinion.

Mrs. Green Pants Suit (Mrs. because of a very large and ugly wedding ring) was talking to a woman who looked fairly normal. Miss Normal wore a nice blouse, jeans, and a hair clip of ivory holding her brown hair in place. The poor normal woman mostly had a glassy-eyed expression and wasn't getting a word in at all. Her head, however, acted like a toy head on a spring, it nodded so much.

Johnson was trying to ignore both the perfume and the one-sided conversation when Mrs. Green Pants Suit finally said, "I wasted my time on Craig."

So Craig must have been the poor sot who had put a ring on her thickening fingers at some point in a remote past.

She started to go into a list of the things this Craig fellow was guilty of, including having toenails far too long and a penis that didn't seem to want to function.

Miss Normal bobbed her head and seemed to not want to look at anyone around her.

That did it. Johnson had had enough.

His lunch was ruined.

He put his napkin over the remains of his wonderful chopped beef like a burial shroud and then stood, adjusting himself to make sure he was in perfect attire.

"Ma'am," he said, turning to Mrs. Green Pants Suit, "if I may say, from the sounds of your one-sided incessant rant about poor Craig, the man seems to have been the one who wasted his time and youth with you. From your smell and looks, you were extraordinarily lucky to get him for even a minute of his time, let alone enough of his clearly precious and wasted time to find out that his penis was not interested in your self-centered way of being."

With that, Johnson turned and walked to the cash register, paid his bill without complaint, and moved onto the sidewalk to make his way the three blocks back to campus. Luckily, the woman hadn't started into her ranting until he had finished enough of his wonderful lunch to last him until dinner.

Since it was Tuesday, he would be eating at Steven's Buffet for Tuesday dinner, as always. The ham if he arrived early was savory.

On the stroll up the crowded sidewalk, he managed to overhear the same phrase twice more in partial statements.

"I wasted my time on that class," one young girl in wide-rimmed glasses and a baggy sweatshirt said to a friend as he passed them.

A man in a business suit, his briefcase at his feet was talking on the phone while standing against the entry to a three-story office building. As Johnson passed, he heard the man say, "Not really a good idea. I wasted my time on him the…"

And Johnson was past the man and didn't get the joy and fulfillment of learning the man's opinion of who was a waste of time.

Johnson was pretty sure, in hindsight, that was when he decided to assign his class to listen for the phrase for one week, categorize the results in groups as to who the time was wasted on, such as a class, a girlfriend or boyfriend, and so on.

The idea had merit. He was not sure of the value, but it would keep the class moving toward the end of the semester at pace and help him fine-tune his grading of the participation.

Back in his office, with his books on walnut shelves around him and his door closed as to not be disturbed by students, he wrote down and worked out the assignment, smiling at his original form of thinking. Granted, this deviated from his intended lesson plan, but only for a week.

Two weeks later, he sat in his office on a Tuesday afternoon, once again just having finished a wonderful chopped beef at Bettie's Steak and Pasta. He felt sated, relaxed, and interested in what the twenty students he had in his second level Human Studies Class had found in their week of listening in on the human condition of others.

He had asked them to turn their findings in to him in an Excel spreadsheet file. And then write a three-hundred-word essay on their opinion of their findings.

He first read their short essays, some of which were surprisingly good on the topic. A number of students put, as he saw it, the problem fairly succinctly.

One said it best.

"In a world with shortened attention spans and far too much to do on any given day, wasting time on something or someone has become the modern mortal sin."

A fascinating observation by his best student.

Johnson sat back and thought about the idea of wasting time as a modern mortal sin. He would have to give that much, much more thought.

Then he opened each student's Excel file and put the files all together in one master file.

One student, the lazy sod of the bunch, only managed to find ten instances of the phrase being heard. Why he thought he would pass this class was a secret of genetics, Johnson was sure.

Most of the others found from fifty to over one hundred uses in the time period allotted.

So with twenty students at an average of sixty-two finds per student, Johnson had 1240 data points. Not a great amount under any circumstances, but a decent test run to what might turn out to be a much larger study at a future time. If he determined this entire subject of wasted time had value.

The results were as Johnson had expected.

Sixty-five percent of the uses of the phrase were aimed at another person. Twenty-three percent were aimed at a major activity, such as a class or a concert.

And eight percent seemed to be aimed at a meal or restaurant, something Johnson understood completely. He treasured his meal times and thus returned to the same restaurants on the same schedule every week. He did not often waste his time on finding a new restaurant.

Two percent of the uses of the phrase seemed to say that a minor online activity, such as a web site or a game, had been a waste of time.

The other two percent seemed to be reporting errors more than anything else, with most of the responses actually stating they had wasted their entire youth or life or vitality or something equally as vague.

He sat for the next hour at his desk, studying the data, and coming to no realizations or, for that matter, finding any hint of any surprise.

The modern world seemed to worship time. He had known that. He was a child of this age, after all.

And any person or event that stepped beyond the perceived value of time to an observer was a person or event the observer wasted time on.

Johnson nodded to himself. Fascinating.

So the time spent, like a currency, on an activity or person, was becoming something to be measured and given an opinion of value.

And clearly, all humans were now being valued by the currency of another human's time-value system. From an interaction between a waitress and a customer to a marriage relationship.

Humans when dealing in any fashion with other humans needed to walk a fine line of perceived value of time in any connectivity.

The base problem with the concept is that every person valued time at a different rate based only on the person's own internal activity value system.

The entire concept was worth more study, Johnson felt.

It fit in the value system he understood.

He noted that the time on his desk clock was fifteen minutes until five. He had spent two-and-one-half hours of his time on this project.

Its value to him at the moment?

Little, beyond a standard assignment to help him weed down the students to a final grade at the end of the semester.

Had he wasted his time on this assignment?

Had he, as one student had said, committed a modern mortal sin?

Possibly. But as with many sins, time would tell if the sinner became a savior or a time-wasting buffoon.

But at the moment, he needed to start his evening walk to Steven's Buffet where if he arrived as the doors opened, the ham would be fresh and juicy, the corn crisp with butter dripping with every spoonful, and the radishes on his salad crisp and sharp to the taste, just as he liked them.

A meal like that had value to him and his time was well spent with such delicacies.

Now Available
from all your favorite booksellers
in trade paper and electronic editions.

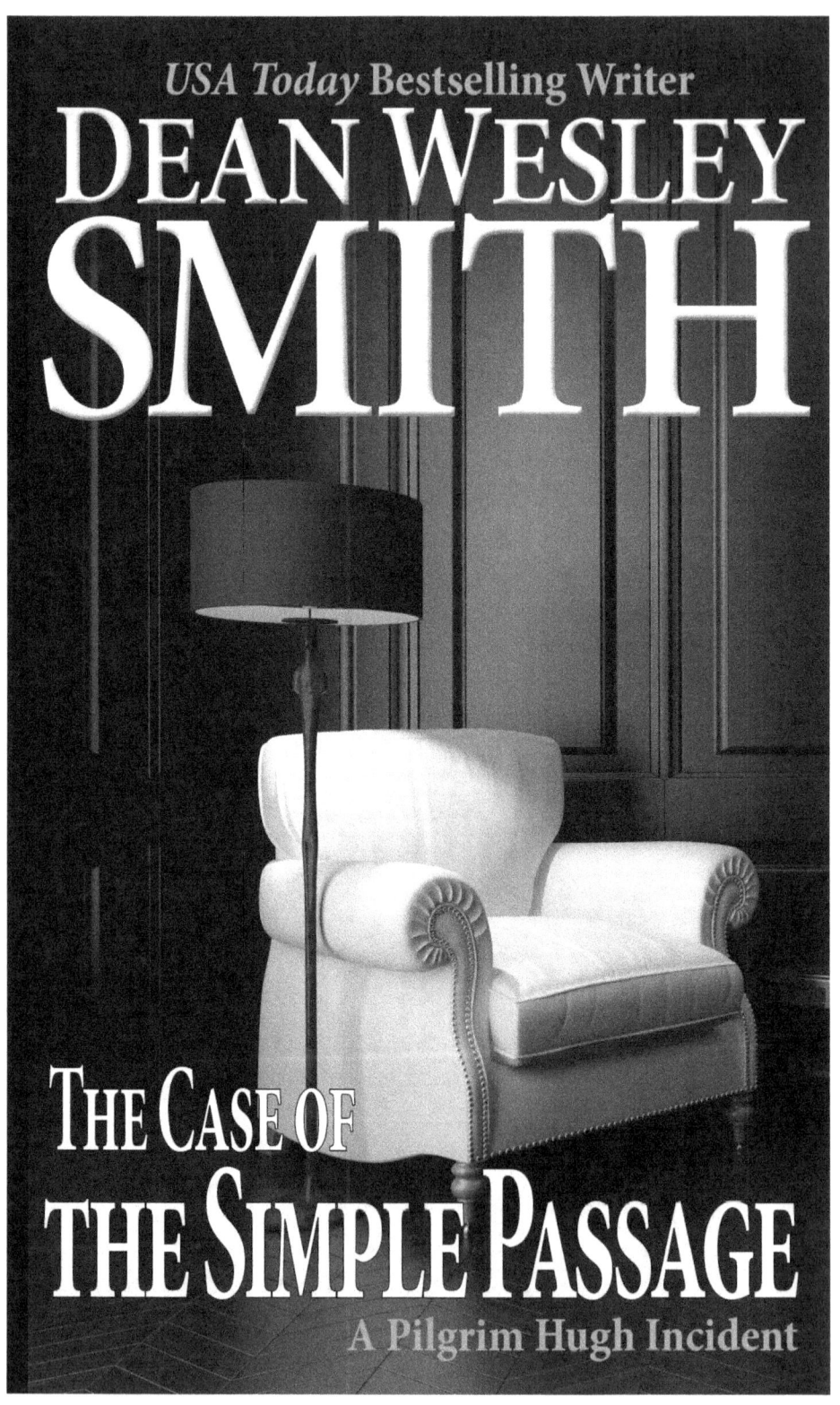

USA *Today* Bestselling Writer

DEAN WESLEY SMITH

THE CASE OF THE SIMPLE PASSAGE

A Pilgrim Hugh Incident

A grandson goes missing in an old house. But he never left.

Impossible. But it happened.

The perfect kind of crazy case for private detective Pilgrim Hugh and his beautiful assistant, Donna.

Another fan-favorite Pilgrim Hugh Incident.

THE CASE OF THE SIMPLE PASSAGE
A Pilgrim Hugh Incident

ONE

DONNA MARKS PULLED Pilgrim Hugh's black stretch-limo up in front of the large Victorian-style mansion and stopped behind the police cruiser sitting at the curb.

"I'll go talk with the chief," she said.

"I'll wait here," Pilgrim said, sipping on a bottle of water. He was clear in the back of the limo and could see out the side clearly even though no one could see in through the bullet-proof glass of the limo windows.

Huge oak trees surrounded the white and gray three-story mansion, casting shadows on it in the warm fall afternoon. Pilgrim had always thought of these old mansions as fun and had considered buying one once until he realized how small the rooms were, how bad the plumbing and electrical was, and how impossible it all was to remodel.

Pilgrim studied the old building for a moment while he waited for Donna. The tall roof looked to be in good shape, but the siding and trim and shutters around the old windows were clearly in need of sanding and paint. He could see evidence around to the side of the house beyond a hedge that workers had been working on the place, but in this neighborhood, they would have come in from the alley and only work on the front quickly.

Pilgrim admired older buildings like this one, but he liked his stuff new and on the cutting edge of technology. His penthouse on the top floor of his law building was state of the art and he spent a lot of money regularly keeping it that way.

And this limo was state of the art as well, with some of the best and fastest computer systems and defense systems money could buy. And with his money, he could buy anything. Thankfully, so far, only the computers had come in handy. They hadn't needed the defense stuff at all, but it never hurt to be safe in his line of work.

He sat parked in front of this Victorian-style mansion because three days before the twenty-four-year-old grandson of the mansion's owner had gone missing and had never left the house in the process.

Or at least that was what the owner claimed.

She was sure he had never left.

Completely positive.

At least that was what Chief Simmons had told Pilgrim over the phone an hour ago. The chief figured after his detectives got nowhere, Pilgrim was the logical choice to figure out exactly what had happened.

And honestly Pilgrim liked this kind of case. The stranger the better, just as the strange way he had ended up being a private detective in the first place.

For a time a decade before, his life seemed to be on a normal track. But then three years of law school and a failed first marriage made him realize he wasn't a normal lawyer.

Or a decent normal husband either. He pretty much sucked at both.

Then his grandmother had died and left him more money than he could imagine. He spent a year of traveling and drinking, finally getting tired of waking up in the morning and not even knowing which country he was in. Fun the first few times, terrifying after that.

So he went back to school, not for yet another standard degree, but to become a private detective. That started off just as poorly as his legal career. Being a private eye wasn't what the fiction books described. He wasn't some dashing Paul Drake, but instead he sat mostly at a computer or did long boring hours of nothingness trying to watch someone without falling asleep or reverting back to drinking.

He finally figured out that he bored easily and needed some excitement and challenges in his life on a regular basis. So with some of his grandmother's money, he set up Hugh and Associates, a combination law firm and private investigative firm.

In essence, he went back to the Perry Mason and Paul Drake image, only in Pilgrim's case, he owned everything, including the massive office building both businesses were in. And he lived alone in the penthouse over both businesses.

Then he had hired a couple great associate lawyers who took all the boring cases and made the firm lots of money and they hired even more associates that he had no desire to meet who also made him lots and lots of money.

And over time, with some help of some smart real estate buys, his grandmother's fortune had gotten bigger.

He had then offered his investigative state-of-the-art services for free to all the surrounding police forces. After a few years, he had solved a bunch of cases and was now called regularly. But only on interesting problems.

He made that clear. His firm would help for a fee on the regular stuff, but he would work for free on the troublesome cases.

Troublesome, like a guy supposedly vanishing from inside an old house without a trace.

Donna had climbed out of the limo and was talking for a moment with Chief Simmons.

For the first two years of being a private eye, his best friend from school, Carrie, had been his assistant, but she had fallen in love with the law side of the firm, gone back to law school, and now worked on the floor below his office doing law stuff that seemed boring to him, but that she seemed to thrive on.

Carrie had trained Donna before she left to be his special assistant. At times he had to admit, Donna was better at her job than Carrie had been.

Donna opened the side door to the limo and Chief Simmons crawled in and moved over to a side seat.

"This moving office of yours gets better every time I see it," Chief Simmons said as he settled into the leather seat and then watched Donna climb in.

Today, Donna had on a tan blouse that seemed slightly too small and she had made that worse by tying the tails of the blouse around her stomach, showing perfect and very trim stomach skin.

She had on a pair of Levi short-shorts and tall brown cowboy boots. From day to day it was impossible to tell what Donna would be wearing, and she never seemed to repeat, which told Pilgrim he clearly paid her too much.

But considering everything that Donna did, he didn't pay her enough.

She punched a button on an armrest as she pulled the door closed, cutting off what little sound was coming in from the quiet neighborhood of mansions. Two large computer screens came up out of the woodwork in front of her and a keyboard appeared from a seat and swung in over her so she could type.

Pilgrim had the exact same set-up where he sat, but didn't need it out at the moment.

After Donna started typing, the chief managed to turn his attention to Pilgrim. "Thanks for coming on this."

Pilgrim nodded. The chief was one of the more competent heads of all the police departments in all the jurisdictions around Portland. He was thin and his tan uniform shirt always looked wrinkled, today being no exception. He had the standard police utility belt with a gun locked down. He wore jeans and also had on cowboy books, showing his Montana background. His hair was so thin and gray, he almost looked bald.

"No problem," Pilgrim said. "So run us through what happened and then we'll go in and take a look."

"The woman who owns this house is named Vista Moulton," the chief said. "She bought the house about five years ago and has had a crew working to slowly renovate it."

Pilgrim watched the chief as Donna's fingers flew over her keyboard, digging up far more information than the chief could ever know. More than likely, Donna was looking into the renovation firm, the contractors and subcontractors and all their legal records and financial records.

"Her grandson, Steven Moulton, a college student at Portland State, was staying in the house and watching it for her. He vanished without leaving the house three days ago and hasn't been seen even in his classes since."

"So why does Mrs. Moulton think he disappeared inside the house?" Pilgrim asked.

"Security system," the chief said. "Everyone who goes in and out of that house is recorded twenty-four-seven. Every door, every window, no exceptions and it can't be turned off."

Donna glanced over at Pilgrim and nodded. Clearly she had backed up the chief's claim by hacking into the security system.

Pilgrim nodded. "So let's go take a look inside. Any remodeling being done today?"

The chief shook his head. "All work was postponed until they found the kid."

"So let's go find him," Pilgrim said, opening his door and stepping out into the warm fall afternoon air.

What he didn't say to the chief was that chances are they were going to find Steven's body. Pilgrim hoped not. But it was a logical conclusion from the facts he had.

Donna was still typing like mad when Pilgrim closed the door and he and the chief started up the old stone sidewalk to the front steps of the stately Victorian mansion.

TWO

PILGRIM HUGH LET the chief unlock the large oak and glass front door and step first into the impressive front foyer. The chief keyed a code into a security box hidden behind a wooden panel to the right of the door as Pilgrim just stared.

A grand staircase fit for a southern mansion right out of a movie started up both sides of the huge foyer and met in the middle, climbing the last ten steps to the second floor landing. From there it looked like a hallway went in both directions.

The staircase had wide dark-stained railings all the way up

The room was meant to impress, from the marble floor and stairs to the massive crystal chandelier hanging in the middle.

And it impressed Pilgrim, he had to admit.

The place had a slight smell of age and another slight smell of varnish. But no smell of death at all.

It soon became clear that the big front foyer was the only large room in the house. Every other room was normal-sized, with high ceilings and wonderful, tall windows. All the heavy drapes were pulled back and open in almost all rooms, letting in wonderful natural light.

A seating area and living room, both with huge stone fireplaces, were to the right of the main entrance and a sitting room and dining room were to the left.

The kitchen beyond a heavy door in the back of the dining room had been modernized, but the tile work and wood on the floor kept the old feeling about it.

The kitchen looked like it had been used regularly and some Diet Coke filled the fridge along with lunchmeat and cans of soup and chips filling two cabinets. Clearly Steven had used the kitchen regularly.

There was a massive island in the middle of the kitchen and a wooden table to one side that also looked to be regularly used.

The kitchen had no windows in it at all as was standard for workers' kitchens back in the time of this old mansion.

Pilgrim and the chief climbed from the kitchen to the second floor on the narrow servants' staircase leading out of the back of the kitchen. At the top, the staircase came out of what appeared to be a wall along the second floor corridor.

No door.

When the wall closed behind them, Pilgrim was stunned that it was almost impossible to see where that staircase was. Pilgrim knew that was standard in these old mansions, but he had never seen it maintained in such good shape as this.

"Hang on a minute, chief," Pilgrim said. Then Pilgrim tapped his ear to talk with Donna who had been listening to their conversation.

"Got a floor plan of this place?" he asked Donna. "Servants' staircase is behind a secret door."

"Got it," Donna said in his ear. "I'll bring it in along with some other things I have found."

"Thanks," Pilgrim said.

He and the chief spent the next few minutes looking in all the rooms on the second floor. The four bedrooms all opened off a wide hallway with a carpet runner down the middle over old wood floors.

Each room was actually a two-room suite and had a heavy wooden door on it. There were two suites to the left of the massive front staircase and two to the right. Each suite had its own bathroom. Everything had been remodeled in the last few years.

The only suite that was actually lived in was the last one on the right, clearly Steven's room. All the rest were empty of even furniture and drapes.

Steven's room had a full living room, drapes closed over the big windows, and a bathroom with Steven's things in them.

Pilgrim only hesitated for a moment, trying to figure out what was missing in the two rooms until it finally dawned on him. There was no computer.

Steven was twenty-four; there should be a computer center stage.

Pilgrim and the chief went back out into the wide hallway.

Antique brass and frosted glass light sconces were spaced along the hallway on both sides, making the hall bright, even though the bulbs in each were low wattage.

The hallway dead-ended in both directions from the staircase. In newer buildings, that hallway would have gone all the way to the exterior wall and would have a window or some sort of emergency escape.

The fact that this massive hallway didn't in either direction bothered Pilgrim, but he wasn't sure why.

The staircase leading upward was to the left, far enough down the hallway as to not be seen from the foyer below.

Donna met them as they moved back down the hallway to the top of the massive staircase.

"Wow, this place is something," she said, shaking her head.

She had her computer pad in her hand and pointed to a painted wall across from the staircase and punched a few buttons on her computer. Then she put her computer on top of a wooden banister for stability.

The floor plan of the house was projected on the wall.

The chief went to one side and Pilgrim went to the other side of the plan to study it.

The servants' staircase was clearly shown.

The hallway dead-ends were also clearly show. The two end rooms on either side of the building shared a wall beyond the end of the hallway.

Nothing at all looked out of place on the plans.

But as a kid, Pilgrim always loved thinking about secret passageways in old homes and that servants' staircase being hidden in the hallway brought all that back.

With one last look at the map, he headed back down the hall toward Steven's room, but instead of turning into the young man's room, Pilgrim went into the empty suite across the hall.

The outer room directly off the hallway worked as a form of living room and a bedroom behind it with a bathroom off to one side. The ceilings were at least twelve feet above Pilgrim and the tall windows let light pour into the spaces.

He studied the door into the hallway, then went to the bedroom door and looked at the wall between the bedroom and Steven's room.

Normally, a person would never see it, but because Pilgrim was looking for it, the space behind that wall became obvious.

The back bedroom was about four feet smaller than it should have been, and if the back bedroom in Steven's suite was the same, the room between the two bedrooms was very large. Bigger than most bedrooms in modern homes.

Now he knew where Steven was. During the day he was hiding back there, then coming out at night, using the servants' stairs to go to the kitchen and so on.

Now to find out why Steven was hiding back there.

Pilgrim glanced back at where the chief and Donna stood. "Did you dig up any information about how Steven was doing in school?"

"Failing," Donna said. "Hadn't bothered to attend most classes and had missed a couple midterms."

The chief shook his head. "Mrs. Moulton seems to be under the impression her grandson is a star student."

"Money missing?" Pilgrim asked Donna.

She nodded, glancing down at her computer. "Steven, over the last year or so, took a steady stream of cash from his account. Totals a few hundred thousand in all, but he did it slowly enough to make it seem he just had higher expenses. Grandmother always made sure there was more."

"Any evidence of family issues?" Pilgrim asked.

Donna nodded. "When Steven's parents were killed when Steven was sixteen, grandmother put all her attention on him. As any young kid would, he rebelled at times. Sometimes those rebellions hit the police reports."

"So we got a guy who wanted out and just ran," the chief said, shaking his head.

"Maybe," Pilgrim said. He turned to Donna. "Any security cameras at all inside the mansion?"

"None," Donna said. "Just on the doors and windows."

"I figured as much," Pilgrim said, nodding. "But there is still something we're missing here and that's the real reason why? Let's head back out to the limo."

"Got a theory?" the chief asked.

"Oh, I've solved the problem you asked me to solve," Pilgrim said as they headed for the massive staircase. "Now I just want to know why."

THREE

THE THREE OF them crawled back into the limo and this time Pilgrim brought up his computer screens around him at the same time Donna did.

The chief just sat, sipping on a bottle of water that Donna had given him.

"With all the computers," the chief said, "this place looks more like a bridge of a spaceship than the back of a limo."

Pilgrim just shook his head and kept focused on the search he was doing as Donna was about to lead the chief to places he mostly likely didn't want to go.

Donna smiled at him. "When was the last time you were on the bridge of a spaceship?"

"Movie spaceship," the chief said, laughing.

"So you really didn't know that this thing can fly," Donna said, her fingers flying over her computer screen. "We should take you for a spin someday."

"You're kidding me?" the chief asked, glancing between Donna and Pilgrim.

Pilgrim laughed. "See what I have to put up with every day?"

"With this rig," the chief said, "I'm not doubting anything."

"So I've got a full report here about Steven," Donna said. "What am I looking for?"

"How were his grades in his English lit classes?"

She glanced down, then frowned. "Only thing he aced. Why did you ask that?"

"I just sent you a list of family names," Pilgrim said. "Run a cross-check on them to see if any combination of them has published work in the last two years."

While she did that and the chief sipped on his bottle of water, Pilgrim ran another check on the wireless service going into the house. There had been activity every night since Steven had left.

Steven had a computer in there, just not in his main living area.

"Bradley Moulton has published three novels and about a dozen short stories in the last three years," Donna said. "His home address is Portland. He's become a bestseller."

"The kid's a writer?" the chief asked.

Pilgrim didn't answer the chief just yet. "Bradley Moulton have an email address and a phone?"

Donna nodded after a moment. "He does."

 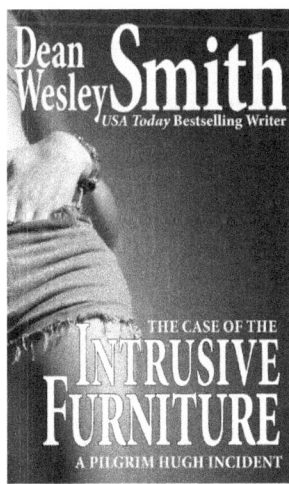 

Three Pilgrim Hugh Incidents
Available at your favorite booksellers.

Pilgrim nodded and pushed the button to let his computers retract back into the seat.

"So where is he?" the chief asked.

"He's upstairs, living and working in a secret room between his room and the other bedroom on that end of the hallway," Pilgrim said. "He never left the house."

"Why would he hide there like that?" the chief asked.

"He had a novel to finish," Pilgrim said.

The chief just blinked in puzzlement and Donna laughed.

"Email and text Mr. Bradley Moulton," Pilgrim said to Donna, "to meet us in the kitchen in ten minutes for a little talk. And call his grandmother to come over as well in about an hour. Seems we need to help in a little communication issue in this family."

"You sure he's up there?" the chief asked. "My detectives saw no sign of him."

"He's there," Pilgrim said. "He's been using the internet connection the last three days."

"How did you get that information?" the chief asked, then waved his hand. "Pretend I never asked that question. You want me there for this conversation?"

"Steven, aka Bradley, replied and said he would be right down," Donna said, punching the button on her computer console to make it retract into the seat.

"I don't think you need to be there, Chief," Pilgrim said as Donna opened the door and stepped out into the wonderful fall afternoon.

The chief nodded. "Good, because I have no idea what has just happened, but I appreciate you have cleared this off my books."

"Actually," Pilgrim said. "It's all about books. I just went to the first logical reason a person like Steven would want to be left alone and to cancel all the construction noises on the house. He needed some peace and quiet to write."

"I'm excited to meet Bradley, actually," Donna said. "I read his first novel and it was fantastic. I just picked up his second and have his third on order."

Pilgrim glanced over at the usually calm and collected assistant who now looked like a flustered schoolgirl.

"Thank you both," the chief said, shaking his head and turning toward his car. "Someday you can explain to me exactly what happened here."

Pilgrim and Donna started back up toward the big Victorian mansion to meet the writer.

"Bradley Moultan's that good?" Pilgrim asked.

Donna just nodded. Then she said breathlessly, "His sex scenes are to die for."

And now it was Pilgrim's turn to be flustered.

Now Available
from all your favorite booksellers
in trade paper and electronic editions.

USA TODAY BESTSELLING AUTHOR

DEAN WESLEY
SMITH

LAYING THE MUSIC TO REST

A former college professor turned bartender, Doc finds himself trying to save his friends from a ghost under a lake in the wilderness of Idaho.

From diving into a ghost town buried under a lake to trying to stay alive on the sinking deck of the Titanic, *this time-travel science fiction novel reads like a roller-coaster ride with all the twists and turns.*

First published in paperback in 1989 from Warner Questar Books, Dean Wesley Smith's first published novel gives a lot of hints of his future series and his bestselling career spanning over a hundred and fifty novels.

Published here in its original form, without any changes, just as Dean wrote it almost thirty years ago.

LAYING THE MUSIC TO REST

PROLOGUE

Roosevelt, Idaho
May, 1909

THE BITING, COLD water of flooded Monumental Creek twisted Gretchen's dress around her legs as she fought to open the front door of the Roosevelt Inn.

"Alex!" she shouted at the wood. "Alex! Open the door."

The black night, the steady drumming of the rain, and the sadistic rustle of the swirling water swallowed her shout as if it hadn't existed. She banged her fist against the wood, but even that was muffled as the dark, empty town seemed to laugh at her.

She took a deep breath, yanked her dress up so that the hem rode around her knees, and braced her left foot against the edge of a board in the sidewalk. She pushed slowly. The door wouldn't move. Frustrated, she rammed her shoulder into the door. Her foot slid on the wood and she went to her knees in the icy water.

"Alex," she called again as the current pulled at her. Her cold fingers found the doorframe and she held on. Alex was waiting for her. She had to get to him. She levered herself back to her feet, then carefully tested the door one last time. Solid.

She took a deep, shuddering breath and tried to make herself relax against the cold. She'd only been wading in the water a few minutes. The sharp, jabbing pain she had felt when she first stepped into the water had faded to a constant dull ache.

She took another breath and forced herself to think. Frank. That was the problem. He must have bolted the front door after they took the last of the supplies up to the tent. He probably figured it would help keep the water away from the piano. The back door was two steps higher and she had been one of the last out that way. She was sure it was open.

She quickly splashed her way along the covered front of the Inn, down the two steps, and into the rain and deeper water. Thick mud from the street oozed up and over her shoes and sucked at her feet, trying to pull her into the muck. Moving carefully so that the mud wouldn't yank her shoes off, she turned into the narrow alley that ran between the south side of the Inn and the next building.

In the summer months, miners too drunk to make it back to their diggings slept along this wall, sometimes four or five at a time. Now the icy water swirling around her thighs tried to push her from between the buildings, billowing her skirt and slips in front of her like sails in a strong wind.

Ahead she could faintly see the dark edges of the two buildings and beyond that the black mass of the steep mountainside. The roar of the swollen creek echoed down the narrow alley, warning her to turn back. But she couldn't. She

had to find Alex. Using both hands, one on each building to steady herself, she pushed slowly forward.

As she neared the back of the Inn, a chunk of wood banged hard against her knees and tangled in her skirt. She reached down to free it, lost her balance, and fell. The cold water closed over her and crushed the breath from her lungs. Her mouth filled with muddy water. The current shoved her back toward Main Street. She jammed one foot down into the mud and pushed herself out of the water.

She pressed both numbed hands against the rough logs of the two buildings and forced herself to wait for her breath to return. She wasn't going to let the water stop her. Not now.

Bracing herself with one hand, she leaned against the Inn, brushed her hair from her face, and then felt for the hand mirror strapped under her soaking dress. Alex's mirror. She had tied it inside her corset against her stomach. It was lucky she had. If she dropped it now, she'd never find it in the black water.

She did a careful check to make sure the mirror was still solidly pressed against her, almost warm inside her soaking dress. Only six hours ago she had seen the mirror for the first time. Six long hours since Alex first pulled out the carved, ivory-framed glass and held it up proudly for her to see. The day might have turned out to be the best day of her life if she hadn't been such a fool.

***

The cold, rainy morning had started with the entire town wild with the rumor that one of the packing outfits had finally made it over the Dewey Summit with supplies from Idaho City. After seven months of being snowbound in the narrow Monumental Valley, that was celebration news.

Gretchen had decided to wear her finest dress for that special night. Alex also dressed for dinner in his finest, coming down to town wearing a Boston lawyer's suit. She thought he looked more handsome than ever, if that was possible.

All the girls said Alex was the best catch in the valley. With his suits, fancy English, and smoky blue eyes, he could have any free woman he chose. But in seven months he had paid attention only to Gretchen. He had been perfectly polite and honorable. And even though she was a saloon piano player, he treated her as if she were a Boston lady.

That night he had come into the Inn at his normal dinner hour and asked if he might have a moment with her after everything had quieted down.

At first the request had excited her. But then, as the evening wore on and she watched him eat his dinner and sip his brandy, she began to worry. What did he want? Was he leaving town now that the pass was open? Why did he seem so serious? Unanswered questions from the winter came flooding back. What was he doing in Roosevelt? What did he see in her? What did he want from her? She was just a saloon girl and he was a Boston gentleman. They could never be together. She was sure he must know that.

But he thought otherwise. He used his grandmother's beautiful mirror to ask her to marry him.

She had said no.

***

She banged her fist against the wall of the Inn and moved carefully toward the back door. Why hadn't she said yes? She had been so afraid and so stupid.

But Alex would not give up. He would come back for her. She knew it. He would be inside the Inn, waiting. This time she would tell him yes.

She reached the back door of the Inn. It stood wide open and the water level was at her knees. The men had better get that mudslide cleared. The water was filling the narrow valley faster than she had imagined possible.

She moved inside the black room and along the wall toward the sink. Jim had left one lantern hanging there in case someone had to come back. She reached the sink and leaned against it for a moment, trying to catch her breath. The cold water had forced a throbbing ache up into her stomach, radiating out under her arms and across her chest in a dull web of pain. She could hardly breathe. She needed to get out of the water and into dry clothes soon. Alex had to be there.

"Alex!" she shouted into the dark, water-filled room. Her voice sounded funny, as if she were in a deep mine shaft. He didn't answer.

He hadn't been in his cabin or down with the men working to clear the mudslide. He had to be at the Inn, waiting for her. That was where he had disappeared, vanished like a wisp of smoke right before her eyes. One minute he had asked her to marry him and the next he had simply faded away, as if he had only been a dream and she was waking up.

But she had not been asleep. He would come back, that she was sure of. She could feel it. He would come back to the Inn, to the very place where he had disappeared. She knew that, too. She didn't know why. She just knew. She touched the hard surface of the mirror. She would have his grandmother's mirror for him when he did. She would wait.

She found the lantern and pulled it from the hook. It seemed unusually heavy in her numb fingers. She held it and felt carefully on the ledge over the sink for the block of matches. They were still dry, so she broke off one match and scraped it against the rough wood of the wall.

The match caught on the second try and the sudden blues and yellows outlined against the darkness blinded her. She lit the lantern, her fingers like logs against the thin chimney glass. After the wick caught, she held her hands over the warmth and looked around the room she had worked and lived in for the past seven months.

In six hours it had become so different. Black water filled the room, with small twigs and leaves floating in quick currents. The four beds that usually stood against the south wall had floated over into the back corner. A blanket lay half on, half off one bed and a black stain showed where the water had soaked up into the cotton.

She lifted the lantern off the counter and waded toward the door leading into the main room. The pain in her legs made her feel as if she were walking on stumps. Only the jarring in her groin told her when her feet touched the floor.

The door to the main room was closed and latched. She fumbled with the bolt before she got it open and stepped up onto the platform that held her piano.

The pale light from the single lantern cast dark shadows across the flooded main room of the Inn. Tables still occupied their correct positions, but every so often the water shifted one of the chairs as if some unseen patron still sat on it.

The potbellied stove against the stairs looked cold and black, its door open, its fire out. The long liquor shelves behind the bar were ugly, empty scars on the face of the north wall. The room was no longer the warm, lively place she had filled with music all winter long.

The table closest to the piano was where Alex had sat. Where he had asked her to marry him. Where he had disappeared. When he had started to fade away, she'd screamed and tried to hold him. But he had been like a ghost. She could see the front wall through his chest and her hands passed through him like a cold draft through an open window.

Frank had been upstairs to allow her and Alex some privacy. The rest of the girls had already gone to bed in the back. Her screams as Alex vanished had brought everyone running. No one believed that he had disappeared. No one.

They had put her in bed by the time the alarm came about the mudslide. Frank had gone to take a look, and when he got back he looked white and scared. There was a huge mudslide coming down Mule Creek from the direction of the Dewey Mine. It was traveling almost as fast as a man could walk.

He had everyone take all they could carry and follow him. They put up a tent about a half mile upstream on higher ground, then made three trips to get the liquor, plates, silverware, clothes, and valuables. By the time they made the last trip, the flowing wall of mud and rock had dammed the main valley a hundred yards below the town and the water from the heavy rains and the spring melt was already a foot deep on Main Street.

Gretchen had wanted Frank to move the piano to higher ground, too. But Frank had decided that it was a better gamble to put all their efforts into trying to clear a channel around the slide. The next few hours had echoed with the sound of dynamite explosions as the men fought the moving mud and rock. Now, except for the rain and the constant roar of Monumental Creek, the valley was still.

Gretchen had been unable to stay in the tent. She knew Alex was out there somewhere. All she had to do was find him and tell him she had changed her mind. She would ask him to forgive her. She would tell him that she would be honored to be his wife and go to Boston with him.

But he hadn't been at his cabin or working at the slide. He had disappeared from the Inn. That was where he would return. She knew it.

She set the lantern down on the piano and held her hands over the flame to get whatever warmth she could. Then she opened three buttons of her dress, carefully untied the corset strings she had used to hold the mirror tight against her stomach, and pulled the mirror into the lamp light.

The ornately carved patterns in the ivory handle and frame seemed to dance in the flickering light as she held the mirror up. It was like nothing Gretchen had ever seen. Alex had mentioned that the mirror had been in his family for generations. His grandfather had used it to propose to Alex's grandmother, and Alex's father had used it to propose to Alex's mother. Tonight, Alex had used it to ask her to join his image in the mirror and be his wife. She had turned the mirror face down on the table. Refused his offer.

"I'm sorry, Alex," she said softly. The room didn't even allow an echo of an answer.

"Please, Alex. Come back."

A fit of shivering caught her. A chair near the front door swung a half turn around, startling her. The building groaned, as if it too wanted to move. She shivered again. If Alex came, he could help her back to the tent and she could get into some dry clothes. Maybe if she played for him, he would hear her.

Using both hands, she slid the mirror face up onto the top of the piano. Then she pulled the bench out. It floated free and started to tip over. She held it against the floor while she moved between it and the piano and sat down.

Carefully she moved the mirror down onto the music rack in front of her, then slid the bench to get into her normal position. Water splashed up on the keyboard. She tried to wipe the drops of water off with the lace on her sleeve. When Alex got back, she would talk to him about getting some men and saving the piano. She couldn't let it get ruined. Not after all the work of getting it over the pass. She had kept such good care of it all winter.

She tried a sample chord with her shaking hands. The sound felt much fuller, louder, as if the watery room wanted to keep the music alive and holding its tone long after she released the keys.

She hit another chord and then tried to run a simple scale. Her fingers were so numb, they got in each other's way. She felt as if they weren't even a part of her body. She couldn't feel her feet and legs.

She pulled the lamp on the piano directly in front of her and held her hands over the chimney. After a moment she could feel the heat biting into her skin. She rubbed her fingers together, then held them over the lamp again. She repeated the process until she could feel tingling in her fingertips. She wished she could do the same for her legs. They were nothing more than logs hanging off her body in the water. She'd have to play without using the pedals.

She sat up straight on the bench, arched her back, and tried to clear the thick fog from her mind. She placed both hands lightly on the keyboard and looked down at the table where Alex had last sat. She tried to imagine him reappearing there, fading back into the room just as slowly as he had faded out. She would play his favorite song for him. Then he would return.

The first note filled the room and the song flowed perfectly. Not once during the entire piece did she look away from the table. And when the last note died in the black of the water, she felt empty. Lost.

She slumped against the piano and looked around. She could feel that Alex was there. She didn't know how, but she knew he was close.

She held the mirror up. He was there, with her, and yet he wasn't. She stared into the mirror until she felt dizzy and had to lean her head against the hard wood of the piano to get the spinning to stop.

The water lapped over the top of the bench. She felt as if her entire body were draining out of her legs. Alex was close. If she played his favorite song once more, he would return and take her to someplace warm and hold her and tell her he wanted her for his wife. She needed to play his song again so he could hear her.

She took a few quick breaths to try to calm the shuddering that racked her shoulders before warming her shaking fingers over the lamp. Then she started the song once more, only this time she looked into the mirror, seeing Alex's face in it.

She played the song. His song. And when she was finished, she started over, playing it again. And then again, until finally her hands would work no more.

She tried to warm her fingers over the lamp, but her head was spinning so much that she misjudged and knocked the lamp sideways, out of reach. She tried to stand and grab for it before it fell, but her legs were nothing more than weights attached to her body. Her sudden lunge shifted the bench and tipped her sideways.

The lamp rolled off the piano, hit the water, and with a hiss plunged the room into total blackness. Thrashing wildly to regain her footing, Gretchen too slipped under.

Her mind screamed for her to find a handhold, get her breath. The cold crushed what little air she had left out of her chest and she tasted the muddy water.

Finally she caught the edge of the keyboard and pulled herself up into the air.

Some Classic Dean Wesley Smith Stories
Available at your favorite booksellers.

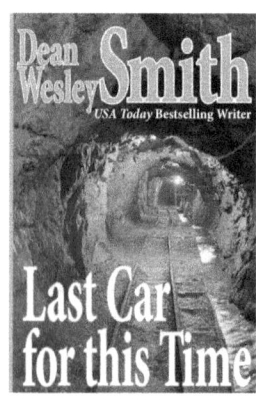

But her legs refused to move under her and her fingers were too weak to hold on.

She slipped a second time. The room held the sound of her struggle like it had held the music moments before, kicking it from wall to wall, savoring it, holding it out for the empty tables and the cold stove to inspect.

She grasped the side of the piano and slowly pulled her head back above the black surface.

"Alex?" she whispered.

But the room refused her, killing even the faintest echo of her plea. Her fingers could not hold on to the polished wood long. After a moment she dropped into the black cold.

Silence again took over the room.

CHAPTER ONE

Boise, Idaho
June 25, 1990

"ALL RIGHT, DOC," Angie said as she pushed open the back door of the Garden Restaurant and Lounge and dropped two grocery sacks on the kitchen counter. "What happened today?"

Not even a simple good morning. I shook my head, trying to contain a smile. "Not a thing yet. But I could cut myself and get it over with." I held up the knife I had been using to slice limes.

"Thanks for the offer," she said. "But I think Tuesday will give us more than enough thrills." She glanced around. "Smells good in here. You must have made it up for the bread."

"Beat the truck by five minutes. I should have slept longer."

She laughed. "I'll be hiding in the office doing the damn withholding taxes. Let me know when the coast is clear."

"Give it time. It's only eleven."

She grabbed the smallest of the two sacks and tapped the remaining one. "Bar rags. Nice and clean. Just like the old man ordered." She stuck her tongue out at me and then turned and headed for the office.

I laughed as she ducked past the sinks and down the back hall, acting as if I might throw something at her at any moment. She loved teasing me about my recent fortieth birthday. Probably because she knew it bothered me.

I loved Angie as if she were my sister. She was single, thirty-two years old, and the shortest woman I had ever met. Well-proportioned, people said. I remember thinking the same thing the very first time I saw her walk into my class.

She'd been a student of mine ten years ago and somehow, over the years, we had managed to become friends. She and my wife, Carla, had hit it off from the moment they met. Six months after Carla died, Angie and I decided to buy the Garden. It was one of those "what-the-hell" decisions. Angie had money to invest from her divorce settlement and I was sick of teaching at the university. We both needed the change and the Garden had looked like the ideal way to do it.

So for the last five years, I had done all the day bartending, becoming more and more bored and set in my ways. Even more than when I was teaching.

Angie's side of the partnership was to do the books and help out Friday and Saturday nights. In five years she hadn't missed a weekend and I'd never asked her if she was bored. And every damn

Tuesday over those years something had gone wrong. Sometimes only little things. Sometimes major, like the Tuesday a year ago when we had the grease fire in the grill hood. Shut us down for over a week.

Besides all the happenings, I had another good reason for not liking Tuesdays. They delivered the bread on Tuesdays at nine in the morning, one hour before I usually had to be at work. One very long, very annoying hour. Someone had to meet the truck to give the driver a check. So Angie and I had agreed. She washed the bar rags. I met the bread truck. I swore every Tuesday morning as I climbed out of bed that I was getting the raw end of the deal.

This week it wasn't until after the lunch rush that Tuesday struck.

Angie had gone home for the afternoon "to hide," and the normal lunch crowd had left. I had just finished cleaning off the last table, had put a good jazz tape on the sound system, and was sitting at the bar reading the morning paper and eating my normal French-dip sandwich when the front door opened and Constance walked in.

Alone.

Just as simple as that, Tuesday struck. The little bit of the sandwich I had already eaten suddenly felt like a hundred pounds of rock pressing me into the bar stool. Something had happened to Fred.

I swiveled off the bar stool and went to meet her as she weaved her way in and out of the plants and tables. Constance was a robust woman, not really tall, but the way she held herself made her seem tall. She had a full head of curly gray hair, a deep, rich voice, and a smile that made others around her smile without reason. Today she wore tan slacks, a blue work shirt with the sleeves rolled up, and a blue ribbon that held her hair back away from her face.

Fred, her husband, was my best friend. We'd known each other since we were in the first grade. Believe me, I can't go back much further than that and still remember things.

Fred looked like a bald flagpole. At forty, he maintained his wiry look and incredible strength. Above my fireplace I had a picture of the three of us that Angie took a few years back. Constance, the shortest, was on the right. I was in the middle, wearing one of my usual thick sweaters. I had my beard and mustache trimmed a little closer then and my hair still had a lot more brown in it than gray. Fred, three inches taller than me, clean-cut and bald, was on my left. I always had the feeling that the picture was tipped slightly because of the way we were standing, short to tall.

During the winter, Fred and Constance both taught at a local high school and were regulars at the Garden. Every summer they would pack up and disappear into the rough central Idaho primitive area to work on small mining claim and some land they'd bought up there before the government locked it all up into wilderness. They were putting a lodge and six small cabins on it. This summer was to be their first season with what they liked to call "guests."

For the past three summers I had promised I would go in with them to take a look and maybe help out a little. Every summer something had come up. And not once in all those years had they come out of the primitive area until the week before school started. Yet suddenly, here was Constance without Fred. Something was big-time wrong.

I gave Constance the best rib-compressing hug I could, and she gave me a quick answer to my question—yes, Fred was all right and had just stayed back up at the lodge to watch the guests. I pointed to the stool beside mine and moved around behind the bar.

"You had lunch?" I asked as I poured Constance her regular drink—vodka Collins, only half the ice, lime garnish—then slid it in front of her.

She nodded. "In McCall. Two hours ago." She held up the drink. "Thanks." I nodded and then built myself an orange juice and soda and moved back around the bar.

I pushed my unfinished sandwich down the bar, out of the way. "I give up, I can't stand the suspense. If Fred's all right and you're all right, just what are you doing here?"

Constance laughed her deep, full laugh. "Always right to the point," she said. "One of the many things I love about you." She leaned over and kissed my check, the first time a woman had kissed me in a long time.

"Well, I'm here for three reasons. One, to talk to you. Two, to get supplies. And three, to place some new advertising. Always use more guests, you know."

"You been getting some?" I tried to keep the disbelief out of my voice. I had always thought the idea of a lodge twenty miles inside the most rugged primitive area in the lower forty-eight was something on the other side of crazy. Of course, being crazy was part of Fred. But this idea was beyond even Fred's normal sense of looney. Hell, from the maps and pictures they had shown me, there wasn't a stretch in that valley wide enough or long enough to put a landing strip. The ranches down on the Salmon River at least had that. All of Fred and Constance's guests had to pack in on horseback. Or worse yet, walk.

Again Constance laughed. "Of course we are. At one point we had nine guests. Not bad for our first year."

I nodded, but I could tell now that Constance wasn't giving me the entire story. She had that little wrinkle above her eyes that she always used to get when she worried about Fred and me doing something stupid. Carla used to just frown and shake her head. I hadn't seen that look on Constance in years. And it suddenly occurred to me that I had missed it.

"So why advertise? Isn't nine about maximum for what you've got built?"

She nodded. "But we only have two left." She took a long sip of her drink, then turned to face me. "That's why we need your help. Fred wanted to do it alone, but I wouldn't let him. I really don't like the idea of the both of you doing it, but—"

I touched Constance's arm. "Back up a minute. What was it Fred wanted to do alone? And exactly what is this about needing my help?"

"Sorry," she said, then laughed an uneasy laugh. "Fred wants to make a dive into the lake."

It felt as if the air conditioning had kicked on twenty degrees too low. The old mining claim they had bought ran along the side of a small mountain lake. The lake had been formed back in the early part of the century when a mudslide filled the narrow Monumental Valley and backed water up over a booming mining town called Roosevelt. Constance had brought in pictures one September in which you could clearly see a huge logjam that Fred claimed was the remains of the old buildings.

When they had first bought the claim I asked them why no one had ever heard of this huge disaster. It seemed to me that losing a town of over five thousand people would be a big deal. Yet the fact that it had happened had become one of those forgotten notes of Idaho history. Constance said the people down at the State Historical Society didn't even know much about it. It appeared that only Zane Grey, in his book *Thunder Mountain*, had even noticed and everyone thought that was just fiction.

"Into the old ghost town?" I asked. "Fred wants to dive into the old ghost town?" Fred had said a few years back that to his knowledge, no one had ever made a dive into the lake. The water was too cold, it was too tough to get equipment into the area, and it was just too dangerous. Twenty years ago Fred and I might have tried it. I didn't like the sound of it now.

Constance nodded. "There's not going to be much of any town down there. But he still wants to make the dive."

"Hell, that's crazy. Fred knows better than to think about making a dive alone, especially into a mountain lake like that. Anything could happen." The knot in my stomach that was clamped around the first few bites of my French-dip sandwich wasn't letting go. In fact, it was getting worse and I was getting slowly mad at Fred for even thinking about being so stupid. I'd lost Carla and losing Fred scared me more than I wanted to admit.

"Tell him that."

"I will," I said. "And damn loud. That fool knows better. Jesus, it's been ten years since either one of us strapped on a tank. What could be so important that he'd even think of making that dive alone?"

"Try twelve years," Constance said. "We figured it up one night. The last time you both did any diving was on that rescue operation over near the Snake. Remember?"

I nodded. I remembered real well. How could I forget? It hadn't been so much a rescue mission as pure and simple stupidity. A five-year-old boy went under in a millpond in front of two dozen witnesses. Two days and no one could find the body. Fred and I were called in by a friend of the family to help only because the regular Search and Rescue divers were needed elsewhere. From the report of what the body looked like when it finally did surface, we were damn lucky we couldn't find it. And once Fred ended up tangled in weeds for a good ten minutes before he could work his way free and surface.

For months I dreamed of that boy's bloated face appearing out of the muck of the pond in front of my facemask like some bad special effect in a slasher movie. On top of that, I didn't believe in risking lives in a weed-choked pond just to find a body that was going to float to the surface in a day or two anyway. The only thing that practice did was create more bodies.

Before that nightmare Fred and I had done a lot of diving. We had made excursions in the Gulf of Mexico, Canadian mountain lakes, and a bunch of places in between. Strapping on scuba tanks and exploring was one of the crazy things we prided ourselves in doing, even though it worried the hell out of both Carla and Constance. I wondered what ever happened to our doing crazy things.

"So," I said after a long moment of silence interrupted only by the traffic sounds from Grove Street. "Why make a dive?"

"I'm not really sure, exactly," Constance said. She looked uncomfortable as she twisted her drink slowly in her strong hands. "Professor Jerome says that's what we need to do to help the ghost."

"I—hang on a minute." I swiveled away from Constance and went around behind the bar. She was making no sense at all. I built her a new drink, slid it across the bar, and then sat on the counter behind the bar so I could look directly at her. If whatever brought her into town was as complicated as it was beginning to seem, I wanted to be able to see her eyes. With Constance, everything came through her green eyes.

"All right," I said, "how about you starting from the beginning?"

Constance nodded, then finished her first drink, set it aside, and swirled the straws in the second. "You remember Fred mentioning that the lake was haunted?"

I nodded. A few years back they had returned with stories about a woman ghost walking around the lake. It had been the joke of the bar for most of that September. I remembered being surprised that they would even talk about such stuff, let alone act as if they believed it. That wasn't like Fred or Constance. I ended up not knowing what to believe and they never mentioned it again.

"Well, we weren't fooling," she said, "even though everyone thought we were. The ghost has been there right from the first time Fred and I camped at the old mine site. With all the people who lived in Roosevelt before it was flooded, I guess a ghost or two should be expected. We got used to seeing her walking down along the old mudslide and then into the water. It just never occurred to us that she would be any more than a historical curiosity to our guests."

"She wasn't, I gather?" I didn't know what to make of this story. If it hadn't been Constance and she hadn't been sitting in the Garden in the middle of the summer, I would have laughed. I didn't feel close to laughing right now.

Constance shook her head slowly. "She doesn't hurt anything, except there's this mighty cold feeling if you get too close to her."

"I'll bet. Scared your customers?"

Constance nodded. "We had to refund a lot of money we were planning on using to build a seventh cabin up on the summit. Doesn't seem much reason to now, though. Not if she's going to keep spooking everyone."

"What about using her to bring in people? Seems to me if word got out about your ghost, there would be a lot of folks who would just love to see her."

"Crazies. The wrong kind of people. All we wanted was a place we could enjoy, back away from everything. The kind of people we want staying with us should want the same thing. Hiking. Fishing. Exploring. And lots and lots of quiet. That's not exactly what we would get if we had every weirdo in the country looking at our house ghost. Plus, imagine the fuss there'd be if she suddenly decided to not show up. It's not like we have any control over her."

For a moment Constance had a faraway look in her eyes and then she shook her head like a woman accepting the loss of a dream. "And now, with the guests going home and telling people, we might as well shut down next year."

I leaned back against the liquor cabinet. Constance was serious. I didn't believe what she was telling me, but at the same time I couldn't just laugh at her. "So she scared away all but two of your customers. What happened then?"

"No, she scared them *all* right back up over the summit. We have one new customer, a young woman who we warned about the ghost right up front. She doesn't seem to mind. And then Professor Jerome, who is our guest. He's from the University of California parapsychological studies department. We paid for him to fly into McCall. We picked him up there."

"You brought in a psychic? Fred agreed to this?" I just couldn't believe Fred would go for anything outside the reality of a tall bottle of Bud, a good game of chess, and a turkey sandwich.

"Not a psychic in the way you're thinking," Constance said. "Dr. Jerome is very respected and—"

"I know, I know," I said, waving away the obvious list of credentials Constance was about to spew all over the bar. I had had my share of letters stenciled after my name on my old office door. The only good those letters had done was get me a little more money and intimidate the hell out of students. They might as well have been carved on my tombstone, for all the years I spent buried behind them. Deadly dull years. Fred should have known better than to be taken in.

"So what has this *professor* done so far?" I asked, not really wanting to hear the answer.

"Mostly just study the ghost," she said. "He's spent the last five days following her around the shore of the lake like a little puppy. He must have taken a hundred pictures and done who knows what with a couple strange-looking instruments with names too long for me to remember. He seems to think he knows what she wants."

Now I really wanted to laugh. It was everything I could do not to burst out right then. Constance was serious, I could tell that without a doubt. Her eyes didn't lie. But the thought of a ghost talking to some hokey professor from California was damn near too much. I forced my laughter back down like swallowing a bad pill and

ended up just shaking my head and then taking a long drink off my orange juice. Maybe I was getting too cynical. Fifteen years ago I might have bought this story. Why didn't I today?

Because it was too stupid to believe, that was why. The real question was why Fred was being sucked in by whatever scam this California nut was spouting. Not like Fred at all. No wonder Constance had come down to get me.

I sidestepped the part about the guy knowing what the ghost wanted and went back to my main question. "You still haven't told me why Fred wants to make a dive into the lake."

Constance sighed, stirred her drink for a moment, then looked up at me. "You're not going to believe it."

"I'm already having trouble," I said. "In case you haven't noticed. So you might as well hit me with everything."

"Professor Jerome says the ghost wants to find someone named Alex. There's something in the lake that might help. The professor thinks that if we find it, whatever it is might, as he calls it, let her rest."

"And Fred believes all this?" I had a clear look at Constance's eyes as she spoke. She believed everything she was saying. Everything. And I could tell she didn't like it any more than I did.

"Yes," she said, without hesitation.

"And you want me to make this dive with Fred to keep him from killing himself in that cold water?"

She nodded. "You know we wouldn't ask you to do something like this if it wasn't important."

"Fred would," I said.

Constance started to object until she saw I was kidding. I dropped down off the counter and fixed us both another drink, only this time I laced my orange juice and soda with vodka.

"You know how special the lodge is to us, don't you?"

"Of course," I said. "Hell, I should. Over the last few years it's been about the only thing you two could talk about."

Constance laughed. "It was going to be what got us out of that high school. You know, kind of like this place got you away from the university."

I wanted to tell her that this "escape" had ended up as bad as my original prison, but I didn't.

"With this ghost scaring away our good guests and maybe bringing in all the weird ones, the lodge won't end up being the quiet place we dreamed about. We've got to find a way to get rid of her. Somehow." Her voice trailed off like the end of a song.

"So Fred and I find whatever it is. What then? Does this professor fellow have any ideas?"

Constance shook her head. "None. Fred doesn't like the idea, either. I think that's why he wanted to do it alone. I think he's embarrassed. So am I, really. But we need to try something and we don't have any other obvious roads."

I nodded. There was really no decision for me to make. Three-quarters of my mind was scared silly at the idea of making a dive into a lake that had killed an entire town, especially with a "ghost" close by. A damn dumb thing to do by any standards.

But the rest of me was excited at the thought. Excited at the adventure, like I used to be when Fred and I did something the rest of the world considered crazy. And for some reason, right now that excitement scared me even more.

Scared or not, it was Fred and Constance and I couldn't say no. Besides, if the California professor was pulling a scam, I might be able to spot it.

"How long before the train pulls out?" I asked.

Constance laughed. "Five a.m. tomorrow morning."

"Ouch. Couldn't we at least make it seven?"

Some Classic Dean Wesley Smith Stories
Available at your favorite booksellers.

"Not unless you want to be riding a horse down a mountain in the dark."

"What the hell ever happened to getting up at a reasonable time?" I downed the last of my drink. "You got someone working on the diving gear?"

"Called the dive shop from McCall a few hours ago and gave them the list Fred put together. It will be ready at four this afternoon."

"Good. Then the next step is to call Angie and tell her Tuesday struck again. She's never going to believe this one."

"Tuesday?" Constance asked as I turned and headed for the phone in my office.

"Yeah," I said, trying to calm the twisting fear I felt starting to build in my stomach. "Around here we love Tuesdays."

CHAPTER TWO

Stibnite, Idaho
June 26, 1990

FOR THE LAST five hours I had watched Constance handle her four-wheel drive Jeep as if it were an extension of her right arm. She feathered into graveled corners, accelerated without a jerk, and knew exactly when to downshift to keep the best power to the wheels. In other words, she was a damn good driver.

Five hours of winding, mountain roads from Boise to the ghost town of Stibnite and not once had she taken a corner too fast. And never too slow. Never. There had been a few hundred times when I'd grabbed for the armrest while looking at the fast-approaching hillside

or cliff. But each time she'd known the corner and her speed had been perfect. Of course, it always took me a few seconds to catch my breath after those corners, but I knew an amazing show of driving skill when I saw one.

Now we were on the flat ground of the old town of Stibnite and she was still making me grab for the armrest. She cut close to the remains of a large wooden building, swerved around two weathered piles of rock, and started the Jeep bouncing across a small meadow on what looked like no more than a vague memory of a road.

"Old town hall," she said, pointing back at the building we had missed by a door handle, her voice clear even over the constant drone of the engine and the rattling of our diving equipment. "Last building to be actively used in Stibnite. Abandoned somewhere around 1948, I think."

I nodded. For the last few miles I had been getting a lecture on the history of Stibnite. In its prime, during World War II, thousands had lived here…now it looked like an abandoned battlefield. Tumbled and ruined buildings, piles of dredged rock, and open mining pits half-filled with stagnant water dotted the obviously leveled valley floor. The site of the town itself stretched up the narrow, steep-walled valley. Before the mining boom, the valley must have been spectacular. Now it was nothing more than a monument to what human beings could do to something beautiful if given a free hand. It was no wonder everyone had moved away when the mines shut down. They probably all went looking for other valleys to destroy. With any luck, they'd all left Idaho.

The goat path Constance was using as a road veered suddenly to the right past a stand of pine and merged into what actually was a road, albeit a low-quality logging road. From the looks of it, the road was only maintained for fire access.

"It'll be fairly quick from here," she said. "About eight more miles to the summit. All up hill."

The road stays this good?" I said, joking. The thought of eight miles on this poor excuse for a logging road seemed no small distance.

"It gets a little washed out toward the top. But no worry. We'll make it."

"People find their way into your place?" It didn't seem possible that, even with the best of directions, I would have recognized those faint tracks across the field as a road, let alone the right road in the maze of old buildings and mining pits called Stibnite.

"Oh, really it's simple," she said. "I just took you on the scenic route. We tell our customers to stay on the main road heading up the river out of Yellow Pine. The gravel turns into this logging road about a mile beyond the point I turned and went into Stibnite. There are real clear signs pointing the way. Haven't had anyone get lost yet. Of course, customers we sign up pretty much know what they're getting into. That's why they want to stay at our place. It's away from things."

"I'll drink to that," I said, and Constance laughed.

"See what you've been missing not coming up all these summers?"

I glanced out over the tops of the pine trees as we climbed away from the valley floor on a road that was becoming no wider than the Jeep plus two door handles, with dirt brushing the handle on Constance's side and high-flying eagles pecking at the one on mine. There was no doubt that the stunning beauty of the Idaho mountains could make a person stop and stare for hours. But like all beauty, danger went hand-in-hand with it, and right now I was more concerned about the wheel on my side not dropping off into space.

I did the only thing I could do without letting Constance know how scared I was. I grasped my seat belt just below the seat on my door side while forcing my left hand to stay calmly on my leg. And the higher we climbed, the more I hoped she knew how to fly a plane.

Constance didn't seem to notice the road any more than she had the paved, two-lane road out of Boise. She took each corner at what seemed to be the maximum possible speed, her left hand steering and her right hand resting on the stick shift.

"You know, don't you?" she said, "that Fred's really happy about you coming up? I think if this mess with the ghost hadn't come up, he would have invented something just to drag you away from that plant-filled bar."

"Did he invent the ghost?"

Constance turned to look at me for a quick moment before darting the Jeep through a dry streambed. "No, I'm afraid it's there," she said. "And it's as real as a ghost can be."

She didn't look happy. This ghost thing had her worried far beyond anything I had ever seen Constance concerned about before. I forced myself to look out over the valley without glancing at the edge of the road flashing by, inches from the front wheel.

These were my two best friends and they were hurting. I wanted to help, but what could I do against a ghost? What could anyone do?

Especially this far from anything. It suddenly occurred to me that in the last three hours of driving, we had not met a single car. Not one. As Constance said, this was away from things. A long damn way away.

Below I could see the faint outline of a mountain stream as it cut through the pine and brush. Back down the valley I could see a mountain range that faded into the distance on the clear, summer day. Ahead, there was only up.

***

My ears popped seven times in eight miles.

And, as Constance had warned, the road didn't get better, it got worse. At one point we had to get out and move fallen rock out of the way. At another tight switchback, Constance had to back up two nerve-destroying times to keep the front end from banging into the hill. The second time she ground into reverse I swore she was backing right out into space.

"Last switchback and we're on top," Constance shouted over the noise of the engine as she cut the corner hard and at the same time shifted into low and let the Jeep's tires eat at the road, spraying dual fishtails of sand and dirt out behind us.

I had completely given up on hiding my fear and was holding on to the dash with both hands. I always thought that as I got older, I would fear death less and less. That basically had come to pass, but what I hadn't counted on was my increased fear of accidents. Death no longer bothered me. Accidents scared me something awful. Especially when I wasn't in control. This road would have bothered me even if I had been driving. But sitting in the passenger seat, the eight miles had been pure and simple torture.

I glanced at my watch. Forty-five minutes since we had left Stibnite. We must have gone through twenty switchbacks, across five streambeds, and straddled six miles of washed-out gullies down the center of the two tire tracks. From the first mile I had kept looking up thinking that the summit was only a little bit farther. But with every turn it never came any closer. The mountain just seemed to grow as we climbed it.

But finally, mercifully, the road widened and then cut up on top of the ridge. Constance leisurely wound the Jeep in and out of trees. The summit could have passed for Mid-western flatland, if not for the fact that if I looked real hard through the trees on either side, I could see blue sky and mountaintops for fifty miles in all directions.

The road ended in a widened turn-around with a large Forest Service sign blocking the remains of a trail continuing off through the trees. The sign said, FRANK CHURCH SALMON RIVER PRIMITIVE AREA. NO VEHICLES ALLOWED PAST THIS POINT.

Constance pulled the Jeep off under the pines to the right. Two other rigs were parked among the trees. One I recognized as Fred's rebuilt pickup truck. The other was a blue Ford two-door sedan. It looked like any standard airport rental car and felt incredibly out of place sitting up here on the edge of the primitive area. I had trouble believing that anyone could even get it up the road. But, short of having it airlifted in, someone must have, because there it sat.

Constance honked two long blasts on the horn, then cut off the engine. The silence seemed louder than the engine. I let go of the dashboard one finger at a time as Constance laughed, then unsnapped my seat belt, and pushed open the door.

The mountain air was as welcome as opening a refrigerator on a hot summer day. I took a deep breath of the freshest-tasting air I could ever remember and let it slowly out, along with five years of built-up tension. The crisp, cold feel of the air let a flood of memories back in. Memories of dives into cold Canadian lakes and the taste of hot coffee while sitting beside the fire afterward. Memories of camping as a kid, helping Dad put up the tent while Mom fixed lunch. Memories of the first nights with Carla at the retreat and how golden her skin looked in the faint starlight.

I took a few more deep breaths to let the memories drift their natural course, then did a few deep knee bends to loosen some of the tense muscles. Ten seconds of mountain air and I was starting to understand why Constance and Fred came up here every summer.

Constance scooted around to the back of the Jeep and started unloading the equipment, piling it on the thick carpet of pine needles.

"It'll take Fred a few minutes to get the horses and get them here," Constance said, as I joined her. "I hope he heard us coming up the mountain and got them ready."

"You weren't kidding when you mentioned me riding a horse, were you?" I pulled one of the double scuba tanks out of the back and stood it against the wheel of the Jeep. "You know how long it's been since I rode a horse?"

"Do I win something if I guess right?"

"No."

"Then what's the point of guessing?" she asked as she pulled out a large sack of groceries.

"So you won't laugh when I fall off."

"I'll still laugh."

Before I had a chance to answer, there was a loud snapping of branches and Fred appeared out of the trees on the left side of the clearing. He was riding backwards on a medium-sized brown horse while leading seven other horses.

It was the funniest sight I had seen in a long time. His long legs dangled down the side of the horse, his feet only loosely caught backwards in the stirrups. He looked like Ichabod Crane, except he had on blue work jeans, a red plaid work shirt, and the most beat-up excuse for a baseball cap I had ever seen. He even had the damn cap on backwards.

Constance looked over at me. "He does that all the time. Says it works better when he has to lead more than three horses. I'm waiting for a low tree limb to knock him on his nose."

I just kept laughing. Fred smiled and tipped his cap as the train of horses filled the small turnaround. He was still the same old Fred. Down in town, he had lost some of his craziness over the past few years. But up here, it was clear that he was his old self. Probably the thin air did things to his brain.

Constance moved to help him with the horses and I followed.

"Glad to see you could make it, barkeep," Fred said as he dismounted, somehow without kicking the horse in the head. His handshake was firm. His skin felt hard and calloused against my bartender-soft hand.

"Wouldn't have missed seeing your trick riding for all the money in the world. Besides, that Sunday drive up the mountain is a real thrill a minute."

Fred chuckled as he unhooked two horses from the string and tied them to a tree. "Constance doesn't believe in wasting any time, does she?"

"It wasn't that bad," Constance said as she led two other horses toward the Jeep.

I held up my hands, fingers curled. "Permanent white knuckles."

"Comes with age," Constance said. "And you certainly aren't getting any younger. Besides, I got us here, didn't I?"

"And just in time," Fred said. "Lunch is cooking and I wasn't planning on waiting for you two."

I glanced at my watch. It was only eleven in the morning yet it seemed like we'd been on the road a full day. Or more like a full lifetime.

We spent the next half hour packing all the dive gear and supplies on the horses while chatting about everything except the ghost and the lodge. By the time we were done, I was sweating and a little out of breath from the high altitude. But I felt better inside than I had in years. There was something about being out in the mountains with close friends that surrounds a person with a warm glow of belonging. Maybe it was the openness of the air and the trees. Or maybe it was

the lack of the confines of buildings that reminded us of our pasts. All I knew was that working there with Constance and Fred made me feel good.

Fred's "cooked" lunch consisted of ham sandwiches and cold lemonade, with the promise of a better lunch once we reached the valley floor. We ate quickly and before I knew it, I was on a horse for the first time in too many years and headed off into the Idaho primitive area.

***

Two and a half hours later we reached the Monumental Valley floor. My back ached, the insides of both legs were rubbed raw, and my face felt as if it were coated with three inches of dust. I had completely lost any feelings of wellbeing I had had about the trip. Now all I wondered was why anyone would want to do something like this for fun.

Not that it hadn't been fantastic at the start. The trail along the summit had stayed wide, winding its way along

the ridge for about a mile through open meadows and stands of pine. The clear smell of the air, the warm sun, the power of the horses had made everything seem so easy.

The trail had turned to the right and headed down the side of a ridge into a picture-postcard valley. The steep walls on both sides cut upward to end in linked chains of rocky mountain peaks. Patches of snow still dotted the walls of the valley, reflecting the sun like slivers of mirrors. Far below I could see flashes of deep blue as a stream wound its way through the trees.

At that point in the trail I could look back and see where we had been riding. The cars were parked on a low saddle between the mountain ridges. The valley we were dropping into seemed to dead-end into that saddle.

"It's nothing but downhill from here," Fred had said at that point. He hadn't been kidding. The trail became so narrow and so steep, that I found myself leaning into the hill for fear of sliding off the horse and not hitting the ground for hundreds of feet. Fred and Constance didn't seem to mind, even the two times we had to stop, dismount, and lead the horses across places where mud and rocks had slid down the mountain and wiped the trail away.

About a hundred yards beyond where the trail bottomed out, Fred led us down into a small meadow beside what he said was Monumental Creek. I let Fred take my horse and the packhorse I had been leading and tie them up while I found a nice, solid rock next to the stream and proceeded to alternate taking a drink and washing my face off with the icy water. By the time I felt refreshed enough to wander back up to the meadow, Constance had a fire going in a ring of rocks near a small grove of trees and Fred had a hammock strung and was already stretched out in it.

"Looks like you two stop here regularly," I said, pointing at prerigged hammock hooks on the trees.

"Every time," Constance said. "We take turns cooking and lying in the hammock. Doing the entire trip to the summit is just too much without a rest. We usually stop here for an hour or so. Gives the muscles time to loosen back up. Plus we figured our guests would like it here."

"And the creek there has a little color in it," Fred said. "I show the guests how to work a pan. They get a kick out of it."

"You're kidding," I said, glancing back at where I had washed my face.

"Don't let Fred get you going," Constance said. "There's very little gold left in that stream. And besides, the water will freeze your hands blue after only one try."

"Not if you do it right," Fred said. "Trust me, there's gold in there. I don't have the source spotted yet. It's somewhere above here, but I haven't had the time to go searching, what with building the lodge and everything. Bet you haven't dipped a pan in years. You want to give it a go?"

"Next time," I said, more interested than I let show. I sat on a cut-off stump and watched as Constance expertly built us a quick snack.

"You know," I said, finally breaking the unspoken rule that we wouldn't talk about the ghost or the dive until later. "What I would really like to know is more about this old town. What are we going to find down there? You got any idea?"

Fred shook his head. "Not much, I'm afraid. They didn't believe in securing buildings to foundations in the old mining towns. And since all the buildings were made of logs, everything floated, broke apart, and jammed into where the stream topped over the slide. There's a huge log-jam there. The water is as cold as that stream and with the long, frozen winters, I doubt if there will be much down there but old foundations and a lot of junk.

"So what's the point? Won't the old site be covered with two or three feet of silt?"

Fred shrugged. "Most of the town site is in about seventy to eighty feet of water. There's going to be some silt, but not as much as you might guess. The lake is relatively near the top of this valley and the stream doesn't have much time to pick up the mud and sediment that would fill in the lake. What sand and stuff the stream does pick up is dropped near the upper end. There's a pretty good sandbar built up there over the years. It has some color in it too."

"So how big was this town?"

"During the peak mining seasons," Constance said, "over five thousand people. The last few years before the flood, the gold boom had started to die off and on the day the slide buried the town, there were less than seven hundred living there. Of course, that was in the spring and the summer influx of miners hadn't yet returned."

Fred shook his head and the hammock with him. "That town was an amazing place. It was famous for its saloons, wild summer nights, and pianos."

"Pianos?" I asked. "Why would a town be famous for its pianos?"

"Because there were seven of them in town," Fred said. "All in the main saloons."

"So?" I couldn't figure out why pianos in a 1909 town were such a big deal. I always figured there were a lot of them around.

"You just came down the main trail," Fred said, gesturing at the hill above us. "That trail hasn't changed much in

seventy years. Can you imagine getting a piano down that?"

"You're kidding?"

"Nope," Constance said. "There are two other trails in the area. Both worse. One comes in over the summit up Mule Creek. That's where the Dewey Mine was. The other comes up Monumental Creek from the River of No Return area of the Salmon. There was never a wagon in Roosevelt that wasn't built there. Yet somehow they had seven pianos."

"Amazing," I said, glancing up at the tall mountains that towered above us like huge walls.

"Sure is, isn't it?" Fred said. "And the music's pretty amazing, too."

The voice in the back of my head screamed at me not to ask. But I was already into this mess past the point of turning back, so I did anyway. "Music?"

"Damn it, Fred," Constance said. "Give him time to get used to the ghost before springing anything else on him."

"It's part of the ghost," Fred said.

"There's more than the ghost?" I asked. I didn't like the sound of that.

"We're not sure the music is caused by the ghost," Constance said.

"I think it is," Fred said. "Makes lots of sense."

"Would someone please tell me about this music?"

Fred looked at Constance and then smiled. Constance shook her head in disgust and went back to working at the food. "Every so often," Fred said, "usually in the evenings, someone starts playing a piano."

"And I assume you're going to tell me you don't have one and neither do the neighbors." This entire thing was starting to stretch even my belief in Fred. They had to be suckering me into some big joke that they'd spring when we got to the lodge. Angie was probably involved in it too, and they would be laughing at me for months.

"That's right," Fred said with the straightest face I had ever seen. He had a good poker face. But after all the years, I knew when he was wearing it. This time he was being dead serious. And he looked embarrassed about it.

I turned to Constance. "Is he kidding?"

She shook her head no. I could see in her eyes she too was telling the truth.

I just sat there. A ghost that roamed around a lake. And someone playing piano music in the middle of the Idaho wilderness. It was all too much. If it hadn't been Fred and Constance I wouldn't have listened to it for a moment.

Constance handed Fred, then me, a cup of coffee. The smell was like a comforting hand that said I hadn't yet left the world of reality. Coffee was civilization and civilization was still here, at least for the time being.

"Why don't you tell him about the legend?" Constance said.

"There's a legend, too?" I asked. "No, don't tell me. Big Foot drops by every twenty years and he's due this week. Right?"

Fred laughed. "Believe it or not, there really is a legend about the music. Constance found it down at the historical society after our first visit up here. It's in some book—"

"*Legends of the Frontier*," Constance said, "by Nelson. A great book."

"Yeah," Fred said. "It is. The one about the music is called *The Legend of Lake Roosevelt*. I got a copy of it here somewhere. It'll be just as easy if I read it to you." Fred climbed out of the hammock and rummaged in one of the saddlebags they'd brought over to the clearing. After

a short moment, he pulled a few folded sheets of paper out and opened them up. He didn't get back into the hammock, but instead sat in it like a chair and rocked as he studied the paper in his hands.

He took a sip on his coffee, then looked up. "You ready?"

I shrugged. "Couldn't be any wilder than some of the things I've heard so far."

He laughed. "True. Here goes: 'To hear the pianos of Roosevelt, the listener must follow instructions.'"

"A legend with instructions?" I tried not to snicker. "What do you have to do, climb the third tree from the lake and put your ear to the trunk?"

"You really don't have to do anything," Constance said. "You can hear the music all over the valley."

She said it so matter-of-factly, it made me shudder. I suddenly had a great desire to stand and move back out into the warm sun of the meadow and let the heat on my shoulders remind me I really hadn't gone crazy. But I sipped my coffee instead as Fred started reading again.

"The listener is to make camp at the upper end of the lake where Monumental Creek has laid a fine carpet of sand and rock, overgrown in places with light brush. The valley walls on both sides will be steep, climbing almost vertically for thousands of feet. The slope to the left as you face the lake will be tree-covered and thick with brush."

"That's where the lodge and cabins are," Constance said. "About three hundred feet above the water. Had to clear a massive amount of scrub."

"She's not kidding there," Fred said, holding up his hand. "Remember those thick calluses we used to show you every fall?"

I nodded.

"Bush and logs," he said. Then he went back to reading.

"The slope to the right, the West, will be mostly free of tall pine. Instead it will be covered with large rockslides and cliff faces."

"Is that where the slide came from?" I asked.

Constance shook her head. "Nope. It was on that side of the canyon all right. But the slide was completely mud and whatever else it picked up along the way. The slide came down Mule Creek which drains into Monumental right below the town. A lot of the mining was up Mule Creek, so that's why they built the town where they did. Besides that, it was the widest place in miles."

"You know," Fred said, "there's still two cases of dynamite unexploded under that slide? They tried to blow it to stop the slide, but it didn't go off."

"You mean they had time to fight it?"

Fred nodded. "Lots of time. The accounts of what happened that night say the slide was moving about as fast as a man could walk. It started three miles up Mule Creek, right below the Dewey Mine."

I just shook my head. "Could the dynamite still be dangerous?"

"I doubt it," Fred said. "Would take something pretty strong to set it off, even if it was still any good after eighty years in the ground."

"Amazing," I said, again.

Fred nodded and went back to reading the legend.

"The sand flat above the lake will be marked with stone fireplace rings, black pimples against the white sand.

The listener should choose to camp to the right of the trail that leads to the lake from Monumental Summit and at the nearest fireplace ring to the lake and the rock slope."

"A few people still camp there every summer," Constance said. "But they rarely stay for longer than a night. The place spooks them."

"I can understand that," I said. "It spooks me and I haven't even seen it yet."

"The listener should have dinner early. Then, as the light slowly drains from the sky between the towering ridges the listener should let the crackling of the camp's fire die down."

Fred looked quickly up as Constance set his lunch beside him on a stump.

"The listener should then beware. His ears will pick out other sounds from the forest twilight. Birds fluttering in the branches. Fish jumping after one last insect. Maybe even the sound of a

chipmunk clattering up among the rocks. The listener must try to push those sounds into the background."

As Fred read, I found myself becoming aware of all the sounds around us. The fire's soft cracking as it licked the bottom of the large water pot Constance had sitting across two rocks. The slight breeze clipping the tops of the trees with a light brushing sound. The clear, but distant background bubbling of the creek as it tumbled over rocks on its way toward the submerged town. And every so often, the cawing of a distant hawk cut through the clear air of the valley and echoed off the mountain walls.

"The listener must now try to focus his attention completely on the cold water of the lake. He must try to imagine the old Main Street spread out at his feet. He must see the miners as they celebrated the end of the day and their success or failure in the saloons that framed the street like nails in a coffin lid. Then, and only then, will the listener hear the music of Lake Roosevelt."

Fred looked up at me with a raised-eyebrow sort of look.

"Some crazy legend." I took another sip of coffee. Damn, it was getting cold in this shady little nook. The sunlight that filled the meadow looked like water to a thirsty man. I took a big gulp of the hot coffee and let the heat work its way toward my stomach. Fred and his damn ghost stories. If this was all a joke, I was going to kill him.

"There's still more to it," Fred said as Constance handed me a plate filled with corn, potato chips, and a great-smelling hamburger.

Constance filled her plate while Fred and I took big bites of our hamburgers. Then Fred went back to reading from the papers in his lap.

"If the listener hears the music, he must understand the reason is a simple one. The town submerged before him prided itself on one aspect more than even the gold it fought out of the hills and streams. Its pianos."

Fred glanced up at me, then over at Constance. Then he continued.

"Seven pianos, one for each of the famous saloons along Main Street. Every night, the seven battling pianos filled the narrow valley with sound, pouring from their gun-barrel saloon doors. And for years, the pines took every song and held it in their sap and their needles. The rocks let the notes seep into their cracks and crevices like water, then trapped them. The great mountains, Thunder to the west, Monumental to the east, took the music and laid a net of echoes between them until the songs supported themselves in the night without touching the stars.

"The listener must be alert, for the concert only lasts a short time. The mountains and the rocks and the trees are jealous of their songs. Also, the listener should not be surprised if all but one of the pianos drops out of the musical war. The listener who hears this should consider himself treated to a special concert, for the remaining piano's music will be clear and crisp, as if the listener were standing right outside the saloon door. The playing will be fine, practiced. But the song will feel sad and somehow lost. The listener should look around as the dim night shadows of the pines will seem to sway to the melody of the solo.

"And, if the listener still has the courage at this point to not throw an extra log on the fire and start whistling his own tune, he just might recognize the song."

Fred stopped reading and folded the paper.

"You might get to hear the music tonight," Constance said.

"Lovely," I said. "Just lovely. And we're going to make a dive down into that lake?"

Fred nodded. "Crazy, huh?"

I nodded and took a bite of my hamburger. Crazy didn't even begin to describe what we were going to do.

CHAPTER THREE

Monumental Lodge
June 26, 1990

"ALMOST THERE," FRED said over his shoulder as we rounded a curve and started to climb. "You'll be able to see the lake in another hundred yards or so."

I nodded and tried to adjust my position in the saddle for the thousandth time in the last four miles. There wasn't a spot left on my ass that wasn't sore or bruised. Four o'clock in the morning had been a long time ago.

The sun had dropped below the edge of the high mountains and over the last few hours the line between bright light and dark shadows had worked its way up the steep slopes like the waterline in a filling bathtub, leaving the tops of the mountains tinted pink. The moment the direct

sunlight had left the valley floor, the air had turned a crisp, biting cold. Three miles back I had put on both my sweater and light jacket, and if the ride went on much farther, I was going to ask Fred to stop so that I could dig out my ski parka.

The main trail branched to the left and climbed hard up the left side of the valley away from the streambed we had been following. Fred took the high road and after a short distance pointed down. Through a gap in the trees I could see a small section of the lake and the part of the sandbar the legend had talked about. In the shadow-filled light, the water looked black, as if the valley was filled from side to side with a pool of ink. Every so often a ripple spread out on the glass surface as an insect or fish broke the calm.

At first nothing about the small lake seemed unusual as I studied it through the branches of the trees. No ghost walked its banks. No music stirred from its black depths. It seemed like any of the hundreds of other small mountain lakes I had seen over the years.

Almost. The more I studied it, the more the lake felt different. Colder. Alien.

I pulled my jacket tight in front and tried not to shiver. The thought of diving into those black waters seemed ludicrous. Granted, Fred and I had pulled a lot of crazy stunts over the years. And by and large got away with them. But somewhere, sometime, there was going to be one we couldn't do.

Up ahead, Fred turned left off the main trail, kicking his horse to move straight up the steep slope. The two packhorses he was leading scrambled to follow.

Through the trees farther down the main trail I could see a two-story log structure built into the side of the steep hill. Two large windows on the main floor stood guard over a wide clearing and the black lake. Both windows gave off a yellow glow that lit the deck railing around the front of the building. Smoke curled from the top of a rough stone chimney on the near end, giving me a sense of warmth that cut through the chill.

At the same spot, I turned to follow Fred. As firmly as I could, I coaxed my horse up the steep slope, at any moment fearing that either a cinch would come loose and I would slide right off the back to be trampled by the packhorse, or that my horse would just tip over from being on too steep a slope and smash down on top of me. I'd seen that happen in a dozen old movies and it always made me flinch.

Miraculously neither happened and I made it up to the log stable behind the main building, breathing hard, but still seated on all the spots the saddle had rubbed raw.

Fred dismounted and tied his horse to a long bar outside the back door of the lodge. I nudged my horse into place beside Fred's packhorses and then did my best to dismount without kicking anyone or anything.

I'd thought I was sore while sitting. Getting down, I felt so stiff it was a wonder I could move at all. My legs felt weak, almost as if my weight was too much for them. I leaned against the horse and took turns shifting from one foot to the other to give each a fair shot at recovery.

"Here we are," Fred said. "That wasn't so bad, now was it?"

Constance moved her horse into place beside my packhorse and slowly dismounted, obviously feeling some of the same aches that I did.

"Ask me in the morning," I said. "Assuming that I live that long." I rubbed the back of my legs and then my shoulders. My body was so full of kinks I didn't know where to rub first. My face felt like it had two inches of dust on it and if I smiled too hard, it would all cake right off, taking the first four layers of skin with it.

Fred moved around to help Constance with the two packhorses she had been leading. "Believe it or not," Constance said, leaning against the rail and brushing one layer of dust off, "we feel exactly the same way the first few trips in and out every spring. But you almost get used to it."

"Don't let her kid you," Fred said. "You'll be able to hear her groan clear across the valley when she crawls out of bed tomorrow morning."

"It will be a duet, I'm sure," I said.

Both of them laughed. The thousand aches that made up my body didn't think it was so funny.

"Twenty minutes to get this all unloaded and the horses taken care of." Fred said. "Then you can hit the hot shower. Guaranteed to work wonders on

horse-type aches and pains." He looked over at where Constance was pulling a saddlebag off one horse. "Whose turn is it to cook?"

"You know whose turn it is," Constance said, as she carried the saddlebag over and dropped it with a loud thump on the wooden back porch of the lodge. "And it's not going to even get started until I get into a hot shower and then some clean clothes. Besides, if I cook, you do the horses. Remember?"

Fred patted the neck of the horse he had been riding. "How could I ever forget?"

***

It took closer to an hour before we had all the gear stored, my bag up in my room on the second floor of the lodge, and my body standing under a hot shower washing away the smell of horses. Fred made me promise that no matter how good it felt, I would make it quick. Hot water was scarce since all they had was one water heater powered by a generator. He didn't want to take a cold shower.

I promised him. But it was a hard promise to keep.

After far too short a time, I fought my way out of the shower, put on a fresh pair of cotton work pants, my most comfortable shirt, and a thick wool sweater. I carried my shoes and padded in my socks down the wooden stairs.

The Monumental Lodge was one of those big, open-roomed places where the minute you walked in, you just knew deep down inside that you'd found the home you'd always wanted. The walls and rafters were all made of large, rough logs, filled in between with a light brown chinking. The kitchen sat in the right back corner as you entered from the main door.

Directly to the right of the main door, in front of a large, small-paned window that overlooked the lower end of the lake, was a huge wooden table with a dozen chairs around it.

A stone fireplace filled the left wall, surrounded by a number of handmade couches and chairs padded with an abundance of throw pillows. The stairs went up the back wall to the one bathroom and two bedrooms upstairs. I dropped my shoes by the front door and walked slowly around the room, glancing at a few of the old pictures and odd knickknacks. The room made me feel cozy and warm, even with only a small fire in the massive mouth of the fireplace.

Constance had been first in the shower and she was now preparing dinner.

"Feel better?" she asked as I wandered into the kitchen.

"Six thousand percent," I said. "Anything I can do to help?"

"Sure is. See that cabinet there beside the back door?"

I nodded. It was a rough wood cabinet with no sign of a lock. An old picture of six miners standing with shovels in front of an open mine shaft hung beside it.

She slid a ceramic mug across the counter. "Pour a little rum in that for me. Then fix yourself whatever you want. Figure I might as well let you do what you do best."

I picked up her mug, enjoying the heavy feel of the stoneware in my hand. "What's this for? Rum toddy?"

"Hot buttered rum."

"Sounds too good to pass. Toss me a mug too."

She slid another across the counter and I went to the well-stocked liquor cabinet.

"You folks sure know how to spend your summers," I said, inspecting the supply of booze that would have made a small public bar proud.

"It's been a lot of work."

"Obviously. All a person has to do is look at this place to see that. Have I told you how impressed I am with all this?"

Constance looked at me with one of those very serious expressions reserved for marriages, funerals, or corporate boardrooms. "You mean it?"

"Of course I do. This place is fantastic."

"That means a lot to me," she said. "Really. Make sure you tell Fred. He's afraid you'll think this is all stupid. What with the ghost and all."

"It's far from stupid. And I'll make sure Fred knows that. All right?"

"Thanks," Constance said. She gave me one of her light-up-the-room smiles and went back to working on dinner.

"In fact," I said, "even if you can't think of a better way to get me in here than on some stupid horse, I think you've made a regular customer out of me. Assuming, of course, I survive the ride out."

"You will," Constance said. "Wait until you see the cabins. They're really cozy. Perfect for that getaway with your current lady. And that reminds me, just who is your current lady these days?"

"No one," I said, and then kneeled down in front of the liquor cabinet. That was one topic I really didn't feel like talking about. In the years since Carla had died, I had spent very little time with any other woman. Somehow, I would end up comparing every one to Carla and that would be the end of that. For most of the last year I'd been keeping company only with myself and almost enjoying it. At least, that's what I kept repeating to myself. Just as I kept telling myself I enjoyed tending bar at the Garden.

I finished putting the rum in the two mugs and went back to the counter. "Mix?" I held up the mugs.

"In the fridge. And the water should be almost boiling."

I dug the mix out, added the hot water, and then sat down on one of the bar stools facing across the counter into the kitchen as Constance began her standard quiz about my invisible love life. For years she had been trying to set me up with one woman after another. None of the ones she had picked had ever lasted more than a date or two. But she showed no signs of giving up.

Fred came down the stairs at the same time footsteps sounded on the front deck, the front door opened, and two people came in without knocking.

I turned around on my stool, cradling my hot buttered rum in my hands, and studied the two new arrivals as they took off their heavy jackets and hung them on hooks beside the front door. They did it without hesitation, as if they were very used to doing so.

The man looked to be in his late thirties, about my height, maybe six foot one, with a full head of graying black hair, and a sincere smile. Clear across the room, I liked the guy. I didn't want to like him. But for some reason, on first glance, I did. Annoying. Damned annoying.

That happened once in a while with a customer in the Garden. I would like certain people even before they said a word. The ones that I had been lucky enough to get to know ended up following along with my first impression. It had also happened a lot back when I was teaching. There was always one, sometimes two, students in the class that I would instantly like. It had been hard not to give the favorites too much extra attention. Angie had been one of those students.

The woman was young, maybe middle twenties. She had striking silver hair, cut in a short, page-boy haircut. She wore a "University of Idaho" sweatshirt and Levi's as if they were the most natural things in the world. I could tell that her small green eyes didn't miss a thing. The feeling I had about her was one of distrust. No more reason for it than for my liking the guy.

Fred, now wearing a thick baggy sweater and a wool stocking cap on his bald head, did the introductions and I again assumed my role as bartender. Susan Rule wanted a touch of gin with a lot of soda. A very unusual combination. Professor Steven Jerome wanted scotch, a splash of water, lots of ice. He was a drinker's drinker. Another reason I liked him.

I handed Steven his drink, then slid Susan's across the table to where she had sat with her back to the now-dark window. As I did, I noticed she was staring at me as if trying to remember something and not really being able to.

"Fred said your name was Kellogg Jones?" she asked after I sat back down on my stool at the counter. "Do you happen to go by a nickname of some sort or another?"

I nodded.

"Sure," Fred said as he sat down at the table with a can of beer. "Everyone calls him Doc. Why?"

Susan's face drained of color and she looked quickly down into her drink. Then, as if deciding that the drink would help, took a deep gulp of it.

"Why?" I asked, after I got over shuddering from the thought of how bad gin and soda must taste. "Have we ever met?" I knew we hadn't. I'd have remembered her. With or without the silver hair.

"No, we haven't," she said after a quick moment in which all of us looked at her. She smiled a weak smile. "The name reminds me of someone out of my past, that's all."

"I hope it's not a bad memory," I said. Judging from her reaction, there didn't seem much hope of that.

"No, it's fine. Your name just caught me a little off guard, that's all."

I nodded, not believing a word she was saying. "I'd change it if I could, but you know."

She laughed. "No, really. I like the name a lot. Honest." She looked me square in the eye and we held the pose for a moment. I didn't know what to think by the time she looked down into the depths of her drink and her own thoughts. There was a lot more to this woman than what showed through the surface. And she was not as young as I had thought. No one had old eyes like that without having lived awhile. No one.

***

The rest of our informal cocktail hour and dinner was filled with laughing conversation and short history lessons about everyone involved, except Susan. She steered the conversation expertly away from anything about herself, always directing it back to someone else. She was a master at it, like a good teacher who could keep the students talking.

The meal was one of those fun meals between friends and strangers where everyone was relaxed and seemed to share a common sense of adventure. Being that far back in the wilderness made everyone friendlier, more open. In my trips to mountain lakes, I always found that occurrence interesting. And I was not immune to it.

It wasn't until after Fred and I had the dishes cleared up and everyone was sitting in the big living area around the built-up fire that the topic of the ghost came up.

I started it.

"Steven," I said, trying to keep my voice as conversational as I could, "what do you think of this ghost I've been hearing about?"

Steven shrugged and took a sip of his after-dinner drink, Constance's lodge-made eggnog. He looked no more concerned about the question than if I had just asked him what time it was. "She's just a trapped spirit," he said. "And damned unhappy. One of the clearest cases in recorded study."

"Clearest what?" I asked.

"Oh, sorry," he said. "She makes more obvious appearances than any other spirit I have ever seen or read about. Very regular and very consistent."

"So this is a real ghost, then?" I asked, then glanced over at Constance and shrugged. I couldn't help it. She smiled at me.

"In the common definition of the term ghost, yes. She is very real. By the way, her name is Gretchen."

I didn't want to ask how he knew that yet, so I turned to Susan. "And you've seen this ghost? She's real as far as you're concerned?"

"Very much so," Susan said. "And anything possible should be done to free her so that she can move on. It makes me really sad every time she walks."

I sat back against the pillows of the couch and stared into the fireplace. My intellect was saying go ahead and buy it, but my stomach and all my years of believing in only the here and now was yelling at me.

"I know it's hard to understand," Steven said. "Especially when you haven't seen her yet. You obviously don't believe in ghosts. Am I right?"

I nodded.

"What kind of afterlife do you believe in?"

"None," I said. "When you're gone, you're gone. Six feet down and cold. Nothing more." I told him the truth, but lately I had been wondering. I had figured that the questions I had been asking were a natural function of getting older and having that cold end come closer and closer. But there was no way I was going to get religion. To me it made no sense. I had lived a good life. If some God did exist, and was even half of what all those churches claimed, He or She would see that. If there wasn't a God, then I certainly wasn't going to go wasting time on an insurance program of pray now, collect later.

"The simplest way to understand a habitual spirit, a ghost," Steven said, "would be to give the brain some credit. From what Fred has told me, you spent a lot of years teaching college. Right?"

"Too damn many."

"I'll drink to that," Fred said.

"So then," Steven said, "just think of a spirit as a brain that's too powerful to die. For some reason, a spirit usually has such a strong feeling for something that the power of that feeling alone does not allow the essence of the person to either dissolve, as you believe, or pass on to the next life, as the religions teach."

I had to give him credit. What he was saying made an odd sort of sense. "So then why is this Gretchen spirit still hanging around here?"

"Something happened to a man by the name of Alex and she felt he would return for her. She's been waiting since the day the town was destroyed."

"You'd think she would realize that this Alex is, in all likelihood, dead."

Steven shook his head. "Maybe not. There's a lot of evidence that trapped souls have no sense of time. And no idea who has died and who hasn't. In a few cases in the past, it has been necessary to summon spirits from the other side to help the trapped soul."

"I bought your 'power of the mind' idea," I said. "But now you're getting way past my gag level."

Steven shrugged. "Doesn't really matter with Gretchen. But I'd be glad to show the facts of other cases where such an occurrence has happened. That is, if you're interested."

I wasn't. "Maybe sometime," I said. "So tell me, why the dive into the lake?"

Steven looked over at Fred and Fred nodded for him to go ahead. "As I said, this spirit is waiting for someone named Alex to return for her. I got that much from her just in thoughts. She radiates it over and over. There is something down in the lake that is very important to her and to her search. I am unable to sense what that something is, but know for certain it is there."

"Do you believe her?" I asked.

"I have to admit," Steven said, "that I do."

"You think we might be able to help her?" Fred asked.

Steven shrugged. "We'll have to see what it is that's so important to her. If you can find it."

"What about the chance this may be some sort of trap?" I tried to mentally stop the shivers from running up and down my spine from the thought. I could see Fred shift on his seat. He didn't look too happy with the idea, either.

"I doubt it," Steven said. "But, of course, there's no way of knowing. It's not like habitual spirits to take any kind of action against the living. When some harm does come to someone, it's usually because the spirit is doing something related to its own time and the living get in the way. Evil spirits are the invention of fiction."

"But you said this Gretchen was different. Right?"

Steven nodded slowly while looking first at me, then over at Fred. "That she is. But I got no sense of animosity from her. None. She's just lost. And waiting."

I looked over at Susan and Constance. "Any opinions?" I asked. Both women shook their heads. I could tell that Constance was upset, but she wasn't going to say anything. I could imagine the arguments she and Fred must have had over this.

I turned to Fred. "What do you think we should do?"

Fred shrugged. "Doesn't seem like there's much choice. We don't stand a hell's chance of keeping this place the way we want it without getting rid of the ghost.

It looks to me like the best hope we have of doing that is on the bottom of that lake."

"It's been a long time since we've made a dive," I said. "Think we're up for it?"

"Why not?" He smiled the half-smile that I knew meant we were in trouble. "Besides, when were we ever known for doing sane things?"

"Ten years ago, almost never. And this time certainly won't be any exception."

Fred nodded as his smile disappeared. "That it won't be."

An uneasy silence dropped over the room, leaving only the crackling of the fire and the very loud stillness of the mountain night. I listened hard, expecting to hear the faint sounds of piano music drifting in from the direction of the black water.

It was obvious I wasn't the only one listening.

CHAPTER FOUR

Roosevelt Lake
June 27, 1990

"YOU GETTING CLOSE there?" I asked Fred as Susan handed me my mask and then moved back across the coarse sand of the lakeshore to talk to Constance.

"Almost," he said. "Two more minutes."

I watched him as he checked over his regulator and double tanks as I had done a few minutes before. In the old days, he had been faster at that predive routine than I was. But this time I was so nervous I did my equipment checks twice and still beat him.

I glanced down at the dive watch strapped to my wet suit. It was a little past noon. The day was one of those perfectly clear summer days in the mountains. The kind that a person always hopes to stumble across on a vacation, but never does. The lake had a deep blue tint and the fresh smell of pine was in the air. Even the sandbar beside the lake was warm. A complete switch from the way it had looked the night before.

We'd planned to start the dive around midday when the lake would be completely in the sun. Better light that way. More chance of seeing whatever it was we were supposed to find. So far, we were right on time.

But it had been one very busy morning getting ready. After breakfast, bundled against the early morning chill, we had set up a temporary camp on the sandbar twenty feet from the water's edge. Then we hauled all the diving gear down on horseback. It had taken most of two hours to get set up for just one dive for the day. We talked about the possibility of making a second dive the next day, depending on what we found. I really didn't want to think about that. This one dive was going to be more than enough as far as I was concerned.

After we had set up the gear, Fred had taken me on an exploratory walk around the lake. He used an old photo of the main street of Roosevelt to make wild stabs at where things used to be.

The photo looked like any other old photograph of a mining boomtown. The street was mud. Wood and log buildings lined both sides and all the buildings in the center of the town were two stories tall and had covered sidewalks.

As we walked along the single-file trail around the lake, I somehow kept expecting to see the ghost come shimmering up out of the water. Three or four times I caught flashes of something down through the water and swore to myself it was the ghost. Yet each time I knew it wasn't. After a while I started reminding myself that I didn't believe in ghosts, habitual or otherwise.

In the daylight, the lake looked a little bigger than it had through the trees the evening before. It filled the valley from side to side, a distance of maybe a football field. From end to end it ran a quarter of a mile, with a little twist to the left at the bottom end where the stream cut up and over the mudslide. The slide was now covered with an eighty-year-old forest and looked exactly like the rest of the mountain. Of course, Fred had to remind me, just as we were walking along the slide, about the cases of dynamite buried somewhere among the trees.

Where the water had gone over the slide, there was a huge logjam filling the upper section of the lake. The trail ended right at the logjam and started again thirty yards away on the lodge side. Fred didn't even hesitate. He walked right out on the logs, skipping and jumping from one log to the next like a six-year-old child walking along a curb.

To me, the logs didn't look that solid, even though they weren't sinking at all under Fred's weight. He stopped in the middle, straddled an open water space with each foot braced on separate logs, and motioned for me to come on.

"Take a look at this," he said, pointing down.

I eased out on the nearest log. One end was jammed into the mud of the bank. The other end disappeared twenty feet later under two other logs. It felt solid enough, so I worked my way out toward Fred. The farther from the bank I got, the more apparent it was that I was walking on the remains of broken up buildings. The logs looked like giant Tinkertoys jammed in solid from the floor of the lake all the way to the surface. Down through the clear water I could see layer after layer twisted and turned in all directions like a mixed-up spider web.

I made it to Fred's location, braced myself so that I wouldn't slip, and took a look at what he was pointing at. It was an open space of water running like a well down through the logs. I figured I could see maybe fifty feet down with no sign of the bottom. A large trout swam lazily out of the shadows of one of the logs and then disappeared under another.

"I tried to fish here once. Hooked a good sized rainbow and immediately lost it in the logs. Dumb thing to try." Fred laughed as he looked around. "A bunch of timber, huh?"

"That it is," I said, trying to get an idea of just how many buildings it would take to jam this much of the lake solid. "Think there's much left standing down there?"

"From the looks of this," Fred said. "I doubt if there's anything at all. You ought to see the pictures in the historical society, taken on the day the town was flooding. Some guy took it from a place back up there." Fred pointed up the mountain wall across the lake.

"It shows most of the large buildings on Main Street twisting and floating as the lake got deeper and deeper. Hell, an entire area of town was just tents laid out in rows like in the army. Can't imagine spending a winter up here in one of those. But I guess some people did."

"Does seem amazing, doesn't it?" I looked down through the layers of toy-like logs, each one obviously hand cut. The entire valley was amazing. No wonder Fred and Constance had picked it. There was more than enough history and exploring to do here to keep their guests interested in the Old West for weeks on end.

***

"I think I got it," Fred said, patting the top of his tank. He looked over at me. "Ready?"

"No. But when did that ever matter?" The butterflies were having a great time in my stomach. I wanted to go back up on that huge front deck around the lodge and sit, stare off at the mountains, and drink.

"Tanks," Constance said as she held up Fred's dual scuba tanks so that he could slip his arm through the straps. Susan moved over and did the same for me. Carla used to help me, but that seemed a lifetime ago. I couldn't imagine what she would have said about this nutty dive.

I let the tank's vaguely familiar weight nestle down against the middle of my back as I tightened the straps into place. I had to admit, it almost felt good. For the first time in years, I could feel my heart pounding from something other than bending over to move a beer keg.

Susan turned my air valve on with a quick turn and then slid the mouthpiece over my shoulder. "You're on and ready," she said. I glanced back at her. She obviously knew diving.

"Good luck," she said. She wasn't smiling.

I slipped the regulator into my mouth and bit lightly. It tasted of disinfectant and rubber. An odd, but familiar, taste from my past. I took a couple of deep breaths to check if everything was working properly, then glanced at my gauges. Right on the money. I picked up my fins from the log beside my dive pack. "All set?"

Fred finished a check of his regulator and nodded.

I worked my way across the sand and rocks to the edge of the water, sat down, and let my legs float. Damn, it was cold. I could feel it right through the wet suit. I wasn't looking forward to letting the water trickle inside my suit, let alone trying to let my body warmth heat that water up.

"Cold, huh?" Fred said as he sat down on the sand beside me and kicked his legs a few times.

"Maybe we should wait until we get some dry suits," I said. I could feel the water starting to trickle down into my boot lining. It felt as if the lake were trying to pull my body heat right through the rubber.

"I think we'll be all right," Fred said. "For as short a time as we're going to be down there."

"Just make sure that if you start getting too cold, you signal for the surface. I'll do the same." I looked Fred square in the eye to make sure he was hearing me.

"Deal, partner," he said, then smiled. I knew he was serious. He was as concerned about us making this dive as I was. He wasn't going to be doing anything beyond his limit. That made me feel a little better. Not much, but a little.

I turned to Constance, Susan, and Steven. "Any sign of the ghost yet? We could use a tour guide."

All three of them glanced out over the lake and then shook their heads.

"Just kidding," I said and turned back, facing out over the water. "Not funny, I guess," I whispered to Fred.

He chuckled, then pulled his mask on.

I pulled the hood of my wet suit up into place, inflated my flotation vest enough to keep me afloat, grabbed my mask in one hand, and pushed off into the water with the other.

The biting sting of the water cut at my skin as the first trickles seeped into my wet suit. For some reason, the first drops that got inside the wet suit always went right down my spine and into my crotch, a feeling I had never gotten used to and always dreaded. This time was no different. Maybe even worse. I suddenly felt short of air and forced myself to take longer, deeper, and much slower breaths.

I floated, half-turned up on my back, working on making sure my mask would stay clear, then getting it snug down onto my face. We stopped thirty feet out from the shore, facing the three watchers.

"Follow our bubbles along the trail there with the extra tank," Fred yelled, pointing to the path along the right side of the lake. "We have any troubles, we'll surface and go that way."

Constance nodded. We'd worked the plan out beforehand, but for some reason, Fred seemed to want to make sure it was clear.

"Be careful down there," Constance shouted.

"We will," Fred yelled. He turned to face me. "Ready?"

I took a couple deep breaths through my regulator, then pulled it aside. "Ready. But let's watch this cold."

He adjusted his mask and gave me a thumbs-up sign.

I quickly dashed water one last time through my facemask. *Here we go, ready or not. Crazy. Nothing but crazy.*

I let some air slowly out of my vest and sank below the surface. I had forgotten a lot of the feelings of being under water. First off, my breathing echoed through my head, making me sound like the villain in a dozen bad slasher movies. Also the feeling of weightlessness returned. A feeling of freedom. How could I have forgotten that?

As my ears popped the first time, the words of a song began to play along in my head in time with my breathing. *We're off to see a ghost. A wonderful, wonderful ghost.* I couldn't get the stupid tune from *The Wizard of Oz* out of my head. Of course, there was no doubt we were off to see something and this sure wasn't Kansas. I tried to clear the song away, but it kept floating around in my mind until I drifted to a stop on the bottom. Amazing what a person thinks about when he's under stress.

My wrist gauge said we were in twenty-six feet of water. The bottom was smooth and sloped quickly away toward the lower half of the lake and the slide. From the looks of the slope, the main site of the old town might be in eighty or ninety feet of water instead of only sixty. I hoped not. At that depth, the light would be bad.

I shot a little more air back into my vest so that I couldn't stand on the bottom, but not enough to send me back to the surface. Then I looked around.

Fred was holding onto the stump of an old tree to my right as I faced down the slope. He worked for a moment on adjusting his vest, then looked up at me and gave me the okay sign.

I pointed down the valley and he nodded. We started slowly swimming through the clear water, side by side, about eight feet off the lake floor and an arm's length apart.

Down the slope stood an underwater grove of a dozen or so old pine trees. They had most of their branches and looked dark and eerie in the shimmering light. Tucked in below them were the foundation of a small building and the stones of its fireplace and front step.

As we passed the small grove, the bottom leveled out and it became apparent that we were swimming over what was once the town's main street. Probably its only street. On both sides of us now were mounds, buried foundations of buildings lost under eighty years of silt. Shallow holes marked others. It seemed that the entire town was part of the logjam. Nothing but old trees and a few stone fireplaces broke through the silt bottom.

We drifted over one of the foundation mounds. Besides the fireplace stones and a few other lumps covered by silt, there was nothing to see. I swam over to one of the lumps and brushed aside the four or so inches of silt. It turned out to be an old bucket, upside down and so rusted that it came apart in my hand.

I shrugged at Fred and swam back up out of the drifting cloud I had stirred up. We had no hope of finding anything down here. That was becoming very clear.

He pointed down the valley and I nodded yes.

It was then that I saw the ghost.

She was twenty yards away, in the middle of the old road, walking away from us. She wore an old-fashioned light blue dress with lace around the neck. Her hair was tied back and there was a feeling of determination about her.

I grabbed Fred's arm and pointed, but he had already seen her. All I wanted to do was head for the surface. Fast. Damn fast. I didn't want anything to do with a woman who could walk under forty feet of water. No damn way.

After a moment, I calmed down enough to take a breath and slow my heart so that it wouldn't come flying right out of my wet suit. After all the talk about her in the last few days, I thought I was going to be prepared when I finally saw her. How stupid that though had been. No one can be prepared to see something so obviously not a part of the world as we know it. Her very presence blew apart everything I had ever thought about death. Forty years of believing one way and suddenly a woman walks along the bottom of a lake and it's all shot to hell.

At that moment, it took every ounce of hard thought and concentration to not go

madly streaking for the surface. I desperately wanted to be out of the lake, out of that cold, and a damn long ways away from that ghost. But somehow I made myself hold still until I was under control. Then I glanced at Fred. Through his mask I could see that his eyes were as big as I imagined mine were, and he'd seen her hundreds of times before. After a moment he seemed to shake his head and then turn to me and give me the question sign. Were we going to follow her or head for the surface?

Follow her, obviously, was the answer the little voice in the back of my head said over the top of the wall of fear that was freezing my arms and legs. We were doing this dive because of her. Just because we were now faced with actually going swimming with a ghost was no reason to stop now. My mind laughed at that one and another song from *The Wizard of Oz* popped back into my head. *Lions and tigers and ghosts, oh my.*

I made myself take slow, measured breaths as I watched her walk away. She seemed to walk on a surface that was five to ten inches below the lake bottom. She left no footprints and stirred up none of the silt. As Steven had said the night before, she wasn't really here. She was still walking the road of the old town.

After watching her for a moment longer, I finally calmed my breathing and my heart rate enough to give Fred the shrug sign. What the hell. We'd come this far. Of course that kind of attitude was the same as throwing good money away on a poker hand you know you should have folded right at the beginning. Sometimes you have to keep on and see what turns up. Stupid, I think was the word for it.

Fred nodded and we swam to a position about twenty feet behind her, square above in the middle of the main road and about ten feet off the bottom. Ahead, I could see where the main part of the town had been. Large, flat areas framed the sunken street. A few broken logs jutted out of the smooth surface of the silt. A small school of fish swam around the remains of an old stove. Two rails where horses had been tied still fenced one side of the street. And hundreds of small mounds indicated junk buried under the silt.

The ghost angled left and stepped up on what must have been a wooden sidewalk. She paused and went through motions as if she was tugging on something, banging her fists against an unseen wall.

Fred and I stopped over the middle of the street and watched her pantomime. My stomach was clamped up tight and I had to remind myself to slow my breathing. Otherwise I was going to suck down the entire tank of air in the next five minutes.

There had been a building there and she was trying to get in. After she seemed to slip in the silt, yet no silt was disturbed, she moved to the right, down a few steps and around the side of the flat area, using her hands to steady herself on unseen walls.

I caught Fred's arm and gave him an arms-up question sign. He shrugged and shook his head. He didn't know any more about what she was doing than I did. Whatever it was, it was damn creepy to watch.

She moved around to the other side of the flat area, up a few more unseen steps, and onto what must have been the floor of an old building. The floor had stayed, but the building and everything in it had floated. Her feet seemed to walk on the old floor surface, about two inches below the silt.

After a moment she moved toward us, up another unseen stair and then stopped, seeming to touch something. Her actions were so real, so exact, that for a moment

I thought I caught a glimmer of what she was touching.

Then, as she bent over and pulled something out of the front of her dress, the water around her flickered like an old movie and suddenly there was an old upright piano in front of her. I could see the silt and her dress through the piano, but the piano was clearly there. Almost as if it were glass.

She pulled an unseen bench from under it, sat down, and rested her hands on the keyboard. The resulting chord was off key and she pulled back from the piano.

Right at that moment, as that impossible sound cut through my already cold body, it took every ounce of willpower I had to not swim as hard as I could for the surface. I didn't want to see what I was watching. I didn't want to listen to a ghost play a piano where no music was possible. I wanted to sit at the Garden's bar and drink and try to force the image of this woman out of my mind and back into the dark where it belonged.

But instead I floated over the middle of the old street and watched.

She made motions to warm her hands over something on top of the piano, then started playing. The song was beautiful, haunting, filled with desire and feeling.

Fred grabbed my arm and gestured hard for the surface. I didn't need to ask him why. If Constance could hear this music in the middle of the day, she'd think something was wrong. I was right beside him all the way as the impossible music chased us from the dark.

***

Breaking through the surface and into the bright sunlight was like being shaken from a bad nightmare. It felt so good to know it had only been a dream. I pulled off my mask and tried to let the warm rays cut through the first layer of cold. It had felt like a dream, but it hadn't been one. I was still floating beside Fred in the cold water and below us the music was still playing.

"Find anything?" Constance shouted from the bank. I turned around. Constance, Susan, and Steven were all watching us. Steven held the extra tank and looked as if he was about to jump into the water at any moment.

"You hear that?" Fred shouted.

"Hear what?" Constance shouted back.

Fred swung around to face me, his mask pushed up on top of his head. "Jesus, they can't hear the music."

I held my breath and listened closely. The music was a great deal fainter than it had been floating over the main street, but I couldn't believe Constance couldn't hear it either. Strange. Damn strange.

"What do you want to do?" Fred asked.

"Honestly," I said, letting a little more air into my flotation vest, "I'd like to go have a drink and forget the whole thing. But I don't think that's going to help much."

Fred sighed. "What do you think she was doing?"

"I imagine Steven will have an explanation. But I don't have a clue."

We floated there in silence until Constance finally yelled to ask if something was wrong. Fred assured her it wasn't. When he faced me again he had a little boy's grin on his face. The same grin I had seen a hundred times, always right before he suggested that we do something really crazy. Carla used to say that she hated it when she saw that grin.

"Shall we catch the end of the concert?" he said.

"When you said that the water got colder."

"Where's your sense of adventure?" He always used to say that, too. And it wasn't until that moment that I realized how much over the last few years I had missed hearing it.

I grinned back at him. "I hate it when you say that."

He laughed and swung around to tell Constance we were going back down. I watched him for a moment, then cleared out my mask and fitted it back on my head. Even though the music was still drifting up around my feet and my shoulders ached from the cold, I was smiling. A damn stupid smile.

"We only got nineteen minutes," Fred said as he fit his mask into place.

I blew twice on my regulator to clear the water. "Let's try to do this in ten."

He gave me a thumbs-up sign and I let enough air out of my vest to sink below the surface. The music was much louder, more intense, if that was possible.

Fred and I swam at a steady speed toward the bottom. She still sat at the see-through piano, playing while looking intently at something directly in front of her. I motioned for Fred and we swam around behind her, making sure to keep a good distance away from the outer edge of where the old building had been.

As we got behind her, I could see what she was looking at. A hand mirror rested at an angle on the music rack. She was staring into it. I pointed at it and Fred nodded. Maybe the mirror was our item. Or at least the real-world version of it. She sure seemed to be paying it a lot of attention.

She played up to the last few bars of the song, the music getting louder and louder, as if calling frantically for someone to listen. And then, as the last notes faded into the water, so did the piano and the ghost.

One moment she was there, the next she was gone and Fred and I were alone. Watching her fade shook me up as much as seeing her in the first place. My mind had accepted her walking around under all that water. It had accepted the music where no music was possible. But I hadn't expected her to fade away like that.

Fred touched my arm and I swore my heart was going to pound right out of the wet suit. I wanted to hit him for scaring me like that.

He pointed at the place on the old foundation where she had sat, then started in that direction.

I could see what he was after. There was a bump under the silt almost at the very spot where she had played. Careful to not stir up too much silt with the motion of our fins, we eased in and Fred dug a gloved hand down into the muck.

A piece of the piano's music stand appeared from the silt. He studied it for a moment and then dropped it, shaking his head while feeling carefully around in the cloud for anything else.

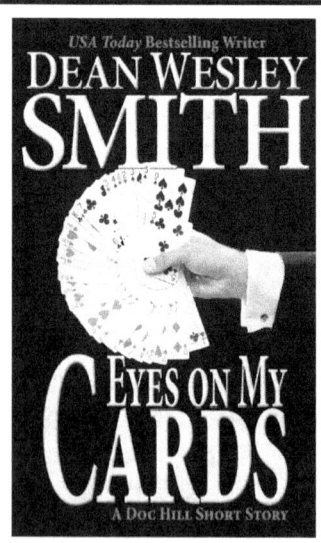

I turned and scanned the smooth lake floor nearby. There were a number of lumps that were obviously things under the silt, but all of them seemed to be too big for a hand mirror.

Fred dug into another of the small mounds and pulled up a bottle. I shook my head as he brushed it off and then tucked the bottle into a pocket of his wet suit. Fred always used to find something on our old dives. None of it had ever been worth anything.

I drifted back about ten feet and let myself sink down so that I had my face right above the level of the silt. From that position I scanned back along the surface, looking for a smaller lump that would indicate the hand mirror.

There were two possible targets. One was about two feet in front of me and the other was three feet to the side of the light cloud of silt Fred had kicked up when he pulled out the music stand.

The one closest to Fred was the one I bet on. I moved up above it slowly, keeping the place marked in my mind. From above it was almost impossible to see. Being careful to not kick up too much silt, I stuck my hand down through the lake bottom.

My fingers touched only wood, slick from the buildup of slime. But then my fingers nudged something hard and smooth. I grabbed it and pulled it out, letting the silt trail along behind like so many streamers.

The hand mirror. It appeared to be the same one the ghost had been staring into during her playing. I held it up for Fred to see and he gave me the thumbs-up sign, then pointed upward.

I was about to nod when behind him, at the edge of visibility, the ghost appeared, walking down the middle of the road

toward the center of town as she had done a few minutes before. It looked as if we were about to get a repeat performance.

I pointed and Fred swung around. He stared at her for a moment as she got closer. Then he turned and gestured upward. I wasn't about to argue I didn't want to be around when the ghost discovered we had her mirror any more than he did. Assuming she'd even notice.

I tucked the mirror in the leg pocket of my wet suit and then followed Fred kicking for the surface.

The second concert of the day started before we reached the surface. And by the time we got to the shore, we could no longer hear it.

CHAPTER FIVE

Monumental Lodge
June 27, 1990

I DIDN'T PULL the mirror out of my wet suit pocket until we had made the climb back up to the lodge and were taking off the suits in front of the blazing fire Steven had built. I doubted I would ever be warm again. Most of the chill was from the drain of body heat through the suit. But part of it was from the music and the feeling that comes when you finish something that's scaring the hell out of you. Not at all like a cold chill. A post fear chill starts right in the middle of your back and makes you shake.

Both Fred and I were shaking so much that Constance and Steven had to help us out of the suits. Of course, Susan,

Constance, and Steven weren't in the best of shape either. They had had to stand on the bank, not knowing what was going on. Steven said at one point he thought Constance was about to strip down and go into the water after us.

I didn't expect anything to happen when I pulled the mirror out of my pocket. I was only getting it out of the suit so I could finish peeling the cold rubber off my skin. I laid it on the coffee table in front of the couch.

The mirror felt very heavy out of the water. It seemed to be made of some sort of ivory, with carved patterns on the back and on parts of the handle. The glass was very clean and clear for being under water that long. An antique hand mirror. A nice find, but nothing that unusual.

But as I laid it on the table, it became obvious that I had found no regular hand mirror.

Steven reacted first. He had been standing near one end of the couch sipping on a drink and laughing at something Fred was doing in trying to free himself from one leg of his tight wet suit. As I set the mirror on the table, Steven's eyes went very wide. He let out a small gasp, took three steps backward, and tripped over a small rug, ending up seated in the middle of the floor staring at the mirror.

"What the—"

"You've got it!" Susan shouted. She jumped up from the overstuffed chair across from the fireplace and yanked a device that looked like a calculator from her pocket. She touched it and the calculator started beeping like a watch alarm going off.

She scrambled over in front of the mirror, punched a few buttons on the calculator, then pointed it at the mirror. It beeped wildly.

"You got it! I can't believe it." She turned, and without a glance at anyone, dashed out the front door, headed in the direction of her cabin.

I stood there with my mouth open, staring out the front door at the running woman. Constance moved over and knelt beside Steven. I don't think he had taken his gaze from the mirror for a moment. Not even with Susan's wild display.

"You all right?" Constance asked Steven as she helped him to his feet.

Steven nodded and Constance led him toward the kitchen table. I watched for a moment and then looked over at Fred. His mouth was also wide open. "I guess they like our find."

"By God, I think you're right."

***

Fred beat me to the shower and by the time I was dressed and had made it downstairs, he was at the liquor cabinet fixing himself a second drink. Susan had returned and was seated in a chair facing the mirror, her full backpack beside her and her coat draped over the arm of the chair. She was fidgeting as if she were a small child waiting for her mother.

Steven sat with Constance at the kitchen table, sipping on a cup of hot chocolate. He looked pale and almost in shock.

"Need something here, barkeep?" Fred asked.

"Same as whatever you're having. Only stronger."

Fred nodded and I went over and sat on the couch in front of the coffee table. In the ten minutes I had stood under the hot water of the shower, I hadn't been able to make heads or tails out of the dive or what had happened afterwards. I kept coming back to how lucky I felt to be alive. Real lucky.

Steven's and Susan's reactions to the mirror made no sense, if you considered the mirror a normal, framed piece of glass. But this was no ordinary mirror. The simple fact that a ghost paid it so much attention made it more. She had a reason. Who the hell knew what it was. But she clearly had a reason.

Fred slid the drink over in front of me on the coffee table and sat down on the other couch in the semicircle of furniture around the fireplace. Constance and Steven moved over from the dining table. Constance sat beside Fred and Steven pulled a chair up at the farthest point away from the mirror. As we had promised on the walk back up from the lake, Fred and I then spent the next fifteen minutes going back over what had happened, what we had seen and how we had found the mirror.

After we finished, I turned to Steven, even though I really wanted to know what the hell Susan was talking about. For some reason it seemed logical to start with Steven.

"What do you think that mirror is?" I asked. "You had quite a reaction to seeing it."

Steven nodded and looked over at where the mirror still lay on the coffee table, glass up, looking polished after eighty years under water.

"It's something of vast power," he said slowly. "I don't know exactly what, but my guess is it's a focus. Or, *the* focus of Gretchen's energies. I would say without much doubt that the mirror is the main reason she has not left this plane of existence."

"She just let us take it," Fred said. "Why would she do that?"

"Maybe the only mirror she sees is the one on her piano," Steven said. "The actual mirror is beyond her time and may well be—"

His voice broke off as right in front of me, and directly in the center of the coffee table, the air started to shimmer and the ghost appeared. So much for that theory.

Now it was my turn to move quickly. I climbed right over the back of the couch and damn near ended up on my face on the hardwood floor. Again I thought my heart was going to come pounding right out of my chest. This just couldn't be healthy.

Fred and Constance both scurried around behind the couch they had been sitting on and Susan and Steven stayed where they were.

As the ghost finished shimmering into what looked like a solid woman, the room temperature dropped as if we were suddenly in a meat locker. I shivered and resisted the impulse to move over to the fire. No way was I going to walk behind that ghost.

She looked exactly the same as she had an hour before. Only this time far less frightening. It was something about her being in our world instead of under forty feet of water that I think made the difference.

She seemed even smaller and frailer than I had first thought. Her blue dress was ripped in at least three places and had brown mud stains around the hem. Her skin was pure white, like fine china. I half expected to see water dripping from her, or to smell a damp smell. But there was no water on her and no smell around her. But did she ever suck the heat from the room. I couldn't imagine getting any closer to her. Not that I would ever want to.

The ghost stood and gazed at the mirror. I glanced over at Steven. His eyes now were glassy and his body rigid.

That did it. I wanted to go home. It was going to take me the rest of the summer to recover from this one day. Not counting the fact that I was still sore from the stupid horse ride in here, today I had been scared so many times my heart was starting to believe two hundred beats minute was normal. I had built up enough excitement to last me through five years of boring teaching or bartending.

The ghost stood over the mirror for a few moments, then shimmered and was gone. That simple. The complete silence in the room seemed to smother everyone's breathing. I'm not sure I was breathing.

Constance was the first one to recover from the sudden appearance and vanishing act. She knelt beside Steven and lightly touched his arm. He groaned.

"This happened to him down by the lake the second day he was here," Fred said. "It was how he learned the ghost's name."

Damn tough way to talk to someone.

Constance helped Steven sit more upright in the chair and then held his drink while he took a very slow sip. I stood and stared at the mirror. Whatever it was, it sure seemed to draw people and things to it.

"Alex is very far from here," Steven said after a moment. His voice sounded very weak and tired. "Very far. That was his mirror. We need to help him find his way back here."

"We could search old folk's homes," I said.

"Did she tell you how?" Constance asked, after helping him take another drink.

Steven shook his head. "It has something to do with the mirror."

"Did she say how he used the mirror?" Susan asked.

"Used the mirror for what?"

Susan ignored my question. Steven didn't. He looked startled and suddenly distant. "Yes, I had a sense that Alex used the mirror to propose marriage to Gretchen."

Susan glanced around the room, her eyes cold and serious. "Anyone have any idea how he might have done that? How could the mirror have anything to do with a marriage proposal?"

"Hell, I don't know," I said. "Maybe—"

"No," Constance said. "Marriage and mirrors used to go together. In fact, my grandfather proposed to my grandmother with a mirror."

"You're kidding," I said.

"How?" Susan asked. "Exactly how was it done?"

Constance shrugged. "Back before the turn of the century, there was a custom that if a man wanted a woman's hand in marriage, he would take a hand mirror, look into it, and then hand it to her. If she looked into it and thereby joined her image with his, she said yes. If she didn't, and turned the mirror over and laid it face down, she said no. Or, as we call it today, she turned him down. I thought the custom had pretty well died out by the turn of the century, though."

"Then that's what triggered it," Susan said softly to herself. She stood there a moment and stared at the mirror, everyone else watching her. Finally, she looked over at me. "I have an idea. Can I touch the mirror?"

My immediate reaction was to say no. But damned if I could figure out why. She certainly wasn't going to get far with it if she tried hotfooting it back up the trail. And damned if I could think of another reason to say no. In fact, at that point, I couldn't see any good reasons for half of the stuff I had seen today. So I shrugged, "Why not?"

She picked the mirror up and studied it, handling it as if it were a fine jewel.

After a full minute of inspection, she laid it on the coffee table, pulled her chair closer to the coffee table and sat down. She pulled her backpack over beside her and made sure it was within easy reach.

Then she picked up the mirror again, looked into it so that it caught her full reflection, and laid it face up on the table.

It appeared she was waiting for something to happen. Maybe, from the expression on her face, something to blow up. Nothing did. After a moment, she sighed and picked up the mirror again.

The silence in the room was too much. I couldn't stand it any longer. I took the mirror from her hands before she had a chance to protest.

"Now, would you please tell us what you were trying to do?"

She sighed and leaned back in her chair. "I'm trying to trigger the mirror."

"Trigger the mirror? What is it? A new type of gun?"

"What do you think the mirror is?" Fred asked Susan.

She glanced over at Constance, then around the room. Then she sat up and held out her hand for the mirror. "May I?"

"If you tell us what you think is going on here," I said as I handed it back to her.

"I guess it wouldn't matter if I told you some of it." She had the pained expression of someone going against the rules. Which rules, I had no idea. But I had seen the same look hundreds of times while teaching.

She held the mirror up reverently. "This is a transportation device. It's what I came here hoping to find. It's a very old device that I think took that ghost's lover. I would like to trigger it so that it will take me to the same place he went."

"And dogs want to fly," I said. This woman was completely crazy.

"I noticed that, too," Fred said, winking at me.

"So don't believe me," she said with contempt.

"Oh, for hell's sake," I said. "You don't really expect us to believe that thing is some sort of bus, do you?"

She shrugged. "In a way that's exactly what the mirror is. There are many more like it scattered around the world, most of them untraceable. This is the third one I have gotten near by following a wave

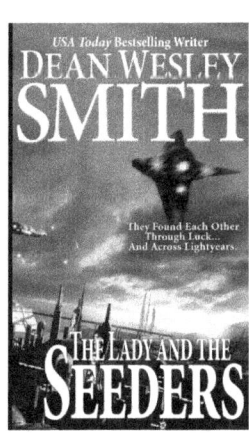

energy they emit. The first two I found I couldn't get close to for security reasons. This is the first one I have been able to actually touch."

"So it's a damn small bus," Fred said. "You mind telling us how it works?"

"It's like on *Star Trek*," I said. "You remember Beam me up and all that."

"In a way," Susan said. "It's more a time machine used for taking random samples from the current Earth society." She held the mirror up in front of her again and ran her hand across the back. Then she laid it down on the table, same as before, and waited, one hand on the pack beside her.

Again nothing happened.

I stood and shook my head. A ghost playing music under water had been enough. Now we had some nut case telling us a story.

"You're a writer," I said. "That's it, isn't it? That's how you know all of this? I bet you even know who would want to take these random samples of our population. Right?"

She shrugged and inspected the mirror again. "Believe what you want."

"Game's over," I said, again reaching out and snatching the mirror from her like a parent would a toy from a bad child. I was damn sick of all this. All I wanted was some simple, straightforward answers.

Now Susan really looked pained. She stood and picked up her pack. "I'll be in my cabin. Would someone please let me know when dinner is ready?"

Constance nodded. "I'll ring the bell."

"Thank you," Susan said, then tossed the pack up on her shoulder on one strap and headed out the front door.

"I think I made her mad," I said as I laid the mirror down in the middle of the coffee table.

Fred laughed as he dropped onto the couch and grabbed his drink. "You just might say that."

Constance patted the still glassy-eyed Steven on the shoulder and sat in the overstuffed chair. "Well, I don't think it's funny at all."

"Women," Fred said. "They always stick together."

I laughed and raised my drink in a mock toast. "I'll drink to that."

***

Susan was good as her word and didn't reappear until Constance rang the dinner bell. I took a two-hour nap and somehow kept from dreaming.

The conversation around the table strayed only a few times onto the events of the day. Mostly Constance, Fred, and I talked about good old times we'd had and other crazy things we'd done. Steven talked about other ghosts he'd investigated and what he was working on in his research at the university. Susan didn't say much at all except to laugh in the right places and make a few mentions about a sister that she used to do a few things with.

By the end of the meal, I knew nothing more about her than I did going in. And I didn't like her much more either. Twice I noticed her glancing at the mirror. It was now sitting up out of harm's way on the fireplace mantel where Constance had put it, glass facing out.

I thought the evening was going to end without anything else wild or crazy happening. Even with the nap, I was feeling damned tired and my body ached in places I hadn't noticed in twenty years. I wanted to finish one last drink and then not wake up until the sun cleared the tops of the mountains. Susan had other ideas. As everyone was getting settled around the fireplace, she asked me if I would take a walk with her. Not far, she said.

What the hell. My poor body had already been beaten by a horse, frozen in a lake, and scared into heart stoppage by a ghost. What could a walk in the dark in the mountains with a crazy woman hurt after all that? Besides, if I worked it right, I might find out a little more about her. Fred gave me one of his raised-eyebrow sort of looks as we put on our jackets and headed out the front door.

We ambled without talking down the main path and then turned toward the logjam. The night was one of those clear, crisp mountain nights that you only see in the city in beer commercials. There were a few night noises and every so often the crack or pop of something in the fireplace of the lodge. Otherwise, the silence overwhelmed even the massive number of stars.

"Let's sit here," Susan said, indicating a log off to one side of the trail that offered a good view of the black water and the opposite dark valley wall. The lake was a giant black hole in the floor of the valley. It was hard to imagine that a few hours before, I had been in that hole. It didn't seem possible. The events of the dive were already fading into one of those memories of something that you remember doing, but never quite believe.

"Nice night," I said, trying to break the thickness between us with stupid chatter. "Cold though."

"That it is," she said. "I love the stars. Where I'm from we can't see the stars like this."

"Can't where I live either," I said. "And that's in this same state. Where exactly are you from?"

Susan never took her gaze off the stars. She sat there and let the question hang in the cold night air until it gathered frost.

But I heated it back up. "Don't want to tell, huh? Is it that bad?"

"No," she said. "It's that you wouldn't believe me. And besides, I'm really not allowed to tell you."

"Why? You a spy or something?"

She laughed. "No, not in the sense you think."

"You know, you sure are a vague woman." It was the nicest thing I could think to say at the moment.

"I thought men found that attractive."

"Not in this case. It's more annoying."

For the first time, she looked over at me. "I really am sorry. I think I might actually tell you if I could."

"Why is it that I don't believe that?" I laughed and looked back down at the lake. "Belief. What a funny word to be using today. I didn't used to believe in ghosts."

She chuckled as she went back to gazing at the night sky filled with dark shadows of mountain peaks and bright pinpricks of stars.

"Look," I said, "that ghost seems to want someone to help her. What I am actually more concerned with is helping Fred and Constance get rid of that ghost so that they can get on with running their lodge here and I can get back to running my own business. If I let you play with that mirror and you end up taking this trip you mentioned, is that going to help either them or the ghost?"

"It might," Susan said as she turned to face me.

"But you don't think so. Right?"

I could see she agreed, even in the faint light.

"Then give me another reason why Fred and I should let you monkey with that mirror."

"Because it's far more important than you think, that's why."

I could tell she was getting angry, so I pushed. "Oh, something like saving the world from a terrible fate worse than death? I think I read about that somewhere."

"Something like that." It was impossible for me to miss the sarcasm in her voice.

She went back to staring up into the night sky and I went back to studying the black lake and thinking about warm things to keep from shaking too much. Finally, after a few long minutes, she spoke up.

"You mentioned beliefs and how you didn't used to believe in ghosts."

"I didn't. And I'm still not completely sure I do. But I'm more open to it now than before the dive and that episode this afternoon."

She smiled. "If I told you the truth, you wouldn't believe me any more than you believed in that ghost before today. In fact, you'll just laugh."

"Go ahead," I said. "It's been one of those days. Try me on part of it. I promise I'll stop you when I think it's getting too deep."

"All right. On two conditions. You let me try to trigger the mirror and you don't tell anyone else."

I shook my head no. "You tell me and you are telling Fred, Constance, and Steven. I can safely say that the four of us will not tell anyone else. But I will not keep secrets from my friends in there."

She thought for a moment and then nodded. "All right, but no one else."

"Promise," I said. "If you promise to not damage the mirror."

"Deal," she said. Then she took a deep breath and let out a long sigh as if some major decision was made and that was that. "I don't exactly know where to start."

"How about where you're from."

She smiled and her teeth seemed extremely white in the dark night. "Get ready, because this is the biggest part that you won't believe."

"I'm ready," I said. And I suppose at that point I really was ready for damn near any wild story she might toss at me. I wasn't going to believe any of it, but I was betting that she would say she was from some high-tech computer firm and they were trying to do something with the space program. Or that this mirror was some artifact from a crashed UFO. Or maybe even Atlantis. Something crazy like that, I was ready for.

"I'm from the future," she said without taking her eyes off the stars.

I was right. Totally crazy.

But I didn't laugh. At least not for the first five minutes.

CHAPTER SIX

Monumental Lodge
June 28, 1990

I AWOKE TO Fred banging on my door and announcing breakfast. I was amazed that I hadn't had nightmares all night. But in fact, I had slept right through and felt something just short of what I am sure death feels like.

Somehow I crawled out of bed without screaming from all the stiff muscles. I felt a little better after a good, hot shower. Not much, but a little.

Fred was cooking the best-smelling bacon I could have ever imagined as I eased my sore body down the stairs. I was the last to arrive. Constance, Steven, and Susan were all sitting at the kitchen table reading newspapers.

"Morning," Constance said as I hit the bottom of the stairs and padded across the room in my bare feet. "Sleep okay?"

"Like a drunk," I said. "How about you, Fred?"

"Didn't even notice Constance's snoring."

"That's because I was awake listening to yours," she said without looking up from her paper.

"Coffee on the stove," Fred said, pointing with a fork at the pot.

I glanced at one of the newspapers as I passed the table. The date at the top was yesterday's. "Where'd you get the papers?"

"Mail drop this morning," Fred said. "Didn't you hear the plane?"

"I didn't hear a thing from the time my head hit that pillow to the time you knocked on the door. Nothing."

"Plane drops off our mail, guest arrivals, and newspapers twice a week in the clearing above the lake. If we're not there to wave at it, or have already put a red flag on one of the small trees beside the meadow, they send in the rescue squad. It's kind of our safety net in case something really bad goes wrong and neither one of us can get to help. The guy lives down in Yellow Pine and he also lets us know when guests are on their way in. He's our contact with the real world."

"Good thinking," I said. "Considering how far out in the boondocks this is."

"Oh, we're not that bad," Constance said. "There are ranches down on the Middle Fork that are a hundred miles from the nearest road."

"But don't they have airstrips?" I asked as I filled my cup and went over to the table. "Morning," I said as Susan looked up.

"Some of them," Constance said.

"Good morning," Susan said without so much as a smile. She went back to reading her paper. She was obviously still mad at me for laughing at her last night. Hell, with a story like her "I'm a time traveler from the future" one, what did she expect? I'd tried to be open-minded. I'd listened as long as I could keep a straight face. If I hadn't been so tired, I might have lasted longer.

I studied her for a moment. She looked tired. Last night, after our "talk," I hadn't told anyone about her strange rantings. I had been too damn pooped to fight it through. Fred had asked me what went on and I had told him I'd give him a good laugh in the morning. I had mentioned keeping the mirror with me, but he suggested a safer place under a floorboard in their bedroom. So that's where we had put it. I noticed that it was now back sitting on the fireplace. I also noticed that Susan's pack was leaning against the wall.

Somewhere in the middle of my shower, I had decided that we should let Susan play with the mirror before I told Fred and Constance her story. It made more sense that way. Let her prove herself nuts without me doing or saying a thing. Maybe then we could get on to something that might help.

Nothing was mentioned about the mirror until after everyone was finished reading the paper and stuffing themselves on Fred's incredibly good bacon, eggs, and home-baked bread. I swore three times I couldn't eat another bite and then found myself, because of the smell of the bread or the taste of the bacon, taking more.

Somehow, I finally pulled myself away from the table and motioned for Fred that he should join me out on the front porch as I staggered for the front door.

The sun wasn't yet above the mountain, leaving the porch buried in shadows and a sharp, cold bite in the air. It felt refreshing. I did a few quick stretches to try to loosen a dozen more sore muscles, then went over to the log rail and leaned on it. This morning the water looked blue-gray. My imagination still could not grasp the fact that there used to be a town sitting there. It was too much a picture postcard lake to have such a strange history.

Behind me, Fred pulled the front door closed. "Great breakfast," I said. I tapped my stomach. If I survived this trip, I was going to be doing sit-ups for a month.

"Thanks," he said. "You find out any more about our guest last night? I noticed you two were being a little cold to each other over breakfast. She turn your pass down?"

"Didn't even give it a try. You know I like redheads. This one is too weird to make an exception."

"That bad, huh? I have an uneasy feeling about her myself."

"Totally crazy doesn't come close. She now claims she's from the future. Or something like that. It all sounded more like the ravings of an asylum escapee. I don't know what to make of it."

"You have got to be kidding." Fred's eyes were wide.

I shook my head. "Nope. She was dead serious. And she wants to try a few things with the mirror."

Fred shook his head. "Not a chance this side of hell. Let's get her on a horse and headed back up that trail."

"Hang on. I was figuring we should let her play with it for a few minutes. Let her play out her fantasy and then send her packing."

Fred laughed. "That does make more sense. But we can't let her hurt it."

"I doubt she would. She seems to think it's incredibly important."

"Hell, what more did she say? The bacon in my stomach is twisting with curiosity."

I laughed. "Do me a favor and let me wait a little longer. I think you'll end up with most of it as she plays with the mirror. Besides, if you and Constance are asking her questions we can twist her up in no time. No one could keep a story like hers straight for long. It was too off the wall."

Fred nodded. "So we let her do what she wants with the mirror, within reason. We'll both stay close to her, in case. She's crazy enough to try anything."

"You called it," I said.

I took one more quick look down at the lake and then held the door open for Fred as we went back inside.

***

I told Susan that we had decided she was free to try her experiments, as long as she didn't damage the mirror. I took the mirror off the mantel and laid it glass up on the coffee table. Then I sat down on the couch beside the table so that I could easily reach the mirror.

"Thanks," she said, and nodded at me as she leaned the pack against the overstuffed chair and sat down.

Fred came over and stood in front of the fireplace with its small daytime fire. When I looked up, he nodded at me and then at the rifle leaning beside the fireplace behind him. He was ready for anything. Smart man.

Constance and Steven sat down on the other couch.

"Exactly what is it you're trying to do?" Fred asked.

Susan glanced at me.

"I haven't told them a thing," I said, and then smiled. She didn't look happy.

She picked up the mirror, studied it for a moment, and then glanced up at Fred. "I'm trying to trigger this device and go where the ghost's lover went."

"And where might that be?" Fred asked. Fred was playing it a lot straighter than I could. He wasn't even smiling.

Susan shrugged. "I'm not really sure. Any one of two dozen or so places." Carefully, she rubbed her hand along the back of the mirror, then looked into the glass and laid the mirror on the table.

We all waited in silence.

Nothing.

"Damn," she said. "There has to be some sequence of events that wouldn't often occur naturally, but would occur with enough frequency to pull the required number of people."

"You know where these places are?" I asked.

Susan nodded. "Of course."

"Then why don't you go directly there, instead of through the mirror? Would seem to make more sense."

"We can't. All the original locations are shielded from us. The only way in is through the original devices."

"Are they all mirrors?"

"No," she said. "But they are all glass of some sort or another. It's the special glass that with a boost of power warps time and allows passage through it."

"So you mean to say this mirror is a machine of some sort?" Constance asked. "I don't see how that can be. It's too small."

"Not really a machine. More like what the doctor said earlier. A focus. In very crude terms, the glass works like a magnifying glass works on the sun's rays. This glass focuses spatiotemporal currents, time waves if you will. Somehow, with the right sequence of events, a burst of power from a source location is triggered and pulls the person who triggers it through the glass and to the source. It's the same principle that our return devices work on. Only hidden."

Some Classic Dean Wesley Smith Stories
Available at your favorite booksellers.

"Your return what?" Fred asked.

Again Susan looked over at me, then back up at Fred. "My people use something similar." She took the mirror and rubbed the handle a few times, then looked into it and again laid it face up on the table.

We waited. I noticed that Susan seemed to be holding her breath.

Again, nothing happened.

"Maybe Gretchen turned down the marriage proposal," Constance said. "Try turning it facedown."

Both Fred and I gave Constance a hard look and she shrugged.

Susan nodded and started to again pick up the mirror. But as she reached for it, the air in front of the coffee table shimmered and the ghost appeared. She spooked me almost as bad as she had the day before. Only this time I kept my seat on the couch near the mirror. As she firmed up, the room temperature dropped twenty degrees. I could see why all the lodge guests had left.

I glanced over at Steven as Fred made a hasty retreat around the back of the couch and away from the ghost. Steven again had that glassy-eyed look and was slumped back against the couch, staring off at the ceiling.

The ghost stood and looked at the mirror for a moment, as if checking to make sure it was all right. Then she faded out and was gone.

Constance rushed over to Steven as he slowly shook his head. I felt sorry for him. It was bad enough having that ghost pop in and out, but being able to sense her, read her thoughts, must have been awful. I was glad it was him instead of me.

Susan stared at Steven. "Did you get anything more from her?"

Steven nodded. "Constance was right," he said, his voice again very weak. "Alex put his image in the mirror, then gave it to Gretchen. She turned the mirror facedown."

"Was there anything else?" Susan asked. "*Just* before he looked into the mirror?"

"No," Steven said after a short pause. "I have this picture of him simply wiping the mirror off, looking into it, and handing it to Gretchen. She turned him down and that was when he left. She wants him to return."

Steven's answer seemed to have satisfied Susan. She held the mirror up in front of her and rubbed the frame along the right side as she kept her image in it. Then she turned it facedown.

And waited. Nothing.

She picked the mirror back up and tried rubbing the left side.

Nothing.

On the third try she found what she was looking for. She held the mirror up in front of her and ran her hand completely around the frame. As if she were cleaning it with a rag, she started at the handle and went clockwise around and back to the handle.

Then she laid the mirror facedown on the table.

Suddenly, she smiled, grabbed her pack, and pulled it up in her lap.

I grabbed the mirror, pulling it out of her reach. She seemed to think she was going somewhere and I didn't want her taking the mirror with her.

She didn't. She saw my action and smiled at me. She faded, shimmering as if we were looking at her through heat waves coming off hot desert sand.

"Thanks," she said to me, nodding at the mirror. "Keep it safe. Others will want to use it very soon." Her voice sounded as if she had shouted it down a long tunnel and the look in her eyes was one of success. An ugly look that chilled me almost as much as the ghost had.

She faded and I could see the chair through her.

Then she was gone.

You could have cut the silence and tension in that room with a dull knife.

"Holy shit," Fred said softly.

I laid the mirror back down on the coffee table, being very careful to make sure it was facing up. Then I stood on what felt like rubber legs and headed for Fred's liquor cabinet. If there was ever a reason to have a drink before lunch, this was it.

I wasn't going to let the opportunity slip by.

CHAPTER SEVEN

Monumental Cemetery
June 28, 1990

ALL PEOPLE IN the world, unless they go through life doing absolutely nothing, and I have known just such people, have a few moments in their lives when their world changes direction. For most, the shifts are gradual, like a slow curve on an interstate highway. The change of direction isn't really noted unless in hindsight. "Oh, hey. Isn't it amazing that I was going to be a heart surgeon and now I'm selling real estate?" People like that never really know the exact time the change took place. It just did.

But changes in my life have been along the line of running into a brick wall. I've run into a number of small brick walls in my life. But only two major ones. The first was the exact moment Fred told me Carla was dead. Killed in a stupid car accident. I knew without a doubt that

at that moment, my life had completely changed. And it had.

The second time was today. When I laid that mirror back on that table and headed for the bar, I knew without a doubt that my life would never be the same. That the easy, don't feel-or-do-anything way of life of the last few years at the Garden Lounge had suddenly ended.

I flopped down on the couch after I had made myself a drink, downed it, made one each for Steven, Constance, and Fred, then made myself a second. Where the hell had Susan gone? I stared at the empty chair and then at the mirror. Was she in the same place as Alex, a man who had supposedly disappeared eighty years earlier? Where the hell would that be? In 1990, there were very few places in the world that could hide a large number of people for eighty years. Let alone a few dozen such places.

Fred dropped onto the other couch and stared at the mirror. "Maybe you should tell us what she said last night."

"You know, I didn't believe one word she said. I do now and I'm scared to death."

"That bad, huh?" Fred asked.

I nodded and motioned for Constance and Steven to sit down. This was going to take a while.

Susan's chair was left open, as if she might appear at any moment. It took about thirty minutes to relay what Susan had told me the night before. Now I wished I had asked more questions, because damned if I could answer half of the ones the three of them threw at me. I just hadn't believed her, so I hadn't bothered. Instead I had laughed.

But I told them what I could remember of her story about how she was from the near future and how all of the people then were descendants of what she called seed groups, people taken randomly from our culture. She had said there were four such main groups. When I had asked her why she had been trying to find the mirror, she'd tried to explain a little about how her world was in conflict, with both sides trying to find the original groups of the other.

When I had managed to ask her what had happened to our present world, she wouldn't say. But she made it very clear that during her time, there were only the seed groups left.

"Pretty farfetched," Fred said after I was finished with the part of her story about how one of the groups called Lomax was a genetically altered group. "What do you make of it all?"

I pointed at the empty chair. "After that, I don't know what to think. It makes sense that something like we witnessed with Susan happened to the ghost's lover. Would tend to shake anyone up, especially someone in 1909. Shook the hell out of me, and I've watched a dozen 'Beam me up, Scotties' on television."

"I agree," Fred said. "It would explain the ghost's lover disappearing."

"And it would also explain," Steven said, "why Gretchen was so traumatized into waiting around for him after she was killed."

"So how come these seed groups are fighting?" Fred asked. "And why are they looking for these mirrors?"

I shrugged. "I didn't let her get that far."

"Do you think we're going to blow ourselves up?" Constance asked, her voice low.

"I read the morning paper. Nothing major seems to be going on at the moment. But you never know. There are a lot of crazies in this world."

"And not all of them are in Russia." Fred said.

"I'll drink to that," I said, and downed half of my drink to try to clear that image from my mind.

We all sat in silence for a few minutes.

"One thing to remember," I said, breaking the silence in the big room. "We still haven't solved the problem of the ghost. And now she pops in and out of here like an unwanted in-law. Anyone got any ideas?"

"Somehow," Steven said, "Alex must return. That is the only thing I am completely convinced will free Gretchen's spirit."

"Lovely," Fred said.

"Maybe Susan will help him get back," Constance said. "If she went to the same place and wasn't lying about all that time travel stuff, she might."

"I doubt it," I said. "But I suppose there is always hope. Assuming that this Alex is still alive after all this time."

I let that sink in for a moment, then said, "I need to take a walk. How about we all do some thinking. Maybe there's something we're all missing."

No one disagreed, so I grabbed my coat and wandered down across the log-jam and up a trail under the trees growing on the old mudslide. I found it hard to imagine that at one time, this entire area had slid down and blocked the valley. I looked up through the thirty-foot-tall pine trees and then back at the smooth forest floor and just couldn't imagine it.

But it had happened, the same as the ghost had led us to the mirror and Susan had disappeared right out of a chair in the middle of the lodge. There was no getting around the reality of it all happening. Maybe I was starting to do what I had always feared most—close my mind to new ideas.

I had hated those who refused to live in the present, but instead stuck to the values of their past without thought or reason. I had prided myself on being able to be open-minded with the kids who sat in my classes and who now came into the bar. But maybe I had been kidding myself. Maybe I was as closed-minded as the next fool.

I stopped and stared through the trees at the lake. Susan had disappeared from the lodge after triggering a mirror she called a transportation focus. That was a fact. And there was a ghost waiting for her lover. That was also a fact. The next question was what to do about it. I was starting to understand how the people of Roosevelt must have felt when they tried to fight the moving wall of mud and rock I was now standing on.

I wandered away from the lake until the trail dropped down across what Fred had said was Mule Creek. The trail forked at that point, one fork going up the Mule Creek valley in the direction of the old Dewey Mine. Fred said it was a fun place to explore. I didn't feel like exploring right at the moment.

I turned and headed down the trail along Monumental Creek, away from the lake. Fred had told me that the trail ran down into the Big Creek valley and then after that into the Middle Fork of the Salmon River. I had thought I would amble a mile or so and then turn back. I didn't make it that far.

About three hundred yards past Mule Creek, in an area of the hillside that was flatter than any other, I noticed the old cemetery.

It was above the trail and fenced off with the bleached remains of a short wood fence. A few of the markers were wood planks on which most of the writing was long gone. About fifteen stone markers dotted the brush and needles under the pines. Most were tipped at odd angles. Another four or five were knocked down. In a few places, the ground had sunk into a grave.

I read a few of the old stones. Just names and dates, mostly from a few years before the flood. One stone caught my attention. It looked newer, a little whiter, as if it had only been there half the time of the others. I walked over to it and read the simple inscription on it.

Richard Haycroft
Beloved Grandfather
1867—1943

The first and only Mayor
of Roosevelt, Idaho. He
loved the town and wanted
to be buried here.

I sat down with my back against a tree near the stone marker and stared out over the narrow valley and the creek below. I knew where I wanted to be buried. Beside Carla in Boise. But now I wondered if I was going to get that chance. Damn it all to hell.

I took a deep breath of the clear mountain air and tried to organize my thoughts into some sort of reasonable pattern. Being able to order thoughts into rational form is a learned skill. Good trial lawyers have it. So do most scientists. Chess and go players also have the ability to see order in things where, to the untrained observer, there is none.

I had learned the trick by doing year after year of lectures. Complex or simple topics, I could always boil them down into hour segments, and then within each hour keep the discussion moving along a certain track. Good note takers in my classes always ended up with clear outlines of the material that needed to be covered. It was a trick I hadn't used in years. Not much need while marking time in a bar.

But now, with so many new things to make sense of, I tried to force my mind to drop back into that organizational frame. I had to sort out some details.

After half an hour, I had the questions and events organized into four main areas. First, I had come to help Fred and Constance get rid of a ghost so that they could keep their new lodge afloat in a way they would like. No solution yet. Even with the mirror and the disappearance of Susan, the ghost was no closer to leaving than before.

Second, I now believed that the ghost did exist and was waiting for someone named Alex to return. The ghost believed that even though eighty years had passed, Alex was still alive. That fact was interesting, considering Alex's probable age. Of course, as Steven said, ghosts seldom are in touch with the current time.

Third, Susan had come here looking for something and that something had

Now Available
from all your favorite booksellers
in trade paper and electronic editions.

turned out to be the very same mirror the ghost had focused on. That Susan said she was from the future and had enemies was either believable or not. However, if there were others looking for the mirror, they might show up. I didn't much like that thought, but Susan had said others would want to use it soon.

Fourth, Susan had clearly done something to the ghost's mirror and disappeared. There seemed to be no way of knowing where she went, short of triggering the mirror and following her.

All four points crossed and crisscrossed and all ended up boiling down to one simple thing. The mirror.

Yet the biggest questions surrounded the mirror.

So, I had a fifth main section. What was the mirror? Susan had said it was a random selector device planted by what she called Seeders. If that was the case, where did the Seeders come from? And how were they planting devices like the mirror at the turn of the century?

There seemed to be no clear answers, especially sitting here in a cemetery. If anything was to be done to help Fred and Constance, then answers were needed. And it followed that the only way to get those answers was to trigger the mirror and see where it took me.

There. I had finally got to the point that I knew I had to get to the minute Susan disappeared. I had to follow her. Simple and crazy as that.

For the next few minutes I sat and thought about being buried beside Carla and how important that had become to me in the last few years. If I followed Susan through the mirror, there was almost certain chance I would never make it back. In eighty years, Alex hadn't. But there was a chance I would. Alex hadn't had Susan to help him eighty years ago. She seemed to know a lot about what she was doing.

But was Susan right? Or was she crazier than I was becoming? I kept picturing her sitting there in that big old chair one moment and then gone the next. If I had to place a wager right now, I would bet on her telling the truth. I didn't like that bet.

There was only one way to find out. I stood, brushed off my pants, and headed back down the trail.

***

Constance was sitting beside Fred on the main living room couch, talking to Steven as he paced up and down in front of the fireplace.

"Ghosts don't lie," he said. "From everything we know about spirits, it would be impossible for a ghost to purposely tell a lie. At times ghosts have been mislead by the passage of events since their death. But no, I would stake anything that a deliberate falsehood would not be possible."

I dropped down onto the couch in front of the coffee table and the mirror. "What's that about?"

Constance shrugged. "I asked Steven if there's any chance that Gretchen was lying about Alex being still alive."

Steven shook his head. "No way. As far as she is concerned, and as far as I can feel by being in contact with her, Alex is still very much alive."

"He'd be at least a hundred years old," I said.

Fred nodded. "At least." He stood and handed me an old eight-by-ten framed picture. "That's one of the pictures we had copied down at the historical society and used to decorate the cabins with. Read the inscription on the back."

I glanced at the picture of seven men standing in what looked to be ankle deep mud in front of a large white tent. There was a sign hung across the peak of the tent: ATTORNEYS HOLBERG & WINSTON. In the background were some of the main buildings of the town. The last thing I wanted to look at was that dead town. I needed another drink.

I flipped the picture over. In Constance's printing it said, *Roosevelt's first law office*.

"It also had names on the original," Constance said, "but I didn't think to copy them down. I do remember that the shortest man there, the one on the left, was named Alex. They put that he was from Boston in parentheses beside his name. That's why I remembered it."

"You think that man was Gretchen's Alex?"

"Possible," Fred said. "Look how old he looks there. Must be at least thirty."

I studied the picture. At least thirty. Maybe more.

"So that makes him one hundred and ten," I said. "Makes the chance of him being alive very doubtful and answers none of the questions."

"Do you think anything is going to?" Constance asked.

"Someone following Susan would," I said.

"I knew it," Fred said, standing and moving around the couch toward the liquor cabinet. "I knew that was what you were thinking. Damn it all to hell."

"You aren't really?" Constance's eyes were wide and staring at me.

I shrugged, but that was as good as screaming a yes to her.

"I won't allow it," she said with a coldness I hadn't seen from her in years. "This lodge is not worth risking anyone's life for. No more than we've already done by having you two make that stupid dive."

Fred fixed himself a drink and returned to leaning against the log wall beside the fireplace. "She's right. We can get by with the ghost. We'll just warn people, that's all."

"Hang on a minute. Why don't we all sit down and talk about this? Let me tell you what I'm thinking and then maybe together we can come up with a better idea. All right?"

Fred nodded and sat down right where he was on the floor, with his back against the log wall.

Steven came over and sat down in the big overstuffed chair Susan had used. For a split second, I wanted to warn him to not sit there in case Susan came back, but then realized how stupid that was.

For the next few minutes, I outlined my five-point summary of the situation, ending with the fact that we had pretty good circumstantial evidence that the mirror worked once in 1909 and we witnessed the mirror working this morning. That alone added a lot of weight to Susan's future new world story.

"But that still doesn't make it safe," Constance said.

"And besides," Fred said, "there's good evidence that coming back ain't so easy."

"So then let me do it," Steven said. I glanced over at him. He hadn't said much the entire day. But I could tell his eyes were blazing with the type of adventure and curiosity that I used to feel before making a dive into a new lake.

"It's logical," he said. "I'm single, have very little family, and am a scientist. The possibilities of this are endless."

"No," I said firmly. "If anyone is going to trigger that thing again, it will be me."

"And why's that?" Steven said. "It makes no—"

"Because I found it. Simple as that."

"Hang on here a minute," Fred said. "Before we go racing to kill ourselves, let's at least try to think this through a little more."

"Good idea," I said and Steven took a deep breath and sat back in the chair.

It was silent in the room for a few moments until I turned to Steven. "Is there anything more that you've gotten from Gretchen that you haven't told us?"

Steven shrugged. "Nothing except that when I saw the picture I knew Alex was from Boston . . . and that Gretchen didn't consider herself a good woman."

I glanced down at the picture on the couch beside me. So that might be Alex after all. I understood what he meant about the "good woman" distinction that divided turn-of-the-century society. Gretchen had been a saloon girl, or as they were called then, a prostitute.

"Do you suppose she knew where Alex got the mirror?" Fred asked.

My mind reeled at what the answer could be. Whoever had been doing the mirrors had been around for a long time. A long time. I didn't like that thought.

"Could you tell if she was in contact with Alex?" Fred asked.

"She believes he is still alive," Steven said, his voice heavy. "But I haven't been able to tell if she had any sense of here and now."

"Same damn problem," I said to Fred and he nodded. The silence and the chill hung over the room while we thought about what to do next. I looked at Fred and Constance, then back to Steven. "Think of anything more?"

Steven laughed a strained laugh. "I know the name of the song she plays.

It's called 'Tonight Has a Thousand Tomorrows.' It was Alex's favorite song."

Constance closed her eyes and shivered.

I felt the same thing. Uncontrollable shivers did a dance along my spine and right up into the back of my neck. A lovely feeling if you're into that sort of thing. I personally was getting damned tired of it.

CHAPTER EIGHT

Monumental Lodge
June 29, 1990

"I THINK YOU'VE finally gone and lost it, old buddy," Fred said. It was almost noon and he was leaning against a handmade wooden dresser in my room, watching me pack what clothes I could into the bottom part of a large backpack.

"You may be right about that one," I said.

"So then what's the point?"

I shrugged without looking up. "Might as well finish what I came up here for."

"Damn it, Doc. You and I both know that's not it. You came up here so I wouldn't kill myself making a stupid dive into a lake. Not to go using some strange mirror to jump you to God only knows where."

"I know." In the lifetime I had been with Fred, I had seen a lot of worry cross his face. Right now it wasn't crossing, it was lodged tight, right out in the open.

"Look on it as an adventure," I said. "Besides, if Susan is right—"

"And if she's wrong?"

"Then look on it as an adventure." I didn't want to think about the obvious possibility that she was wrong. And maybe dead. "What the hell. We've done crazy things before. Like the dive into that lake out there. Remember?"

"That was crazy," Fred said. "This is just plain suicidal."

"You don't know that. And neither do I. But at least give me my choice of going out the way I like. All right? Hasn't that been an understood agreement between us all these years? As long as we went out doing something we wanted to do, everything would be fine. No bad feelings and all that. Well, I want to do this. And see, I'm smiling."

I gave him one of the biggest, phoniest grins I could and he laughed and shook his head.

"Besides, Susan seemed to know what she was doing," I said. "And it didn't look like suicide to me. Admit it. You're jealous. You really want to go along, but know Constance would kill you if you even suggested it. Right?"

Again, he laughed. "Not really. I'm more worried about you."

"Okay for you to worry if you want. But the question is, are you going to help? If so, see how Constance is coming with the food."

Fred shook his head. "I ever tell you that you're impossible to reason with?"

"I learned it all from you."

"I'll check on the food." He turned and went back out the door and I listened as he plodded down the stairs.

He knew I was as worried and afraid as he was. It had been a long night of almost no sleep. I'd thought it through over and over and had kept coming back to the same conclusion. I wanted to see what was on the other side of that mirror. And even more than that, I wanted desperately to not have to go back to that bar and all those nights alone in that house. That was truly the bottom line.

Yesterday, when Susan disappeared out of that chair, I knew that I had found my escape. Not just the pretend escape from a boring classroom to a boring bar. Susan proved her story by proving the mirror was what she said it was. There was a possible new start where she had gone and my little voice was yelling for me to not miss the opportunity. In other words, escape. Run like hell. Jump the wall. Do all those other clichés that come up when a person is trying to rationalize a change in his life. Most people go through life fearing change, hanging by their fingernails to what they know, afraid of the dark, evil "what if" around the corner. I had always scorned those types of people. Yet, in many ways I had done the same thing. Now, finally, I'd found a true adventure. A true chance at change.

I was scared flat silly.

I tucked the last of the clothes into the pack and pulled the zipper tight. Then I swung it up on my shoulder and took one more quick look around the room. There was nothing more I needed here, or for that matter, back in Boise. For some reason, that thought made me feel very light.

I headed down the stairs. Through the front window, I could see that the sun had begun to fill the bottom of the valley in its losing battle to warm the waters of the small lake.

Constance brought the small daypack full of food out of the kitchen and set it on the table beside the other provisions as I leaned the big pack against the wall. She looked up at me. She had the same lines of worry etched in her face that Fred had in his. Of course, if the situation were reversed, I would look the same. And I would be protesting just as much. I also hoped that if they insisted, I would do everything in my power to help. That's the way it had always been between us.

Fred, Steven, and I worked at packing everything and making contingency plans as Constance fixed a huge lunch. Since we had no idea exactly where I was going, we packed every survival type of item the four of us could think of, from boxes of matches to toilet paper. There

---

Some Classic Dean Wesley Smith Stories
Available at your favorite booksellers.

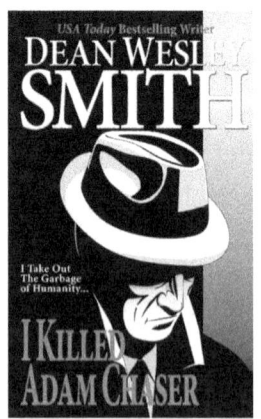
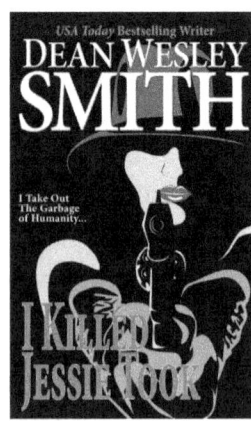

were flints, a mirror, knives, and a string saw. The food Constance packed would last me almost two weeks if I was careful. I also had a medical kit far in excess of what a normal hiker would carry, plus a compass and world map.

After a huge lunch, forced down me by Constance with the rationale, "You never know when you're going to get a solid meal again," Fred and I rechecked the list we had made the night before to make sure everything was included. The pack weighed out at one hundred and eighty-six pounds, sleeping bag, rifle, and all. If I ended up someplace where I had to carry that sucker farther than a few hundred yards, I would be in trouble. Hell, for all I knew, I might end up in an apartment on Broadway. Or maybe in a cave in Africa. Or in a jungle. But, as Fred said, if I was stupid enough to do this, the least I could do was be prepared for almost anything. I could always ditch the stuff I didn't need.

Finally, everything was ready and I had given my last hugs to Constance and Fred. Both Fred and Steven helped me put the pack on. Damned if I knew how, short of falling down, I was going to get it off by myself. I mentioned that to Fred but he didn't think it at all funny.

With the pack, I sat down on the edge of the coffee table and picked up the mirror. "I don't know what to suggest you do with this," I said. "Just make sure you keep it safe. After Susan's comment, there might be others after it. All right?"

Constance had tears in her eyes, but she nodded.

"But do try to keep it out in the open," I added. "I might come back through it real soon.

"You know," Fred said, "I wish you weren't doing this. I mean—"

"Don't," I said. "My stomach is already so damn tight I can hardly breathe. On second thought, maybe it's this pack." I tried adjusting the pack for the show of it, but didn't get much of a smile from the three solemn faces staring at me. "All right, it's not the pack. I'm scared to death. Now, are you satisfied?"

"Not until you change your mind," Fred said.

I shook my head. "Just keep the home fires burning. I'll be all right. And if not, you know where my will is. Just don't give my stuff away too soon."

"Damn it, Doc," Constance said. "Don't—"

I held up my hand for her to stop. "Just kidding. Tell Angie I'll be back before the students return from summer break. And tell her to hire someone to water the damn plants. She always forgets."

Fred nodded.

"If possible, I'll try to get some sort of signal back to you. Maybe through the ghost or something. Damned if I know how."

"I'm sure she'll be around," Steven said.

Again, Fred nodded but didn't say anything.

I picked up the mirror and looked in it. For a brief second, my own image surprised me. I had my navy stocking cap pulled down tight and my parka wrapped around Fred's rifle and strapped across the top of the sleeping bag behind my head.

I looked into the mirror for a moment, then over at Fred. He did not look happy. He looked like any moment he was going to jump forward and pull the mirror from my hands. I winked at him.

I was so scared I could hardly hold the mirror steady enough to look in it. What the hell was I doing? I looked over at Fred and then back at my own image in the shaking mirror. My nerve was fading fast. This was like jumping off a cliff. It was either now or never.

I had started to run my hands along the outside of the mirror, copying what Susan had done, when movement caught my eye.

"Constance!" Fred shouted. "Move!"

Within a foot of where Constance was standing, the air was shimmering. Constance jumped quickly aside as Gretchen took form, facing me. Constance and Fred both moved around to give her room. The ghost stood staring at me. Or more likely at the mirror.

"I'm going to see if I can find Alex," I said after a long moment of silence. The ghost made no motion that she had heard me. Then, as quickly as she had come, she faded.

I glanced around at Steven. He was still standing there with his eyes clear, watching intently.

"I didn't catch a thing," he said.

No one said another word and so finally, I looked into the mirror at my own worry-lined face. If I didn't do it soon, I would never have the courage again.

I took a deep breath to try to calm my shaking hands and sick stomach. Then I looked myself right in the eye and ran my hand clockwise around the smooth ivory frame.

Quickly, I laid the mirror facedown on the coffee table beside me.

For a moment, I thought nothing was going to happen. I was about to reach for the mirror and try again, when I noticed the room seemed to be glowing.

I glanced over at Fred and then up at Constance. They were shimmering, as if I were looking at them through a layer of slightly moving clear water.

"Doc!" I heard Constance shout, but her voice sounded very far away.

"I'll be back," I tried to shout at them. But I think it was too late.

I was in complete blackness.

I had no feeling. Nothing.

No up. No down. No weight. No smell. Nothing.

My eyes were open and I couldn't see a thing.

CHAPTER NINE

Boat Deck
First Cycle
April 14, 1912

THE BLACKNESS FADED quickly, with the light coming back like someone was turning up a dimmer switch.

I was now standing. I couldn't remember straightening my legs, but I ended up that way without a bump or the slightest feeling of movement. As the blackness faded, my weight and the heavy feel of the pack returned.

I was outside, on the deck of a ship, facing over a gray-blue ocean into a setting sun that stabbed streamers of red across the sky. It had been near noon when I left. It was obviously much later wherever I was now.

I took a deep breath and tried to calm down. My heart raced like it was going to explode. That was almost comforting. At least I wasn't dead. Or it didn't feel like I was.

I seemed to be on the top deck of a very large ship. A biting cold wind cut at my face. I could smell the salt in the air as the bow of the ship plowed through the ocean swells, sending huge walls of water crashing off to each side and a fine mist of spray back over the lower decks.

I started to do a quick turn to look around and ended up catching myself on the rail. The damn pack almost tipped me off into the water. The stupid thing weighed a ton.

Slowly, so as not to pull a muscle, I knelt down and eased the pack off onto the deck. Then I unwrapped my coat from the rifle and put it on. The wind was cold and seemed to be getting more so with every passing second. That would figure. I couldn't jump to someplace warm with beaches and lots of sun. No sir. It had to be cold.

I took a pair of pants out of the bottom zipper of the pack, wrapped the rifle in them so it couldn't be seen, and secured it back to the top of the pack frame.

Then I stood and glanced around. No one seemed to be paying me any mind at all. Toward the stern of the ship, a dozen passengers in heavy, old-style coats walked the deck or stood by the rails between the large wooden lifeboats that hung from crane-like arms along the side. The walking passengers turned back at a rope barrier strung across the deck from a lifeboat to a window frame. It seemed that I had landed in an off-limits section of the ship. Maybe this was the normal landing area for people coming through the mirror.

Ocean on the right as I faced the bow meant I was on the starboard side of the ship. On my left seemed to be the bridge of the ship. Seven men in blue, formal-looking uniforms were working. Three stood at panels. Another slowly moved a large wheel while staring out over the rolling sea.

The bow of the ship had to be a good two hundred feet from where I stood.

Behind me, the ship seemed to stretch into the distance. It was one of the biggest ships I had ever seen. Much bigger than any of the transport ships I had been on. I had prepared myself for ending up in a lot of different places. But not once did I think it would be a ship, especially a passenger liner already at sea.

I took another deep breath and tried to force myself to relax enough to think straight. With any luck, Susan was somewhere on the ship, assuming that the mirror had sent me to the same place it had her. I didn't want to think about the chances that it hadn't. I had decided to go through the mirror with the assumption that it would send me to the same place and now it was far too late to start questioning that belief. Susan was here. Wherever here was.

I dragged the pack across the deck and leaned it against the bulkhead, then zipped up my coat and went back over to the rail. The water was a good eighty feet below me. As far as I could see in the quickly fading light, there was nothing but rolling ocean. No other ships or any sign of land. Absolutely no telling where I could be.

I took a few more breaths of deep, salt air and forced myself to calm down as much as I could. I had been so wound up since Susan disappeared, I hadn't let myself stop. And all of this morning I had been plain scared. But now I was here. I was alive. And I had people to find and a thousand more questions to ask Susan.

But first, it seemed the most logical thing I should do was get inside, out of the wind and the cold. I took one more long look at the ocean and then went over to the pack. I grabbed it by the shoulder straps and half carried it, half dragged it in the direction of the rope barrier.

As I came near the rope, a door opened in the bulkhead and two men came out. One was wearing a decorative uniform indicating he was one of the ship's crew. The other wore a thick turtleneck sweater. They were talking about something to do with the operation of the main card room.

"Excuse me," I said as loud as I could, so they would hear me over the wind and the low rumble of the ship's engines.

Neither man looked up.

"Hey! Excuse me!" I shouted again. All I wanted was a little information as to where I might check in. or whatever a person was supposed to do when they came through one of those mirrors.

The two men walked right past me, the officer missing me by less than an inch. Neither gave the slightest notice that I was standing there.

I watched them as they ducked under the rope and went through large double doors into what looked like an open, carpeted area. Through the wooden, paned windows, I could see them move across the room and start down some stairs.

Something wasn't right. I forced myself to stop and really look around. I had seen pictures of cruise ships. They were sleek and modern. This one looked elegant, but in the fashion of an old home instead of a new ship. Those windows had thick drapes framing them. The stairs inside had wrought-iron and wood-sculptured railings. The lifeboats were huge and made of wood. No modern cruise line would do that. Of course, I don't know why I expected this would be a modern cruise line. Alex had been gone since 1909, so it would seem logical that it might be an old ship. But with one glance, anyone could tell this ship didn't show the wear of time. This was a new ship with an old design.

I glanced up at the flags flying in the stiff breeze near the front of four smoke stacks. Four smoke stacks? Something about that struck a bell in my head, but I couldn't quite grasp the memory. One of the flags looked British. The other had a white star.

I dropped the pack and went over to the nearest covered life boat. There, stenciled on the canvas cover were the words RMS TITANIC.

I was going to be sick. I could feel the huge lunch Constance had fed me twisting in my stomach as I tried to deny the possibility of my being on the *Titanic*. I rubbed my hands across the words and then quickly went down the deck and checked the next boat. It was the same. This was either one huge joke or I was on the *Titanic*.

What the hell was going on?

I looked slowly and carefully around. The strange coats and dresses the passengers wore were straight from the early part of the century. So were the ornate wood carvings along the windows, the wooden deck chairs, the thick drapes. And the officers' strange uniforms. Everything fit the *Titanic*.

Except me.

Susan had said the mirrors took people to places where they were held. Why would the mirror stick me on a ship that was going to sink? Punishment? Maybe a test? Or an intermediate stopover?

It made no sense. I must have been sent to a different place, and time, than Susan. What had I done wrong?

Holy Christ, I was on the *Titanic*. I leaned against the rail and looked around at the ship. For me, the *Titanic* had been an obsession. I think I had read everything ever written and watched every movie ever made about the ship and that night it sank. The shock waves of this ship's sinking had been felt throughout the world. I had never stopped being totally fascinated by its myth.

So what was I doing on it? Was this just a trick my mind was playing on me? That was a possibility. Was I really still sitting there in the lodge?

I'd better be finding some answers damn soon.

I went back over and grabbed the pack and somehow swung it up so that both straps were on one shoulder. Then I shifted its weight around so that it rested on my lower back. I could make it a ways, but I doubted if I could walk the entire length of the ship. I figured my best bet would be to go into one of the main dining rooms and find someone who would be willing to answer a few questions. Seemed logical enough.

I followed the same route the two men had taken earlier and went through the huge double doors.

Inside, I found myself looking down at the top of the grand staircase.

The only clear word for the grand staircase was *impressive*. It could easily have been the center of an English castle, or a southern mansion. But instead it had been built on a ship.

Reverently, as if I were a small child entering an ancient cathedral, I moved over and ran my hand along the polished oak and wrought-iron rail. It felt warm and smooth to my touch, almost alive. Below me, the wall above the stair's first landing was covered with a wooden sculpture of two figures holding a crown over a clock. I could remember reading an article about that very sculpture and the story behind why it was there. But right at the moment, I couldn't remember the piece's name.

The clock read 7:30. What day? Another damn important question. The ship sank at 2:20 in the morning on April 15. I just hoped this wasn't the evening of the fourteenth.

I spent the next few minutes easing my way down the huge staircase to the next deck, holding on to the rail to keep the pack from tipping me over. At least a dozen passengers passed me and not a one even noticed I was there, or even glanced at me because of my strange clothes or overloaded backpack. By the time I got to the bottom, I was pretty well spooked by that fact alone. And absolutely convinced I couldn't go another step with the pack.

I moved off to a corner where I figured I would be out of the way and eased the pack down to the thick carpet. I was amazed I hadn't hurt myself trying to carry the stupid thing. I leaned it against the oak-paneled wall. The pack was going to stay there until I found some answers.

I studied the large, high-ceilinged foyer. I was in the first-class section of the ship. On both sides of the foyer were wide double doors that led outside to what must have been the "A" deck. To my left was a five-person-wide, carpeted and windowed hallway. Most of the people seemed to be heading or coming from that hallway, so I dropped in behind a young couple and followed them.

A door to the right opened into what looked to be the first-class reading room. I stayed behind the couple and went through the oak and glass double doors at the end of the hall into a large, open room.

I was stunned by the beauty of the room. Twenty-five to thirty people sat at tables or lounged on couches, talking, laughing, or sipping drinks. Thick, patterned carpet, oak chairs and tables, polished wood columns, and thickly draped, paned windows. I stood there in the doorway with my mouth open, staring. It wasn't until two men rose and started at me that I moved out of the way.

"Excuse me," I said. Both men were dressed in striped three-piece suits. The one on the left was taller, maybe my height. The other man was short and heavyset, with a thick, black moustache. Both totally ignored me.

"Pardon me," I said a little louder as they came near me. "Could you please tell me—"

They walked right on by, the tall man brushing past me and holding the door open for the other man. Neither one acknowledged my presence. It was as if I were invisible. Hell, for all I knew, maybe I was. Or more likely, I was just making all this up in my own head.

I took one more look around the huge lounge and then turned and followed the two men. If they were going to ignore me, the least they could do was lead me around for a while.

They headed down the right side of the grand staircase. I did a quick check to make sure my pack was still where I left it, then followed.

The next deck down looked very much the same as the one above, except without the hall on the right. Instead, across the open foyer at the bottom of the stairs were two wooden doors that led down halls to rooms. The two men went around to the right and continued down. I stayed about five steps behind them, listening as they talked of the medical problems of their wives. It seemed that both their wives were always complaining about some sickness or another.

The next deck was like the one above it and the two men didn't hesitate for a moment before going around and down the right-hand stairway. So far, in two

flights of stairs, I had passed a good fifty passengers and a dozen stewards. Not one of them had looked as if they might belong to a time other than 1912. And not one of them noticed me, or even so much as glanced in my direction.

The next deck was considerably different than the ones above it. The bottom of the grand staircase opened out onto a large, ornately furnished room with at least thirty oak tables surrounded by upholstered armchairs. Less than a dozen passengers sat at the tables, most of them over near the windows on the port side.

The short man made a comment about how their wives must already be seated and both men headed for a double door on the far side of the room. I remembered from my reading about the *Titanic* that the first-class saloon, or dining room, was through those doors.

It was the largest single room on the ship, capable of holding over two hundred diners at one time, all eating elegant meals, served at the highest of society's standards. I almost beat the two men to the door in my eagerness to see that famous room.

And it was everything I had ever imagined it to be. Handcrafted oak chairs, linen-covered tables, ornate wood columns, deep oak paneling on the walls. The air was full of rich food odors and the sounds of people talking, silverware clinking against plates, and ice swirling in fine crystal.

I moved out of the doorway and stood and watched as an army of waiters catered to every whim of over a hundred people at once. The two men I had followed went to a table near the center of the room and sat down with two women. After a few minutes, another party of six people entered from the port-side entrance and were seated at another table near the center. The maitre d' who had seated them headed in my direction, looking stern. Finally, someone had noticed me.

But I was wrong. He walked right past me and through the doors into the waiting area and the grand staircase. That scared me. The way I was dressed, in a ski parka and jeans, I should have at least gotten a dirty look from a man used to everyone wearing fine clothes to dinner. I quickly followed him back into the waiting area to his small desk.

"Excuse me," I said, standing in front of his desk. "Could you tell me what day this is?"

He didn't even look up.

"Hey, I asked you—" I reached forward to touch his arm. My hand went right through him and touched the desktop ledger instead.

I thought I'd been shot.

Not only did my hand pass through him, but he must have been wired with electricity. I got a jolt that sent me staggering back across the room and into a table. I suppose I should have sat down right at that moment, caught my breath, and thought everything through. But I didn't. It didn't even cross my mind.

Instead, I turned and ran.

It took me no more than ten seconds to cross that large room and get up those stairs. At the next deck, winded, sweating, scared, and my heart again threatening to jump out of my chest, I slowed down to a walk. But I didn't stop until I got back to my pack two more decks up. There I slumped down on the carpet with my back against the oak paneling.

I wasn't moving until I got my head clear and I felt rested. For the next half hour I sat and watched the steady stream of ghosts climbing up and down the grand staircase.

Or was I the ghost? Either way, I had gotten myself into big trouble this time. It hadn't just been the shock from the maître d' that had sent me running. As I reached for him, I had caught a glimpse of the date on his ledger.

April 14, 1912.

Unless the mirror pulled me off real soon, in a few hours I was going for one very cold swim.

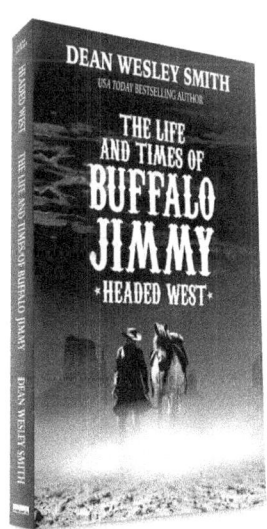
CHAPTER TEN

Boat Deck
First Cycle
April 15, 1912

THE *TITANIC*'S BAN, tucked back in an alcove beside the first-class entrance to the boat deck, played ragtime as the ship sank. Upbeat, happy music to cheer the passengers as they prepared to die.

It wasn't cheering me at all.

I didn't plan on dying just yet. I threaded a rope through the wooden slats of a chair, wrapped it around the legs of the other four chairs in the bundle, then yanked on it hard to pull all the chairs tightly together. Hard to believe I had been dumb enough to get into this. Going through the mirror had been a risk. I had known that. But I never expected anything like this. In all my forty years, I had never been this confused.

Or this scared.

Or this damn cold. The hair in my nose had frozen into needles the minute I stepped back out on the wood-covered boat deck. My ears ached, my knees were numb from kneeling, and I had lost track of any feeling in my fingers two minutes after starting this stupid raft.

I blew hard on my hands, then stuck them under my jacket to see if I could regain enough touch to tie the next knot. I didn't want to think about what would happen if the raft I was building didn't hold together. Or if Susan didn't come galloping to my rescue. I glanced around. Same thing as the last six hours. No sign of Susan and not a soul paying me the slightest bit of attention.

After getting jolted that first time by putting my hand through the maitre d', I had sat against the wall with my pack until I had calmed down enough to stand up without fear of a heart attack. Then I had gone looking for Susan, being real careful to not touch anyone. I did get one other jolt when a woman in a fur coat turned suddenly and would have bumped my arm, but for the fact that my arm went right through her. Again it felt as if I had brushed up against an electric fence. I couldn't imagine what running into someone head-on would do. Probably be fatal.

I had spent the next few hours going through the halls, dining rooms, libraries, and card rooms, yelling for Susan. I had no idea how big the *Titanic* was until those hours. I wasn't able to cover even a quarter of the decks before there was an ugly rumbling noise deep in the ship and the engines stopped.

The *Titanic* had struck the iceberg.

That was the exact moment, as I felt the engines stop, and then listened to the huge stacks as they started blowing off the steam from the engines, that I decided I wasn't going down with the ship. I had the advantage of knowing what was going to happen and I could figure out a way to stay alive.

I had dragged my pack back up the stairs to the boat deck, only this time I went out on the port side and up about halfway to where there was a large supply of wooden deck chairs. I would build my own raft. Simple as that.

Only the intense cold wasn't making it so simple. I took a few shallow breaths and forced myself to try to relax and listen to the music while my hands warmed.

The small, eight-man band stood fifty feet away on the *Titanic's* increasingly slanted boat deck. They were tucked out of the way in a shallow alcove formed by one of the ship's giant funnels and the entrance to the grand staircase. Their ghost white life jackets gave them a formal look as they stood with their backs to the wall and played to the dark Atlantic night.

They had played right through the madness that had filled the boat deck during the boarding of the lifeboats. There was no doubt they were damn good musicians, but I didn't know how they could play in this extreme cold. I could barely tie a rope, let alone finger an instrument. Yet they had played for what seemed like hours, starting in the first-class lounge, then moving outside on the boat deck. Amazing sense of duty. Legend had it they played right to the final moments. Not one of them survived. It looked like I was about to find out how true that legend was.

I blew on my hands again. My fingers felt like blocks of wood. There wasn't even enough feeling left for them to hurt. I was getting too damn old for this. I should have listened to Dean Haycraft and stayed on at the university. At least my office had been warm. Boring, but warm.

I studied the makeshift raft I had been frantically building as the bow of the ship sank deeper and deeper into the calm, black water. I had figured that if I tied wooden deck chairs in bundles five thick, then tied four bundles together, I might have something that would hold me and my backpack out of the ice-cold Atlantic water. It only had to stay afloat for three hours. If I remembered right, the *Carpathia*, the *Titanic's* rescue ship, would arrive by then. I didn't want to think about the chance that they wouldn't be able to see me either. I'd face that problem when I got to it.

The raft didn't look like much, but it might make the three hours. Assuming, of course, that I could get the raft over the railing and drop it into the water without it breaking apart, then paddle it far enough away from the *Titanic* that the suction from the huge ship going under wouldn't pull both me and the raft with it. Damn big assumptions to be gambling my life on.

It didn't much matter now. In a few minutes, I wouldn't have a choice. The slant of the deck had become far more pronounced and water now rolled over the bow of the ship. The huge ship was about to stand on its nose and unless something

pulled my ass out of here real soon, the raft was going to be my only hope.

I yanked another length of rope free from a discarded lifeboat cover and wound it tightly around the chair legs of one bundle, then in through the seating slats of another. Fifteen hundred people would drown or die from exposure in the next few hours. Yet, as far as I could see, I was the only one building a raft. There was certainly no shortage of rope with all the lifeboat covers tossed aside, and there had to be two hundred deck chairs on this side of the boat deck alone. But not one of the hundreds of passengers left on the boat deck was even tossing chairs into the water. They all just climbed slowly toward the stern of the ship like a death march, making no attempt to save themselves. Made no sense. Hell, nothing on the *Titanic* made sense.

The band finished their song and started another ragtime tune. I glanced down the deck where they played. I hadn't noticed before, but at least two dozen people now stood listening to them, leaning against the rail or standing in small groups. None of the listeners wore life preservers. It was as if they were simply watching a band in their local park on a Sunday afternoon.

Damn strange. Everywhere I looked there were questions. Where had Susan gone? Why had I ended up on the *Titanic*? Why weren't more people trying to save themselves? How the hell was I going to get back home? Questions. Questions. Questions. Not an answer in sight. And no time to do any more looking.

I blew on my hands again, then worked at stacking the last bundle of folded chairs. Maybe I'd tie just one more chair on top of each bundle just to make sure. I'd have to—

"You're wasting your time, you know."

I hadn't heard or seen her come up, so her sudden declaration startled me and I banged together the chairs I was stacking, sending one clattering down the sloped deck.

She stood over me like a teacher over a naughty child. She wore a high-necked black evening gown, elbow-length black gloves, and a small, fashionable black hat perched nestlike on her dark brown hair. I guessed her age to be about thirty-five. She took a sip of a golden liquid from a cordial glass and smiled.

I didn't know what I was more surprised by: what she was wearing, her complete calmness, or that she had spoken to me.

Suddenly, after six hours of saying "pardon me," or "excuse me," or yelling and getting nothing for my troubles but a jolt of electricity, here was this lady talking to me and damned if I could think of anything to say.

"Aren't you cold?" I finally asked, going for the easy question first and indicating her thin dress.

"Do you like it?" she asked, turning a half-turn one way, then back, like a young girl in front of a mirror. "I found it especially for the party. I think it was one of Mrs. Straus's." As she spoke, her breath crystallized in front of her face, glowing in the deck lights and giving her a ghost-like appearance.

"It's striking, but don't you think it a might thin for the weather we're having?" To illustrate my point, I blew on my hands in a futile effort to get some feeling back in them.

She shrugged. "After a few years, you get used to it."

"Few years?" What the hell did she mean by that?

She flashed a smile that made me wish I wasn't about to die, then took another sip from her glass.

I studied my raft and tried to think. Maybe it would hold us both. I could throw a few more chairs over the side and stack them on top of the raft to make up for the extra load. That might make the raft a little top-heavy, but she seemed light enough. Besides, she could help me get the raft over the rail and away from the ship.

"You're new on board, aren't you?" she asked. "This your first cycle?"

"Damned if I know first from last," I said, gathering up the extra chairs and stacking them on top of my raft. "But I've been here about six hours." I wrapped the rope around the chair legs to keep the chairs from scattering.

She laughed softly. "I thought so. Only newcomers do things like this." She indicated the raft. "It's probably quite workable, but—"

"Just what's so wrong with a person saving their own skin?" I demanded. "I don't see you doing anything."

"I don't need to," she said. "Neither do you. Really we don't." She pointed down the slanted deck at the band. They had finished another ragtime song. "That was their last full song. We recycle fifteen seconds after they start 'Autumn.'"

As if she were their leader, the band raised their instruments and began playing "Autumn."

"By the way, my name is Marjorie. Marjorie Thiel. I'm from New Mexico. 1972." She leaned down and extended a black-gloved hand.

I didn't know whether to touch her or not. I doubted if my heart could take many more of those shocks. I decided I didn't really have much to lose at this point.

"Kellogg Jones." I said as I shook her soft, warm hand. "Idaho. 1990. Everyone calls me Doc."

Her soft laugh sent breath crystals swirling in the light from the draped windows. "Tell you what, Mr. Doc. You meet me in the first-class smoking lounge in thirty minutes and I'll fix you a drink. You do drink, don't you?"

I nodded. "But—"

"Good," she said, and took a sip from her glass. "Thirty minutes. I do so love current news." She turned and started down the slanted wooden deck toward the band. I watched her for a moment, amazed that she could keep her footing in such high heels.

She was between steps when everything faded, exactly as it had when I triggered the mirror at the lodge.

Then I was in the blackness again.

No up or down. No light. No sound. No smells.

Nothing. The same feeling of total emptiness as six hours before.

It lasted long enough for me to wonder where I would end up this time. Barely. Then the lights came back up like a curtain on the second act of a play.

I was again standing in the officer's promenade section on the starboard side of the *Titanic's* boat deck. Wind carried the salt spray up into my face as the huge ship raced through the gray waters. The sky was splattered with streaks of red as the sun again set on the *Titanic's* last night.

Everything was the same as it had been six hours before.

Exactly.

I had a full stomach from Constance's dinner, the heavy pack was on my back, and I wasn't wearing my coat. On top of that, I was warm. Warm from sitting in the lodge's big living room.

Had the last six hours been a dream? Or was I really standing here again?

I laughed a strained laugh into the cold North Atlantic wind. And I thought I had been confused the first time around.

CHAPTER ELEVEN

First-Class Lounge
Second Cycle
April 14, 1912

THIRTY MINUTES AFTER I found myself starting my six hours on the *Titanic* all over again, Marjorie Thiel walked through the aft door of the first-class lounge. She was wearing black slacks, a silk blouse, and a long strand of pearls. Her thick brown hair was pulled back and tied with a white ribbon and she smiled when she saw me. I liked her smile.

It had been a long thirty minutes for me, waiting and wondering if she would appear. After I had gotten my bearings again and talked myself into realizing I really *was* back on the boat deck in the same place I had arrived, I eased the pack to the deck and then dragged it over and leaned it against the bulkhead. As I had the first time, I had unwrapped my ski parka from around the rifle, covered the rifle with a pair of pants, then put on the parka. In a daze, I had gone over to the railing and stood, staring out over the ocean while trying to make sense out of what was going on around me.

I hadn't gotten past the first twenty questions when behind me a door in the bulkhead opened with a loud clang and two men came out and turned toward the entrance to the grand staircase. One wore a turtleneck sweater and the other a ship's uniform. They were the same two men who had almost run into me six hours earlier. Only this time I was standing farther up the deck as they repeated their exact motions, ducking under the rope barrier, going inside and down the stairs. I felt as if I were watching a movie I had just seen, only from a different seat in the theater.

It appeared I was about to repeat the same six hours. But this time I would get to do different things while the ship and its crew stayed on their original course.

I followed the two men inside and spent the rest of the thirty minutes standing near the bow entrance to the first-class lounge, leaning against an oak column, and watching the passengers.

When Marjorie finally came through the stern door, I acknowledged her smile with a slight wave, then moved across the room to meet her. Most of the room was now empty. The two men I had followed down to the dining room the first time around had already left, passing me as I stood beside the door.

Marjorie pointed toward a booth under a port-side window and I headed there as she seated herself.

"Pretty shocking, isn't it?" she said as I got to the booth. No hello, how are you. Nothing.

"What's that?" I studied her face as I slid into the booth across from her. She was a much more striking woman in the light than she had been outside in the cold Atlantic night. I reduced my estimate of her age by a year or so, and even that might have been a little high. She had intense green eyes and lots of smile lines in her face. I liked her right off.

"All this," she said, sweeping her arm around at the lush room and the furnishings that by 1990 standards would have cost a fortune. "Being on the *Titanic*, time repeating itself over and over."

"Time doing what?" She ignored my question and went right on.

"I'm new enough on board that I remember how shocking it can be the first few times. Not like some of those rude ones who were on deck listening to the music. They were laughing at you. That's why I went up to talk to you."

"I'm glad you did," I said. "But I don't understand why they were laughing. I was—"

She held up her hand. "Lots of time for that. I promised I'd make you a drink. What would you like?" She slid out of the booth and stood waiting for my answer.

After the last six and a half hours, I felt I needed something strong. Real strong. "Scotch. Rocks. Splash of soda, if you can."

She laughed. "Practiced drinker, huh?"

"Bartender," I said. "Mind if I tag along?" I really wasn't a practiced drinker like the scotch implied. I used to drink scotch a lot, but I hadn't had one since the month after Carla died in that car wreck. Of course, during that month right after the funeral I had drunk a lot of it while trying to forget. The scotch hadn't helped.

"Sure," she said, turning and heading across the lounge's plush carpet toward the oak bar built into the center wall. "Just be careful of the passengers and crew. In case you haven't noticed yet, touching one of them gives you a real jolt."

"I noticed," I said. "Twice."

"Don't worry. After a few years you know exactly how they're all going to move, right down to who's going to pick their nose when. You get real good at avoiding them. Mostly the prisoners stay in areas where there aren't too many passengers."

"Years? Prisoners?" My voice must have sounded as shocked as I felt. The full reality of being stuck on the *Titanic* for years was finally starting to hit me. I didn't want to think about what she meant by prisoners.

"That's right," she said softly. "What was the date before you got pulled here?"

"June twenty-ninth, 1990."

I was cleaning my grandmother's hand mirror on August third, 1972, and found myself here. Almost eighteen years at four cycles a day. How many would that be?" She stared off at the ceiling trying to figure the math, then gave up. "I never was any good at math. You'd better stay here and watch how I do this. I know how this guy moves." She laughed. "I ought to. I drink here often enough."

I stood near the entrance as she ducked around behind the ornate oak and maple bar and moved toward the well. She waited for a few moments until the bartender, a man in his early forties,

draped his bar towel over his shoulder and moved down the bar. Marjorie stepped into position at the well and, with practiced ease, pulled two crystal rocks glasses off the overhead rack, scooped ice into both, filled one with a brand of scotch I didn't recognize, and then filled the other with what looked to be a brandy. She then grabbed a bottle of soda out of the area below the ice and added a touch to mine.

She had my drink in my hand before the bartender even stopped walking away.

"Fast," I said, holding my drink up with a nod of thanks.

"Bartender," she said, smiling. "Flagstaff for a few years, then Vegas. I was back in Flagstaff helping with my grandmother's estate when I was pulled here."

I followed her back over to the same booth under the port-side windows. Through the paned window was the first-class promenade and beyond that the dark waters of the North Atlantic. I slid over the cloth seat of the booth until I had my back to the water. I'd have to face that again soon enough.

Some Classic Dean Wesley Smith Stories
Available at your favorite booksellers.

"Where'd you work?" she asked after a sip of her drink.

"Boise. A place I half owned called the Garden. Taught at the university before that."

"Professor type, huh?" She laughed.

"That's why the name Doc. Too damn many degrees."

Again she laughed. She seemed to be the type of woman who enjoyed life. Every time she laughed, her face would almost glow. Infectious. I found myself relaxing around her.

"So, Mr. Doc. Tell me what you were doing when you ended up here?"

"Being stupid, from the looks of things."

"Huh?" she said, stopping in the middle of a sip of brandy and looking up at me.

"I came here on purpose."

"You did *what*?" She shouted the last word and I glanced around the room to see if anyone noticed. Of course, no one did. "Why would you do that? I don't understand how you even knew. No one I've talked to has come here on purpose."

It was my turn to laugh. "I didn't know where I was heading. Not really. I was following someone who triggered the mirror right before I did and might be here. You seen any other newcomers besides me? A woman with short, white hair named Susan?"

Marjorie shook her head. "You're the first new person I've seen in the last six months. But that doesn't mean anything. It's a big ship. I can't believe anyone would come here purposefully. Do you have a way out?"

"That's exactly what I'm starting to hope Susan has."

Marjorie had put her glass down and was staring intently across the table at me. "For God's sake, would you tell me how you got here?"

"Sure, if you promise to answer some questions for me when I'm done."

"Deal," she said and we shook hands on it. Her hand was warm and smooth and I didn't want to let it go for fear she too would simply vanish. But I did and she settled back into the soft seat.

I spent the next forty-five minutes going over the story about the lodge and about the ghost named Gretchen. I told her about Constance and Fred and about how much the lodge meant to them. I told her about Susan and her strange story about this being a group collected by some unknown people she called Seeders to give mankind a second chance after humanity pulled the plug on itself. That part sounded stupid the minute I said it, but at least Marjorie was nice enough not to laugh.

Then I found myself telling her about how bored I had been teaching and how dull it was in the bar and how stagnant my life had become. Admitting that part to her surprised me. I ended my story with the weak rationale that I came through the mirror to look for the ghost's lost lover. She didn't laugh at that one either, which meant she was a nicer person than I had hoped.

"You need another drink?" I asked at the end of my story.

"Sure thing," she said. We crossed the distance over the thick, patterned carpet to the bar in silence.

"What will it be?" This time I went around behind the bar while she stayed at the edge.

"Brandy," she said. "You'll find it to the left. The scotch is above it." The main bartender was standing down the bar talking to one of the waiters.

I watched him out of the corner of my eye as I grabbed two rocks glasses off the rack and filled them. I stayed with the same scotch she had poured for me. It had tasted good after the first sip or so. A light, smoky taste that I knew I could grow to like very quickly.

"How come he can't see the glasses move?" I said as I slid her drink across the end of the bar. "It's obvious we're invisible to them, or something like that. But shouldn't he be able to see the glasses move?"

She shrugged. "They can't. I don't know why. I remember someone theorizing it had to do with us touching it. And them being locked into exactly what happened in their time frame. Something about solidarity of time. Or something like that."

She shrugged and tasted her drink. "I don't know how it all works, but it works for everything. In fact, I'm wearing a passenger's clothes right now." She indicated her blouse and pearls as we headed back toward the booth. Before she sat down she pointed at her slacks. "A man's pants. I was in my bathrobe when I arrived and every six hours I end up back in my bathrobe."

"Where? I didn't see you anywhere on the boat deck when I came through."

She laughed. "I end up down on E deck near the engineer's mess. Gave me a real start the first few times, let me tell you."

"I know the feeling."

Her face went serious again. "You think this Susan's story is true?"

"When I saw her pop out of that chair, I started thinking it just might be. And after the last few hours, I don't know what to think. Someone or something has a reason for setting this up. What little bit she told me makes as much sense as anything else I can think of."

Marjorie nodded. "Then she's probably here somewhere. And if she knew what she was getting into, she wouldn't do all the newcomer's stuff that would make her stand out."

"Like building a raft?" I said.

"Like building a raft." She touched my arm. I really enjoyed the light feel of her fingers. "At least you tried to save yourself. I went down to the main first-class dining room and threw plates at people to try to get someone to talk to me. It's real unnerving to watch a plate hit someone in the side of the head and not even have them flinch."

I laughed. "I can imagine. I tried and failed to get someone to listen to me a few hours ago. How about answering some of my questions, now?"

"What I can," she said.

I looked across the table at her. There were so many questions, I didn't know where to start. And the funny thing was that even though I was so confused, I found myself wanting to ask her questions about her life and what she liked and didn't like. And if she had been married.

I forced my thoughts back on questions that had been plaguing me the last seven hours and picked the first one that came to mind. "From what I've gathered, you've been on this ship since 1972. Right?"

She nodded.

"And every six hours you find yourself back in your bathrobe in the same place you started. Correct?"

"I'm afraid so."

"And you can remember all of the six hours before?"

Again she nodded. "Our minds remember, but our bodies don't."

"I don't understand," I said. "How can your body not remember?"

"I don't know how it works. But our bodies repeat. I still look exactly how I did when I arrived here in 1972. Same number of gray hairs. Same exact wrinkles. Everything. I've talked to people who look twenty and have been here fifty years."

"Back up a minute. You mean we don't age?"

She nodded. "That's right. And if you were hungry when you came through, even if you eat right before the cycle, you're hungry again." She laughed. "There's a guy named Greg who was drunk when he was pulled here. Every six hours he's drunk again." She laughed again and I couldn't help but join her. "He's hungover four times a day and he's been here longer than I have."

That would explain why I had been warm and full again on the boat deck after being so cold moments before while building the raft. And if what she said was true, then it was possible that Alex might still be alive, and looking exactly like he had in 1909.

"So everyone who was ever brought here is still here?"

"Afraid not. Quite a few flip out and kill themselves, or go over the side and drown before they cycle. Death stops the cycle. So far, it has been the only way to escape the *Titanic*. However, the good side is that if you're injured, you come back healthy the next cycle."

I took a long sip of my scotch and let the chills from that news finish doing their tap dance along my spine.

"So how many people like us are there?"

"We call ourselves the *Titanic* prisoners. Last time someone tried to count, there were over four hundred. There could be more, though. That was a few years back."

"Where are they?" I fanned my arm at the almost empty lounge.

"Everywhere. In case you didn't notice, this ship is huge. There are over

two thousand original passengers and crew, and not even close to all the rooms are full. In fact, someone did some figuring once and came up with the fact that the first-class section was only half-full and second class was closer to only one-third full. Lots and lots of room. Most of us prisoners stay in the cabins and just sleep or read. Especially at the beginning of the cycle when most of the passengers are out and about. Another hour or so, when the passengers start turning in for the night, more prisoners will be wandering around. Then, when the ship hits the iceberg, we all go back into hiding until the next cycle. Unless, of course, there is a party like there was last cycle."

I sipped my drink and tried to scramble my thoughts into some sort of form. Impossible task. The more I saw what I had gotten myself into, the less I wanted to know. And the more I wanted to find Susan and figure out a way off this doomed ship.

"You know," she said. "Hearing that there might be a purpose to all of us being here sort of feels nice. All these years, I've been going along hoping that I would get back in time to see my mother alive and thinking this was all some big joke or dream I was going to wake up from and laugh at. But if that woman's story is true, and we're the ones to start over for mankind, that adds a reason for living. Know what I mean?"

I nodded. I was starting to. Three days ago I would have laughed at her and called the idea of starting humanity over a wish-fulfillment dream. But after yesterday and the last few hours, I had a much more open mind. But I couldn't imagine the boredom of being on the same ship for years and years. I didn't like the thought of having to completely start over every six hours. I'd only been on board eight hours and I knew I couldn't understand what she felt.

But she looked like she wanted to help. And help was what I needed. "Think you might want to see if we can find Susan, if she's on board? And maybe this Alex guy while we're at it?"

"I'd love to." She smiled at me with a smile I knew would stick in my memory for a long time. All the years since Carla died I'd never found anyone who interested me even in the slightest. Now I'd met someone who just might, and it was on a sinking ship. Figured.

"Then let's get going," I said as I downed the rest of my scotch and slid the glass into the center of the linen-covered table. "It's your turn to pour. Only this time make it a vodka soda with a squeeze. That scotch tastes just a little too good."

"Ask and you shall receive," she said, standing and heading for the bar.

I followed along behind her, hoping it was going to be that simple.

CHAPTER TWELVE

First-Class Stateroom E-7
Second Cycle
April 14, 1912

MARJORIE SAID SHE knew exactly where to start looking.

She led me aft to the rear first-class staircase, a staircase almost as ornate and beautiful as the grand staircase. The stone-tile stairs clicked under our heels and the thick oak railing felt smooth under my hand.

We went down two decks, along a carpeted hall lined with wooden doors, and out onto the second-class promenade on C deck. Twice along the way we had to stop to avoid passengers. The fear of getting shocked had me spooked. From the way Marjorie avoided the passengers, I wasn't the only one. There weren't many passengers out. The clock over the stairs said it was 11:00 P.M. ship time. Forty minutes until the ship was due to hit the iceberg. I didn't want to think about what I'd do then.

During one of the quick stops, I asked Marjorie what would happen if one of us ran into a passenger head-on. She said she'd only done it once and didn't wake up until cycling. She said it hurt enough that she didn't want it to happen again.

As we stepped outside onto the second-class promenade, the cold hit me like an unexpected punch, knocking the air from me and making it hard to breathe. The wind from the ship's fast pace swirled around the sheltered deck and cut through my shirt. I had been carrying my jacket and swung it around to put it on.

"Don't bother," Marjorie said. She led me to the starboard side and into a foyer with a simple staircase in the center. Even with the door closed behind us, I wanted to put the coat on. I had been too damned cold too many times over the last few days. Instead of getting used to it, I was becoming more sensitive.

I thought Marjorie was going to start down the stairs, but she didn't. We waited to one side until two men came out a wooden door opposite the stairs, then she held the door for me.

This is the library," she said, leading me across the large room filled with stacks of books and assorted tables and padded chairs. "Amazing, isn't it?"

I had to agree. The room was large enough to handle a large city's entire library, building and all. I could see at least two dozen people and the room looked empty. Yet it had a comfortable feel that made me want to stop and browse. I ran my hand along the spines of some of the fine, leather-bound editions. The only thing missing was that it didn't smell like an old, comfortable library. This room had the smell of new books and polished wood. A comfortable smell all by itself.

"You'll end up spending a lot of time in here," Marjorie said. "Only annoying thing is that if you're right in the middle of a book when you cycle, you have to go back to the shelf and get it again. Never have to worry about books getting shelved wrong, though."

"Living here has some wild drawbacks, doesn't it?"

Marjorie gave me a smile as she continued to lead me across the room. "Yes, it does. The one that bothers me the most is that it's senseless to write anything

Now Available
from all your favorite booksellers
in trade paper and electronic editions.

down. It won't be there in six hours. Does wonders for your memory, though."

"I'll bet," I said.

We wound through the books until finally Marjorie said, "Ah, there he is," and headed toward a table occupied by a middle-aged man. She started the introductions while we were still a good ten feet away.

"Craig," Marjorie said, "I'd like you to meet Kellogg Jones. Otherwise known as Doc."

Craig stood and reached out his hand to greet me. "Medical doctor?"

"University," I said, as I shook his hand. His grip felt solid, confident. He stood maybe six foot, had a large beer gut and wore World War II-style navy pants with a pullover sweater. I instantly liked him and had the feeling that he would be someone I'd want on my side, whichever side that may be.

"Craig's the unofficial prisoner historian," Marjorie said. "If anybody would know who you're looking for, he would."

Craig frowned as he sat back down and pointed at chairs for us to join him. "Looking for someone? I know you're new on board. Saw you building the raft last night."

Neither Marjorie nor I moved to accept his offer to sit down. I laughed. "Real new. About nine hours now."

"Thought so," Craig said. "You have that look. Marjorie must have filled you in on how things run around here. Most newcomers are yelling and screaming at about nine hours."

"I'm still giving it some thought."

Craig and Marjorie both laughed. "So tell me," Craig said, leaning back in his chair and putting his hands behind his head, "why are you looking for someone? How could you even know anyone that's here?"

"A very long story," I said.

"Very long," Marjorie joined in. "Too long to go into right now. Do you know of a prisoner by the name of Alex? I vaguely remember the name but can't place it. He's been on board a long time. Seems I remember—"

"There's only one Alex in all the prisoners," Craig said. "He's been here since around the turn of the century. He helped me once with some history about Boston. Short, reddish brown hair. That the guy?"

"Seems like it might be," I said. "I obviously have never met him. You know where we might find him?"

"Sure do," Craig said, looking up across the table at me and smiling. "But I'm real curious as to why you want to find him."

"I got a message from an old friend of his."

"Back real world?" Craig asked.

I nodded.

"For the life of me I can't figure out how you knew he was here."

"Just a hunch, more than anything else," I said. I didn't really want to spend the next hour or more trying to explain my story over again. "Tell you what, after we find him, I'll tell you every little detail. Promise." I gave him my best smile.

"You're not going anywhere, so I suppose I can wait. Toss in some current real-world news and you got yourself a deal."

"With pleasure," I said.

Craig nodded. "Try the first-class reading room. He spends most of his time up there. If he's not over near the windows there, try E-seven."

"Thanks," I said. "One other question. Have there been any other new arrivals the last few days?"

"You mean cycles?" Craig said. "No. Not that I know of. Why?"

"Part of that same big story. If you happen to see a white-haired young woman named Susan, please tell her I'm looking for her?"

Craig nodded, looking very serious. "I sure will. And I'm going to be waiting very impatiently for this story."

"It's a whopper," Marjorie said. "I can promise you that."

We beat a hasty retreat back through the library. "Reading room is right back up where we were," Marjorie said.

"I know," I said. "Saw it the first time around."

We retraced our path, only this time we didn't have to stop for passengers. The halls were almost deserted except for an occasional passenger and a few stewards.

We cut back through the first-class lounge. Only a few men were still there. In one corner, a loud group of seven younger-looking couples were laughing and drinking. One of the women waved at Marjorie as we went by and she waved back.

"They party almost every cycle," she said over her shoulder as she led me toward the bow door of the lounge. "Not much else for us to do."

I didn't like the sound of that one bit. I never was one for parties. Carla always had to drag me to the required university functions and I always managed to drag her out early.

The first-class reading room was deserted and felt cold. Ornately carved wooden tables and padded arm chairs were spaced at comfortable distances around the high-ceilinged room. We walked all the way into the middle of the room and stopped. I felt like I had stumbled into a huge, oversized version of someone's fancy living room that was used only for show. I couldn't imagine how anyone could be comfortable in here.

"Let's try E-seven," I said.

Marjorie glanced over at the old grandfather's clock against the wall. "We're going to have a hell of a time getting there."

"Why?"

"I'll show you." She led me back out into the warm, carpeted hallway and we stood looking out the draped window over the starboard side of A deck. After a moment's wait she pointed toward the bow of the ship.

At first I couldn't see what she was pointing at. Then slowly, out of the dark, a vague, gray shape started to form on the black water, growing in size and heading at the ship. Or I guess I should say the ship was heading at it. It was the iceberg.

As if the world had shifted into a slow-motion silent movie, the ship plowed through the calm sea toward the gray mountain. Finally, when it seemed a direct collision was imminent, the bow of the huge ship slowly moved to the left. The mountain towered above us as the ship slid by the rough wall of ice. I took an unconscious step away from the window. It felt as if the entire side of the iceberg was going to come crashing down at any moment. Deep inside the ship I could feel a low rumbling. The drapes beside me shook. Then, just as quickly as it had appeared, the wall of ice was past the ship and receding into the dark.

Except for the constant background hum of the engines, the ship was quiet.

"Going to be passengers everywhere very shortly," Marjorie said. She took me by the arm. "Let's get moving. It might take us a little while to find his room."

I nodded and followed her down the hall toward the grand staircase. My mind felt numb. I had just witnessed the event that had killed over fifteen hundred people. And it had happened so fast, it felt almost like an understatement.

The low, background hum of the engines stopped, leaving the air with a heavy feeling of something missing.

"Heads up," Marjorie said as we started down the right side of the grand staircase. She went to the right and I went to the left rail to get out of the way of two officers running up.

"We have about fifteen minutes before all hell starts breaking loose in the lower halls. We've got to be in some room out of the way before that. Keep an eye out for anyone. They all seem to be in a great hurry and act very erratically."

"Wouldn't you?"

She nodded. "I did."

We made it down to D deck, as far as I had gone the first cycle, before we met anyone else. On D deck we had to move over into the first-class reception area to get out of the way of a dozen passengers. The grand staircase narrowed between D and E decks and we only made it to the landing before we had to retreat in the face of eight passengers all heading upward, laughing as if nothing were wrong.

The next try we only had to dodge one steward.

"This way," Marjorie said and headed through a door and into a wide hall. Closed wooden doors lined the inside of the hall, with electric lamps in the shapes of lanterns on each wall. Twenty-five-foot-long dead-end corridors led off at regular intervals on the outside. Stewards were busy toward the aft end of the long main corridor, knocking politely on doors, starting to wake the occupants. A few of the doors near us stood open as passengers moved into the hall to see what was wrong.

"Got any ideas?" I asked.

"I think lower numbers are usually nearer the front and to the outside. But that pattern doesn't hold for all decks."

"Sounds as good as anything." The floor was starting to tilt noticeably down toward the stern and starboard side. We headed *down* the hall. The first door on the left was E-42. The first door in the nearest side passageway was E-19.

In the next side passageway, the closest two doors were numbered E-17 and E-14.

"We're going the right way," I said as we stopped to let two stewards move quickly past. "About three more side hallways."

"Good," Marjorie said as she watched more passengers file out of the rooms and start for the stairs. "I don't want to be out here much longer."

I agreed with her there. But I also didn't want to be six floors down inside a ship when it sank. Not my idea of giving myself a chance to survive. And I didn't fully believe I was going to end up out on deck again, safe and sound. I knew it had happened once. But I still didn't believe it.

"Here," Marjorie said as she cut down a side passageway and stopped in front of the door labeled E-7.

"Hope someone's home," I said as I knocked on the door.

"Come in," a muffled voice said from inside. "It's open."

"You ready?" Marjorie whispered.

I wasn't' sure that something new wouldn't send me screaming back down the hall, but I nodded anyway, and she pushed open the door.

The room was gigantic by a 1990 cruise ship's standards and small by hotel-room standards. A diamond-patterned carpet covered the floor. The walls were half oak paneling and half elaborate wallpaper. A small couch with throw pillows was built into the wall beside the door, and a bed was built into the far wall. Sitting in the room's only chair, his back against the bow wall and his feet up on the edge of the bed, was the same man I had seen in the photograph of Roosevelt, Idaho. He looked up over the edge of the book he was reading and without even a smile said, "May I help you?"

I stood there too stunned to move. My mind wouldn't accept the fact that this was the same man that was standing in front of that tent in that picture, even though he looked like he was, right down to the turn-of-the-century style pants and shirt.

He had a rugged, hard face, accented by a short handlebar mustache. His blue eyes cut at me with a look of annoyance.

Marjorie pushed me far enough into the room to get the door closed behind me. Then she turned and faced the man.

"Alex?" she said.

He nodded, looking first at Marjorie and then back at me, with the same annoyed look.

"My name is Marjorie. This is Kellogg Jones. He's new on board and was looking for you."

"Looking for me?" Alex asked. He got a puzzled frown on his face that cleared his eyes. He stood, closed his book and laid it on the bed. "Do I know you?" He reached out to shake Marjorie's hand, then mine.

I shook my head. "No. But I know of you. And in a fashion I have met Gretchen."

His face seemed to drain of color and he sat down in the chair, his eyes focused on something not in the room. After a moment he came back and looked at me. "That was a long time ago," he said. "Have a seat and tell me about her.

There's an extra chair in the room across the hall."

I went across the small side hall and into a matching room. The chair was solid, heavy wood and I ended up dragging it back into Alex's room instead of carrying it.

Marjorie had already sat down on the couch, her legs curled up under her and the pillow behind her back against the wall. I slid the chair over so that we formed a triangle in the small room. I was facing down hill, and if the tilt to the floor got much worse, I wouldn't be able to sit in the chair. I could see why Alex had his chair against the forward wall and his feet up.

"So tell me, Mr. Jones," Alex said, "how you came to meet Gretchen."

"Call me Doc. Everyone else does."

Alex nodded.

I didn't know where to start, so I figured I might as well get the worse part over. "Gretchen is dead."

Alex nodded thoughtfully. "I assumed she would be by now. She must have lived a full life to have met you. I'm glad to hear that."

I looked over at Marjorie and she nodded.

"She died the night you were pulled here," I said.

"But how—" He stared at me with a cold, intense stare. "If this is some sort of joke, I do not find it the slightest bit funny. I was very much in love with Gretchen."

"I'm afraid it's a fact," I said. "Gretchen is the main reason I'm here. She died the night you left. The same night the town of Roosevelt flooded. She has been waiting for you to return."

"Waiting?" All these years?" Again his eyes focused on another place and he had to shake himself to return. "How? How can she be waiting? And what do you mean the town flooded?"

Again I looked over at Marjorie, but she didn't offer help. "She's a ghost."

"A ghost?" he asked. "A spirit? Now I know you are making fun of me. A ghost seems a little farfetched, wouldn't you admit?"

"I didn't believe it either, but I'm afraid it's the truth. She can be clearly seen, and she seems very centered on having you return."

Alex shook his head. "I'm getting very confused."

"I don't blame you," I said. "Let me back up and tell you everything I know. It might make more sense that way."

"A very good idea," he said. He laughed softly. "A very good idea."

I started by telling him about what happened to the town of Roosevelt and what was left of it after eighty years. I told him about Constance and Fred and how Gretchen was hurting them without meaning to. I told him about the dive and about Gretchen playing the piano. Then finally I told him about Susan and how she had come through his grandmother's mirror before I had.

During the entire story, he just nodded, or added a detail about Gretchen or Roosevelt. After I finished, he sat there, his legs up on the bed, his eyes glazed over in thought.

I couldn't tell if he was accepting my wild story or not. But I was having different troubles. The floor of the cabin was tilting more and more. Halfway through the story I had abandoned the chair and sat down on the carpet. Now I was feeling very trapped. Claustrophobic. I didn't like the idea of being so far inside a ship while it was sinking, even if the two people in front of me were living proof that I would survive it. I would much prefer my chances at swimming.

I looked over at Marjorie. "Think it might be possible to go up and listen to the band?"

She smiled and checked her watch. "Don't think we'd make it."

Alex checked his gold vest-pocket watch. "Just a few more minutes." He looked directly at me, his blue eyes now very clear, even more intense. "Do you think there might be a way back?"

I fought down the fear building in my stomach and tried to give him a straight answer. "I got the impression that Susan thought there was. But we'd have to find her."

"I'd like to help," Alex said. "It's been a long time since Gretchen, but I still have memories of her as if it were yesterday. Before coming here, I would have laughed if you had brought up the possibility of a ghost existing. After eighty-one years on this ship, I tend to believe you."

"Fine," I said. "But couldn't we talk about this up on one of the decks? Doesn't the water come up this high?"

Again Alex checked his watch. "As a matter of fact, it does. Have a look down the hall." He smiled at Marjorie as if they shared some stupid joke.

I opened the door and scampered down the narrow passageway into the very tilted main hallway. No one was in sight. Water swirled one corridor away, rising toward me incredibly fast.

I ran back to Alex's open door. "There's water in the hall. I'm going to try to —"

"Come back inside and close the door," Alex said. His voice was firm and left no room for argument.

I glanced back toward the main hall and then did what he said. Somehow I had to believe this man. If he was wrong,

it wouldn't matter much longer. Even if I didn't believe him and tried to make a run for it, it was doubtful that I could make it up those stairs in time.

"Sit here," Alex said, swinging my chair around so that its back rested against the bow bulkhead. "Stick your feet up there." He pointed at the end table beside my chair. Then he sat down and put his feet up on the bed.

I did as I was told. It was like sitting in a chair that had tilted backward and rested against a wall. Only the entire room was tilted, like we were in a carnival fun house. I was not having fun.

"Where we going to meet?" Marjorie asked.

"In heaven, no doubt," I said.

Both laughed.

"How about the first-class lounge?" Marjorie said. "I think Doc just might need another drink."

She was right. I wished I was there having one right now. Water was swirling

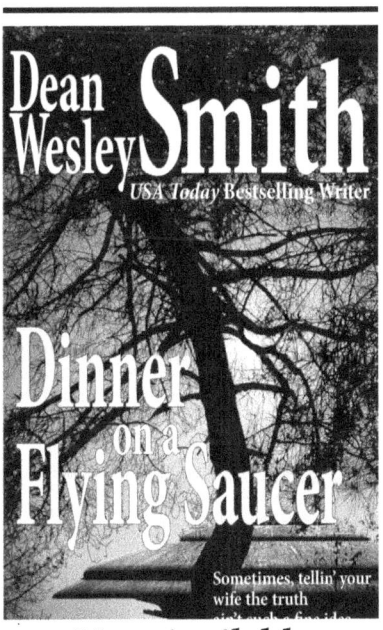

and bubbling under the door and a wet stain in the carpet was moving across the room lightning fast.

"How deep does it get in here?" I asked, trying to make my grip on the arms of my chair relax before my fingers went completely numb.

"Not very," Alex said as the water started to bubble up under the door like an artesian well.

"Good to hear," I said.

Again they both laughed.

"The first-class lounge would be fine," Alex said. "It will take me a short time to reach it."

"Thirty minutes, then," Marjorie said.

"Don't you think we might want to get started now?" I asked.

Both were laughing at my gallows humor when the room faded and I found myself for the third time in total blackness.

This time, the weight of the backpack felt heavenly against my shoulders and the cold wind felt like my first kiss.

And I was never so glad to see a sunset in my entire life.

CHAPTER THIRTEEN

First-Class Lounge
Third Cycle
April 14, 1912

AS I HAD last time around, I beat Marjorie into the first-class lounge. Only this time I didn't stand and wait for her. I went straight to the bar, watched until the bartender was down the bar and all of the stewards were serving, then jumped

in and made myself a drink. Scotch again. My nerves deserved it.

I poured Marjorie a brandy, then went over to the same booth and tried not to gulp my scotch while I took stock of myself and tried to sort out all that had gone on.

First off, I had survived twelve hours of the last six hours of the *Titanic*. I wasn't tired and I wasn't the slightest bit hungry. In fact, I felt full, as if I had just eaten the huge lunch Constance had forced down me. If I got stuck here, that meal was going to do me for years. Constance would be happy to hear that, I was sure.

Not being tired seemed even more amazing, considering that over the last few years I had been getting tired much faster than I used to. If the last twelve hours had been in straight time, I would have been a walking zombie by now. Of course, I had gotten tired a lot because I was bored. The last few days had been anything but boring.

It was fairly obvious that I was in what was called a time loop. But a loop where not everything repeated. In each of my three cycles so far, I had done different things. I wasn't forced to follow the same path. My body started over but my memory didn't. I didn't have the foggiest idea how that could work and the more I tried to figure it out, the more my head ached. Maybe Susan could explain, assuming she was on board and assuming we could find her.

Even if she could explain the time loop, it was going to be one damn long time before I really trusted the cycle to work each and every turn. Just my luck that the one time there was a malfunction I'd be trapped down in a cabin with the water swirling around my toes and a drink in my hand.

"Already fixed yourself a bracer, I see," Alex said as he came up from behind me.

"And one for Marjorie. Didn't know what you were drinking. Want me to make something for you?"

"Thank you, no," he said. "Been pouring my own now for years." He laughed softly to himself as if he'd said something funny, then moved toward the bar.

I watched him as he went behind the bar and worked around the bartender. Alex seemed to know every move the bartender was going to make and was always a fraction of a second ahead when the guy made it. It didn't seem possible that he was the same Alex who had lived in Roosevelt, Idaho. What had kept him going for eighty years? Why keep living? This was only my third cycle, but I could already tell how life would be if stuck here. And he'd been going around and around for over three hundred cycles.

He ambled back across the lounge, his walk light, almost bouncy on the thick carpet. "You recovered your wits yet?" he asked as he set his drink down on the linen tablecloth and slid into the booth so that he sat facing me.

"Going to take some getting used to."

"I'm afraid you're right about that."

"I imagine you've seen a few over the years."

Again he laughed his soft, easy laugh as he leaned back and twisted his mustache. "That would be an understatement of large proportions. There have been more than I can remember. A large number don't make the transition."

"Transition?"

"They go insane," he said. "Go over the side, kill themselves in some fashion or another. Sometimes they take some of us with them. I'm surprised Marjorie talked to you. Those of us who have been on board a few years have learned to stay clear of the newcomers for a few cycles."

"So that's why no one here has formed a welcoming committee. I was wondering about that during my first cycle."

Alex shrugged. "All of us have helped others at one time or another, as Marjorie obviously helped you. But to my knowledge, nothing organized has ever been done. There is very little organization on any level among the prisoners. We're all stuck here and everything stays the same every six hours. What is there to rule? There's just no need for it."

He looked away into the distance for a moment, then went on. "Except, of course, when incidents occur, such as those murders back a few years." He laughed to himself. "Dreadful episode, that one. We actually had a police force for a short time. It was fun while it lasted."

I was about to ask how murders could be fun when Marjorie came through the stern door to the lounge and waved. I was glad to see her again. I hadn't felt that way about a woman since Carla.

"See you both made it," Marjorie said as she slid into the booth beside me and picked up her drink. "Thanks." She held her drink up and then took a sip. Her smile again made me smile.

She was wearing the exact same thing she had last cycle. So was Alex. It seemed they both had distinct habits they followed. I was learning habits, too. This time I hadn't even bothered to drag the pack over to the wall or put on my coat. Didn't seem to be a need to do either. If one of the other prisoners took something, I'd get it back in six hours.

"Any ideas what we should do next?" Marjorie asked after she took a quick sip of her brandy.

"It seems to me," Alex said, "that finding this Susan should top the list."

"I agree," I said. "But with the size of this ship, that is not going to be an easy task."

"But it is *only* a ship," Alex said. "It would seem logical that since she used my mirror, just as we both did, she is on board somewhere. If that is the case, we will eventually find her or she will find us. We have more than enough time."

"Maybe not," I said.

"Why?" Alex asked, looking directly into my eyes as I'm sure he must have done to witnesses in courtrooms.

"Because we're here," I said. "Someone has gone to a lot of trouble to set this all up and keep us safe and living. Susan said we are all going to be used to start civilization over. My question is, start over after what?"

"Atomic war?" Alex asked.

"How could you know about nuclear war?" I asked.

He laughed. "I've tried to keep up with current news and developments from arrivals. Keep a hand in the real world just in case."

"Makes sense," I said. I took a sip of the smoky-tasting scotch before going on. "Let's stop and logically look at what has happened. First, Susan knew what the mirror was. Second, she wanted to go through it for who knows what reason. Third, she said others would want to use the mirror. Fourth, we are here and cycling around on top of ourselves every six hours. Over the years has anyone on board come up with a reason for all of this?"

Alex shook his head. "None that would hold water," he said. Again he laughed softly at some private joke. I watched him for a moment. I suppose I would laugh a lot after eighty years on a ship. Assuming that I had any sanity left at all.

"Then it might follow," I said, "that no matter how much we don't like the idea, our civilization might come to an abrupt end real soon. Someone set up whatever device it took to guarantee—"

I stopped and smiled at them. It had suddenly occurred to me that I knew exactly where Susan was.

"What's wrong?" Marjorie asked.

"I think I've solved the problem of finding Susan," I said. "She said the mirrors were only triggers and focuses. She said that the real time mechanism would be at the other end. This end. Alex, do you know of anywhere on the ship that seems to be off limits to prisoners? Or that seems in the slightest big different?"

"I see what you're getting at," Alex aid. "The main device would be somewhere on board and Susan would go to it. Very logical thinking. You would make a good member of the bar. But I'm afraid I know of no place on the ship that would even remotely fit your conclusion."

"How about the center?" Marjorie asked. "Wouldn't it be in the center of the ship?"

"Possibly," I said. "But not necessarily. However, it might be in the middle of where everyone cycles. I come out forward on the boat deck. Marjorie, you said you were down below somewhere?"

"Down on E deck on the port side and slightly to the rear."

"I cycle onto E deck, also," Alex said. "Just forward of my cabin."

"Seems that if we got enough places spotted," I said, "we might be able to narrow down this search to an area on a couple of decks."

"Craig has that kind of information," Marjorie said. "It's his hobby. I know he asked me all sorts of questions like that once."

"And he asked me, also," Alex said. "He knows where the plans of the ship's decks are located. But I must say I am hesitant about imparting any of your information to fellow prisoners."

"Why?" Marjorie asked.

I could see why. The same reason I felt hesitant about telling Craig. "We're looking for the way back to the real world. We don't want to get the others' hopes up too soon."

"As well as have them interfere," Alex said.

"Very good point," I said. "Can this Craig be trusted?"

"He seems to be the one most of the prisoners turn to when something needs to be done." Marjorie said. "I guess you could say he is the unofficial leader. He doesn't push it, though. And no one runs against him."

"He can be trusted," Alex said. His voice was flat and serious.

"Well then," I said. "How about someone fixing us all more drinks and we'll go tell the man a story."

"I'll get the drinks," Marjorie said, downing the last of hers and standing. "Alex?"

"Brandy," Alex said. "Porter's, down on the shelf to the right." He laughed softly to himself as we followed Marjorie over to the bar.

I figured that as much as he laughed, there must be a running comic monologue going on inside his head. I didn't want to think about what I'd be like after eighty years on the same ship. I doubted if I would be in half as good shape as he was. I'd probably laugh more to keep from crying.

Marjorie slid our drinks to us across the oak bar and we headed out the aft door of the lounge in the direction of the second-class library.

"That's pretty wild, all right," Craig said after I had finished telling the basic part of my story for the third time in the last eight hours. I was getting it down real pat. A little more practice and I could take the entire show on the road.

"I warned you," Marjorie said. She'd heard the story the same three times and seemed to be believing it more each time.

We had found Craig sitting alone at the same table in the library he'd been at the previous cycle. Again, as we had worked our way toward his table, I had an overwhelming desire to run my hands along the leather books and take deep breaths of the air that smelled of new shelves and new books. So I had done it. Alex had laughed and followed my example. I was beginning to really like Alex.

Marjorie had sat down next to Craig. Alex and I had sat down across the oak table from him. It had taken me about fifteen minutes to tell him the bare-bones outline of my last few days. I hadn't mentioned the part about the world possibly coming to an end. That was one factor I still didn't want to believe myself.

During the entire time, Craig sat with his hands on the smooth table, leaning forward, listening to me. I knew from his eyes that he wasn't missing a thing. Now that I was finished he was going to fill in some holes with questions. "Does this ghost called Gretchen sound right to you?" Craig asked Alex.

Alex nodded. "I'm afraid it does. I did get pulled here as Gretchen rejected my offer of marriage. I've always wondered why she did that."

"She didn't think she was worthy of you," I said, repeating what Steven had found out.

"She didn't?" Marjorie asked.

Alex nodded. "I knew of her fear. I hoped to talk her past it." His eyes seemed to be looking back into another world as he said, "I was not allowed the time."

Craig nodded and turned to me. "I don't understand why you purposely triggered the mirror. Seems like a stupid thing to do to me. No offense."

"It was," I said. "But I had my reasons. Partly to help my friends. I came to take this man back to what's left of the town of Roosevelt." I patted Alex on the shoulder.

Craig laughed a hearty, full laugh. "If you figure out how to do that, please tell the rest of us."

"That's why we came to see you," Marjorie said.

Craig looked at her and then at me, his eyes again intense and very serious. "You have a way?"

"Not yet," I said. "But I think Susan does. We need to find her. But we need to do it quietly. There seems to be no need in getting up the hopes of everyone over what may well turn out to be a wild idea."

Craig nodded. "I agree. But what makes you think this woman knows any more about all this than anyone else?"

I quickly sketched in what Susan had said about this being a reseed group for after worldwide destruction. And I told him what she had said about the main transmitter for all the mirror triggers being here at this end. As I told him that, I saw his eyes take on the look of comprehension.

"Okay," he said. "You obviously have an idea where this device may be. Right? And you're assuming she is there. Right?"

"Exactly," I said. "We were hoping that you might be able to help us pinpoint where people cycle to each time. We think the device might be in the center."

"Makes sense," Craig said. He glanced at his watch. "The plans for the ship are up in the officers' quarters on the boat deck. We've got about an hour before too many officers fill those rooms. I could mark on the plans where everyone I can remember cycles to. I think I can remember most everyone. And even a few who are no longer with us."

"I don't think we need to be that precise. How about doing a rough outline of each deck and marking generally where everyone appears? If there's going to be a pattern, we should be able to tell from that."

Craig nodded, slid his chair back, and stood. "I'll get some paper."

Over the next two hours, Craig proceeded to amaze me with his clear thinking and his fantastic memory for details. He sketched each deck, starting with the boat deck and working downward. He used the grand staircase as his main reference points. For each person, he drew a small circle, stating their name out loud and putting their initials inside the small circle. He remembered hundreds of people's locations. And on four people that he couldn't remember, he knew where they were and sent Marjorie and Alex off to ask them.

My circle on the starboard side, front section of the boat deck was the last circle he put in place.

The pattern was very clear. The seven top decks had circles. The boat deck had six, spaced uniformly around the entire deck and F deck had five, also scattered throughout the deck.

About twenty circles dotted both A deck and E deck. Thirty circles filled both B and D decks, scattered more toward the bow and aft of the ship, with none in the direct center area of either drawing. On C deck, twenty circles dotted both ends of the ship, with not one circle filling the middle.

I kept staring at the large open area in the middle of C deck. It was as if there was a giant hole right in the middle of the ship. It seemed very obvious that whatever device ran the mirrors was somewhere near the center of that hole. Susan probably had had the equipment to find it. We were just going to have to search.

Craig drew a large circle in the center of C deck. "That's on this same deck," he said. "Let's narrow this way down and only deal with the very small center section and forget the rooms along both sides, as well as the areas anywhere near the two staircases. All right?"

I nodded and he went on.

"In the center section between the two boiler casings there are three cross-corridors that run from the port hall to the starboard hall, a distance of over sixty feet." He quickly sketched in the details on his drawing.

"There are maybe thirty first-class rooms in that area, to my knowledge all occupied by passengers. There are also steward service areas and a half dozen small shops."

"What is in the very center corridor?" I asked.

"Only rooms," Alex said. "Four large suites on each side of the corridor.

"Shall we go take a look?" Craig said, and started to stand.

"Caution," Alex said, "would be prudent in this situation."

"I agree," I said. My sixth sense was screaming for us to be careful. I didn't know exactly why. Something about the way Susan had said others would want to use the mirror. I agreed with Alex. We needed to be very careful.

"Why?" Craig asked, seating himself after it became obvious that none of the rest of us were ready to run off and search just yet.

"It would seem logical," Alex said, "that the people who arranged to have us all here also arranged to have their device protected."

"That's a good point," I said. "But there may be more to it than that. Susan mentioned that her goal was to protect this or any seed group from another seed group. And at some point she mentioned one of the groups was called Lomax. I think I was starting to laugh at the moment she was telling me, so I didn't ask any questions. Wish I had now. But you can imagine how farfetched this all sounded sitting beside a lake in the Idaho wilderness. However, she did say that these Lomax are biologically altered in some fashion."

Craig snorted his disbelief. "Are you kidding? Just how would they do that?"

I shrugged. "I don't know how whoever does this does this." I waved at the library around us. "I'd only read about time travel and ghosts in novels up until three days ago. I have a much greater acceptance of the possibility of biologically altered people than I do of sitting on the *Titanic*."

Craig laughed.

"When did you get here?" I asked.

"In 1941. Why?"

"Over the last few years, there have been what was called test-tube babies. Babies that were started in labs and then implanted in women. In 1990, that is an accepted medical fact."

Craig shook his head. "You'd think after being in this craziness all these years, I would be more open-minded. All right. What do you suggest we do?

Marjorie glanced at her watch. "We've only got about twenty minutes."

My stomach clenched up like she'd hit me with a solid right hook. No matter what we found, there was no way I was going to be anywhere but out on a deck when this ship started to go down. I didn't care how cold I would get. There would be no sitting in a cabin with water running around my feet this time.

"My suggestion," Alex said, "would be that we stroll in pairs through the area, noting any circumstance that might seem out of the ordinary."

Craig nodded. "Let's meet in the grand staircase area. Alex and I will go together and take the starboard side. You and Marjorie take port side. All right?"

Marjorie and I waited a full minute after Craig and Alex had left the second-class stairway's foyer before we crossed the cold promenade to the starboard door.

We didn't say anything, but as we passed the first-class stairway, she took my arm. I could feel the tension in her grip. She must have walked these same halls hundreds of times, yet now she seemed afraid. I was too, and damned if I could figure out why. Amazing how I

could create fear where none had existed and not really feel fear when I should have been running like hell.

Just before the first crosscorridor, we had to move out of the way of a steward pushing a small cart. Other than him, the entire port-side hall, a football field long, was completely empty. The brown carpet was soft and the wood panels were again oak. Chandelier-style lights hung like streetlamps every fifteen feet. Walking down that hall was like drifting through a nightmare. And I felt lost and very much out in the open.

The first crosscorridor was also empty. All the doors were closed.

However, one woman occupied the center cross passageway. She was standing with her back against the aft wall, facing stateroom C-85. She had short black hair, wore a pair of brown pants and a windbreaker-type jacket. She stood in a parade-rest military position, hands behind her back.

I guessed her to be barely over five feet tall, with very powerful shoulders and an even more powerful-looking pistol-like device strapped to a wide belt around her hip.

As we walked by, she turned to look at us. I had the feeling she was looking right through me, as if I were nothing more than a piece of furniture. She turned back to staring straight ahead before we passed the hall. We were of no importance and no threat to her.

Marjorie and I walked the rest of the length of the hall in silence, her grip firmly on my arm. It was clear I had seen a second traveler from the future. Whether this woman was a Lomax or not, I didn't know. For some reason I had pictured biologically altered people as being huge, lumbering giants, stomping around scaring us little people. I suppose that was the fault of too many grade-B movies. But just maybe they were and the guard woman was one of Susan's people. Hell, I didn't know and I could think of no good way of finding out. I didn't like that thought one bit.

A few moments later, there was a rumbling deep down inside the ship as the *Titanic* struck the iceberg.

I liked that even less.

CHAPTER FOURTEEN

Boat Deck
Fourth Cycle
April 14, 1912

THE BITE OF the wind against my face and the weight of the pack on my back felt absolutely wonderful as the blackness faded and, for the fourth time, was replaced with the orange and reds of an Atlantic sunset. I took a deep breath of the salty-tasting air, quickly lowered the pack to the deck, and headed at the quickest run I could manage for the doors to the grand staircase.

I was going to try to beat that guard woman to stateroom C-85.

We all were. That was our plan. We had spent the last two hours of the cycle in the first-class lounge, drinking and discussing exactly what we should do next. The first hour we had sat in the same booth. But as the tilt of the ship became more pronounced, Marjorie and I could no longer hold ourselves on the stern side of the seat. We had to move to the bow seat of the nearest booth and then turn around to talk down to Alex and Craig. That kept me continually reminded that I was on a sinking ship.

Outside the windows the passengers scrambled in all directions. I tried not to watch, yet found my gaze drawn to the deck. I kept having a sudden desire to run out on the deck and work at building something that would keep me afloat. But the totally unconcerned nature of my three companions kept me inside. It certainly didn't help my nerves any that during the entire last hour we could hear the clear ragtime tunes of the band from the deck above. I must have had at least six drinks to try to keep from shaking. I hoped I was going to get used to this real soon. Or find a way home.

We ended up not having enough information to form any concrete plan of action or even an educated opinion as to what was actually going on. Everyone had seen the woman standing in front of the stateroom. And everyone had gotten the same impression I had. She was guarding the door and she was not someone to be taken lightly. Susan might or might not be in that stateroom. The controls to the mirror might or might not be in there. The woman might or might not be an enemy. We just didn't know.

So the one conclusion we came to was that we needed more information. We assumed that the woman had gotten here the same way the rest of us had and therefore was governed by the same cycles we were. She too would have to come from outside that circular perimeter and return to the stateroom at the beginning of each cycle. It might be possible to beat her there. Maybe see if there was anyone else in that room.

So, the plan was simple. All of us would rush as fast as we could from our cycle locations and then calmly walk through the stateroom area. None of us were to do anything other than act like prisoners passing through. If there was no one around, someone could take a quick peek inside the room. Alex was going to stay in his original clothes and act like a regular passenger. We'd all meet back in the library as soon as we could afterward.

Running at my fastest, I made it to the A-deck landing without being too winded. At the landing above B deck, where stained-glass panels framed the staircase, I almost bumped into a woman and a small child passenger. By the time I reached the landing above C deck, I was gasping for air. It seemed that five years in a smoke-filled bar had cut down my strength and lung power.

Alex was climbing the stairs from D deck two at a time as I reached the lush C-deck foyer. "You go right," I managed to tell him between breaths. "I'll take the left hall."

"Careful," he said as he jogged past me and through the port-side door. I didn't have the wind to answer him. He was seventy years older than I was. How come I was the one breathing hard?

I paused for two quick breaths to give my heart a chance to catch up, then crossed the wide checkered-tile foyer. I had to wait for two passengers to pass before I could open the door to the starboard hallway. I was about to start down the long, carpeted stretch when I heard Susan's voice behind me.

"You're not going to be able to keep this up," Susan said, her voice nasty and filled with anger. "Not for long. My people will get through and then we'll deal with all of you."

I turned around. Susan was being escorted up the grand staircase by two others. The guard woman was on Susan's right, and a man wearing similar brown slacks and a white shirt was on Susan's left. He looked to be no more than five foot ten, with huge swimmer's shoulders and chiseled facial features. Susan's hands were tied behind her back. She seemed to be offering no physical resistance as she was led along.

As they turned the corner off the stairs and headed across the foyer toward the door I was holding open, Susan saw me. She seemed to almost pause in midstride, but not quite. Amazing control. The only acknowledgment she gave me was a slight shake of her head.

I understood. With one quick look into the man's intense gray eyes, I started down the hall letting the door close behind me. I figured I had about five seconds before they got to that door and got it open. No way could I make the almost two hundred feet to the center corridor in time without looking suspicious. But I could do my best to put some distance between us.

I did my best imitation of a sprinter down the wide hall and past one woman passenger headed in the other direction, counting to five as I ran. Marjorie, dressed in a blue bathrobe, was striding toward me. She was almost at the center cross-corridor.

"They're right behind me," I shouted at her, trying to keep my voice just loud enough for her to hear. She stopped, a frightened look on her face.

"Warn Alex if he's in the hall, then go the other way." She nodded and turned off the main hall into the middle corridor. I reached my five-count and slowed to a walk as I heard the door from the foyer of the grand staircase open behind me. Susan was no longer talking. I was amazed she had even said what I overheard. If I were her, I'd be afraid they'd dump me overboard.

I tried my damnedest to look like I was just another prisoner ambling along, bored, while doing everything I could do to get some sort of air into my poor lungs. As I reached the center corridor, I could see Alex and Marjorie heading for the port-side hallway. Craig was standing at the other end waiting for them. I didn't make even the slightest motion at them, but instead walked right on past the corridor and then did everything in my power not to look back until Susan and her two captors had turned off toward C-85.

The moment I figured they were around the corner, I waited another two counts and then nonchalantly glanced back. No one in sight. I went back and peeked around the corner. I was in time to see the guard woman press some sort of small, calculator-looking device against the door. She made a twisting motion with

the calculator and the door swung open. All three went inside and shut the door.

Alex, acting nonchalant, walked slowly past the other end of the corridor. I was about to signal him that I would meet them back upstairs in the lounge when I caught a glimpse of something.

A tall, very thin man was coming down the starboard hall behind me from the same direction Marjorie had come. This guy was wearing the same type of brown pants with a light brown, long-sleeved shirt. He also had a very wide brown belt around his hip with a gun strapped to it. He looked like a walking skeleton, so tall that if the hall light fixtures had been on the ceiling instead of the walls, he would have had to duck around them.

If I was ever going to have a heart attack, that would have been the moment. I had no idea if he had seen me peeking around the corner, or the start of my signal to Alex. I didn't know whether to run for it down the center corridor past C-85, head back toward the grand staircase,

or walk right at him as if nothing at all was out of the ordinary. I knew right off I couldn't handle any more running for a few minutes, and the thought of walking right at this giant was more than my heart could take. So I took the easiest way. Without looking like I was running, or even in a hurry, I headed back the way I had come, any moment expecting to hear the loud thumps of his footsteps as he overtook me.

Somehow I covered the two hundred feet of nightmarish hall and made the door. As I went out into the foyer of the grand staircase I took my first look back.

He was nowhere to be seen.

Alex and Craig were already in the first-class lounge when I came through the door. Craig was standing beside the bar and Alex was fixing drinks, dodging around the regular bartender like it was a child's game. He still wore his 1909 suit and looked extremely out of place behind the *Titanic's* bar.

I waved at them and headed for the booth, weaving my way in and out of the cloth chairs and intricately carved tables. I needed to sit down. I'd had to make one stop climbing the two flights back up to the lounge and I still felt winded. On top of that I had enough adrenaline pumping through my body to last through a week of horror movies.

As I dropped down into the booth, Marjorie came through the back entrance of the lounge. She was still barefoot, but she'd changed from her bathrobe into a pair of men's slacks and a white button-down blouse. She said something I couldn't hear to Craig and then both of them headed for the booth.

"You all right?" she asked as she slid in beside me and touched my arm. Craig sat down across the table.

"I look that bad, huh? Just a little out of breath is all. Not used to running stairs."

"Who is?" Craig said. I noticed he was breathing a little harder than normal, also.

"Here we are," Alex said, setting four glasses down on the table and then sliding in beside Craig. He placed a double scotch in front of me. "Thought you might need that."

"Thanks," I said. "After that last guy, I sure do."

"He gave me quite a turn," Alex said, laughing to himself.

"What last guy?" Craig asked. "What happened? After you yelled, Marjorie and I didn't dare look back down the corridor."

"Just a second." I took a good solid drink of the scotch and let the flavor roll around my mouth and the slight burning in my throat help clear my head. It was amazing how drinks taste better when you are in stressful situations. It was as if every sense suddenly came out of a dark room into bright sunlight. After a second quick drink, I set the glass down and held it between my hands. It tasted too good to let get away.

"They have Susan," I said. "A man and the guard woman hauled her up the grand staircase. She saw me, but I assume she figures I'm alone. They did something to unlock C-85 and then took her inside. About thirty seconds later this skeleton-like giant came down the starboard hall. He was wearing some type of revolver. I didn't notice guns on the other two. I don't know what happened to the skeleton guy. I didn't want to look back."

"He went inside," Alex said. "After a moment the woman came back out and is now standing guard again."

"Anyone got any ideas?" I asked as I took another drink. I didn't. And I hoped if anyone did, it would be a while. I desperately wanted to rest and sip on a few more drinks.

After all, there were two more full hours until this damn ship started sinking again.

CHAPTER FIFTEEN

Boat Deck
Fourth Cycle
April 14, 1912

WITH COLD FINGERS and while walking as fast as I could toward the entrance to the grand staircase, I clicked the last cartridge into Fred's rifle. I yanked the bolt back hard to pull a shell up into the chamber, then closed the bolt and made sure the safety was on. I was still ten feet away from the double doors.

"Nicely done," Alex said. "Would you like to try one more time?"

I shook my head and handed the rifle to him. "I can do it."

But I didn't like it. All I really wanted to do was get in out of the cold.

After an hour of talking in the lounge, we had formed a plan. We would again try to beat the Lomax, assuming that was who was holding Susan, to room C-85. Using Fred's rifle and a crewman's pistol, we would surprise them at the corner of the starboard hall and the central corridor. With a little luck, we would free Susan.

Simple really, only no way in hell was I going to go pointing a gun at anyone. Not that I didn't know how. The Navy had taught me how to do it in boot camp.

Somehow, I had been lucky enough to get through that. I had never fired a shot since. I even hated the thought of hunting. But Craig and Alex didn't seem to have the same trouble. Therefore, the plan was that I was to load the rifle on my way down, then give the rifle to Alex in front of the grand staircase on C deck. He would do any pointing that was necessary.

I had practiced digging the bullets out of the pack and loading the rifle on the run three times. After my first practice loading, Alex had blown some pretty good-sized holes in a row of wooden deck chairs. He said he wanted to get used to how the gun handled. I felt ready. Alex said he was ready. I just didn't like what we were doing.

As far as I was concerned, we didn't have enough information to go attacking anyone. I wanted to wait and continue to watch. But both Craig and Alex had argued that there was a large chance that they might kill Susan and that the sooner we acted, the better chance she would have. Besides, they said, there wouldn't be any shooting. We would surprise them and do it without a shot.

I argued that if the Lomax hadn't killed Susan yet, they weren't going to. That had sounded lame the minute I had said it. Yet I could think of no reason why they hadn't killed her. Nor could Craig or Alex. And the big question was how they kept capturing her every cycle. It made no sense. Of course, that was nothing new on the *Titanic*.

Alex laid the rifle down on the pack and we headed inside. No matter how many times I walked up and down that staircase, I would never get used to its incredible beauty. The oak rail and wrought-iron balustrades, the carved wood panels on the walls, the carved stone statues at every turn, the glass dome over it all. It made me want to stop and stare.

At the first landing I glanced up at the wall clock. I suddenly remembered the name of that famous clock. "Honor and Glory Crowing Time." It read 11:30. Ten minutes until the ship hit the iceberg. Two hours and forty minutes until the next cycle. A long time and not damn long enough.

Craig and Marjorie stood at the end of the bar, talking and sipping drinks. Craig had gone down to see how long it would take him to get to the crewman's gun. Marjorie had walked C deck to see if anything had changed. I glanced around the lounge. Except for two waiters, the bartender, and two passengers, the lounge was empty and felt cold.

"Any trouble?" Craig asked as we worked our way across the luxurious room, around the empty tables toward them.

"None," Alex said. "Doc had no problem finding the shells and loading the rifle. We shouldn't be slowed down by more than a few seconds over last time."

Craig nodded. "Good. I will take maybe ten seconds longer, but I think I can make up a few of those seconds by coming up the stern first-class stairway instead of the second-class stairway. It might even turn out to be slightly faster."

I went around Marjorie and behind the bar to fix myself a drink. If this kept up, I was going to start enjoying drinking again.

"Alex?" I indicated the well.

"Yes. Thank you," he said.

"Any change?" I asked Marjorie.

"Not that I could tell. The guard is still in the same place." Marjorie looked down into her brandy and swirled the golden liquid around and around in her glass. "I had a thought. If we capture these people, what are we going to do with them next cycle? They'd be prepared for us a second time. And if they keep capturing Susan every time, won't they do it again next time?"

I nodded and so did Craig. The same question had crossed my mind. I hoped Susan would have the answer. I didn't want to face what we might have to do if she didn't. I supposed a ship that size had a lot of hiding places.

"We'll decide that after we see what's inside that room," Craig said. "Everyone agree?"

No one said a word.

Craig nodded. "All right, let's find a seat and make sure we've got this plan straight."

We were halfway to the booth when a faint rumbling shook the tables and lightly tinkled the crystal glasses behind the bar. My stomach again clamped up like I'd been hit with a solid right. My three friends didn't even seem to notice, but I was getting damn tired of this ship sinking.

An hour and a half later I talked Marjorie into going with me up on the boat deck to listen to the last few songs of the band. For some reason, it made me feel better to be out in the open, even though I refrained from madly wrapping deck chairs together.

For three songs, we stood, arm in arm, leaning against the rail, listening to the fantastic music of those brave men. Marjorie felt solid and warm against my side. I wished we had the time to sit and talk and laugh and learn about each other. But we didn't, so we didn't talk. We just stood and leaned against each other and listened. Considering what we were about to try, listening to the band on the *Titanic* seemed somehow very appropriate.

My fifth sunset didn't look anywhere near as good to me as the first four. This time my hands were shaking so badly, I almost couldn't get the pack off. I dropped two shells and it took me until the landing above A deck to get the rifle loaded. From there, to make up for being late, I took the rest of the stairs two at a time all the way down. I reached C deck completely winded, panting, and with my heart pounding like it was trying to hammer out a rock tune on a set of drums.

Alex bounded up the stairs before I even had a chance to slow to a walk. I handed him the rifle and the box of shells as we crossed. He was going to go down the port-side hall and then be in the central corridor when the Lomax holding Susan came around the corner. I was to be near the central corridor and walk back past them so I would be behind them. Craig was to come from the stern along the starboard corridor. That way we'd have them completely surrounded if they came up the same way as last cycle. A good-sized if. All bets were off if they didn't.

Marjorie was to stay over in the port hallway and stand watch in case they came up that way. Or in case we weren't successful. If we weren't, she was to go and tell other prisoners what had happened and try to enlist their aid. That was Craig's idea. I didn't really want to think about what not being successful would possibly mean.

"Loaded?" Alex asked. He didn't even seem out of breath.

"Safety's on," I managed to gasp out. "Be careful."

"You too," he said.

Twenty seconds later I was leaning against the wall at the intersection of the center corridor and the starboard hall, desperately trying to get some air into my lungs. Without warning the door from the grand staircase opened and the two Lomax with Susan between them came through.

Alex was in place in the center corridor, Fred's rifle ready. Craig would reach the ambush corner at exactly the right time. Acting as nonchalant as the lack of air in my lungs would let me, I ambled down the hall directly at them, keeping my gaze locked on the carpet and the line where it met the oak panels on the right side of the hall. I kept telling myself I wasn't frightened. And I kept not believing it.

I met Susan's group halfway between the door and the central hallway. I moved against the right wall to let them pass and I purposefully avoided looking at Susan, but did glance up and catch the guard woman's glance. She nodded a slight hello and I found myself nodding back, as if we were simply meeting on a park sidewalk.

The moment they were past me, I stopped and pretended to be checking a cabin door on the left of the hall. At the moment I figured they would be reaching the corner, I turned around and headed toward them. Damned if I knew what I was going to do to help, especially against guns, but I figured I might as well be close.

As the two Lomax and Susan started to turn the corner, I heard Alex shout "Halt!" Craig, who was within a dozen feet of them in the main hallway, pulled his gun out of the back of his pants, dropped into a combat firing stance, and pointed it at the guard woman.

Everything froze, as if someone had turned the world down to ultraslow motion. Nothing more would have happened if everyone had stayed put as Alex had ordered. That was the plan and for an instant it seemed it was going to work.

But we didn't count on Susan.

Without warning, she shoved the guard woman hard with her elbow, then tried to yank away from the other Lomax.

The guard woman hit the side wall, rolled toward Craig, and came up with a gun in her hand. Craig never stood a chance. Her low, muffled shot opened a wide gash across his chest. He jerked backward against a door and dropped with a hard thud to the carpet.

A moment later, a deafening explosion filled the hall as Alex fired Fred's deer rifle. The Lomax who had been struggling with Susan spun twice and smashed hard into the wall, then crumpled. He was facing me and I could see the life leave his body as his open, shocked eyes clouded and became frozen in a death stare.

The high-powered rifle bullet had passed through the Lomax and slammed Susan backward. Her head cracked hard against the oak paneling and she slumped to the carpet. Blood pumped from the large hole in her stomach, soaking her blouse and pants.

"Don't!" the guard woman shouted in very clear, very understandable English. She was lying on the carpet in firing position, her gun pointing down the central corridor at Alex. I couldn't see Alex, but I doubted if he had had time to pull another shell up into the chamber of the rifle. I also knew she would not hesitate in killing him if he tried.

"Drop the rifle!" Her command didn't allow room for argument.

I heard a dull thump as Alex dropped the rifle to the carpet.

"Back up," the woman ordered Alex. Then she glanced my way. I had taken a half-dozen steps toward the fight and then stopped. "Come down here." She motioned with her gun where she wanted me to be as she slowly got to her feet.

I moved down the hall toward the bloodstained carpet and wall. Alex's shot had sent both Susan and the man spinning and their blood had covered the walls and carpet like a splatter painting at the fair. I had to walk right through the middle of that painting.

A large, brown stain was forming under Craig's body. From the way his body lay, twisted unnaturally, he too was obviously dead.

It was everything I could do not to gag. The huge lunch Constance had fed me wanted to climb back up my throat. The copper smell of the blood mixed with the thick odor of gunpowder made me dizzy. I forced my attention on keeping the contents of my stomach in place as I neared the corridor intersection. Somehow I made it through the blood but I felt numb. My hands were tingling.

The guard woman backed up enough to let me into the central corridor. Alex was standing there, his face completely drained of color, his hands in the air. He was staring at the bodies of Susan and the man he had killed.

The rifle was lying off to the right side of the corridor. I went and stood beside

him and she motioned for us to move on toward C-85. We hadn't taken more than a few steps when the tall skeleton man came around the corner from the port hallway pushing Marjorie in front of him. He held a small gun in his right hand and looked upset.

Marjorie was still in her bathrobe and seemed unhurt. Her eyes were wide with fear. As she got closer, she looked past us to the bodies and the blood-covered walls. For a moment I thought she was going to do what I almost had done. I could see her choking, fighting to regain control. Finally, she closed her eyes and let out a deep, shuddering sigh. I moved forward to support her, but she was holding her own. I put my arm around her shoulder and her arm went around my waist. I wasn't sure who was holding up whom.

"What happened?" the skeleton man demanded of the guard woman.

"They attacked us. Lawrence is dead," she said. "The Lomax is dead. I hit one of their members. He is around the corner to the right." She motioned back down the hall without taking her eyes off of us.

"Craig?" Marjorie asked. Her weight against my arm suddenly got heavier.

I hugged her arm and could feel her shudder as she tried to hold together. In all the last few hours of planning, we had not considered it could possibly turn out like this. I had felt there was a chance someone might get hurt or killed, but when I thought that, I didn't have a full realization of what it meant. It's one thing to see death all the time inside a nineteen-inch box sitting in your living room. It is quite another to smell the blood and feel the responsibility as a person dies.

I didn't want to watch, but I made myself as the skeleton man went down the hall and checked out first his own named

Lawrence, then Susan, and then finally out of sight down the hall to look at Craig.

It was as we were standing there waiting that what the guard woman had said finally sunk through the fog in my mind. She had called Susan a Lomax. I had been assuming they were the Lomax.

The skeleton man came back around the corner and held his gun on the three of us until the guard woman got the door open and then stepped back, holding her gun trained evenly on us. It was very clear she was a soldier. She didn't seem the slightest bit shaken that she had lost one of her own and killed another man. One cold woman.

"Inside," the skeleton man ordered, his voice unable to hide a tone of disgust.

Alex led the way, followed by Marjorie and then by me. The room looked very much like Alex's room down on E deck. There was a built-in couch and bed, one padded chair, a small table, and a dresser.

"Search them," he said to the guard woman, "then take care of the bodies before they are discovered."

While he held his gun steady on us, she patted us down like an expert, not missing an inch, then took short pieces of twine and tied our hands. She made mine painfully tight. So tight that I knew there was no way I could pull out. I hoped blood could get to my hands.

She pointed to the couch. I sat on the left side nearest the door. Marjorie was in the middle and Alex against the wall.

As soon as the guard woman had gone out the door, the man sat down on the bed across from the couch and looked at us. "Who are you?" he asked. His voice sounded tired, as if he was facing a task he didn't want to face. "You first." He pointed at Alex.

Alex shook himself and then took a deep breath. "Alex Meredith, formerly of Boston."

"And you?" He pointed at Marjorie.

"Marjorie Thiel. I'm from Flagstaff, Arizona."

The man's eyes took on a shocked look of surprise which he quickly tried to mask. "And you?" He pointed at me. Now his tone was different.

"Kellogg Jones. Boise."

This time he made no effort to conceal his surprise. He shook his head and muttered a soft "Damn."

I wasn't real sure I liked the fact that my name was causing a stir. It had done the same with Susan and I had no idea what it meant. I had a feeling it wasn't good.

The skeleton man got to his feet and paced back and forth in the limited space. Up close, he looked even more like a skeleton. He was unbelievably thin and tall. His skin was pure white and his clothes hung loosely on him.

"I'm afraid to ask this," he said after a few moments of pacing, "but who was your friend?" He made a slight gesture toward the hall.

I looked over at Marjorie. I had never known Craig's last name.

"Craig Kendall," she said. "I'm not sure where he was from. I never heard him say."

For some reason, the tall man looked relieved. He went out into the hall, pulling the door closed behind him.

"Are you both all right?" I asked.

Marjorie nodded. "I think so. What happened?"

"Alex and Craig surprised them as we planned, but Susan spoiled things by jumping in the middle of it. The woman shot Craig and Alex hit their guy. The bullet went through him and hit Susan."

There was a long silence in the room. I went back over the disaster in the hall. How could we have been so stupid as to think surprising them would work? We had jumped into a situation that we knew nothing about and now Craig was dead. And Susan was dead. My one hope of getting back. I pushed that thought away and turned to Marjorie. "How'd you get caught?"

She shook her head. "I was so stupid. When I heard the shots, I glanced around the corner. I saw she had Alex and was motioning for you also, so I turned and started to run. He was coming in the stern door. He just pointed his gun at me. I guess he heard the shots and figured I was in on it. If I would have not panicked and walked. . . or gone the other way. . ."

"Don't worry about it," I said. "This entire thing was a mistake. A big one. Alex, are you all right?"

Alex blinked a few times and then looked over at me. "I will be fine," he said softly.

It was obvious he was in a light shock. We sat there in silence for another minute. I tried not to think about how I would feel if I were Alex and had killed two people. I wouldn't be handling it even as well as he was. To try to stop my mind going over and over what had happened, I concentrated on the room.

There seemed to be nothing that would make it special. It was as lush as any of the first-class rooms on the *Titanic*. But I couldn't spot one extra panel or closet. Absolutely nothing. We had probably guessed wrong—there wasn't one main device in the center. Yet, why would they guard this room? And why had he called Susan a Lomax? If she was, why had she even mentioned the Lomax in the first place? Just for one minute I wished I could start getting a few answers to questions instead of getting so damn many new questions.

I turned on the couch so I could see Marjorie and Alex better. Alex looked very pale and his eyes seemed unfocused. Marjorie gave me a half-smile.

"Any suggestions?"

Marjorie slowly shook her head, then squirmed, trying to pull her hands free. "I wish they'd loosen these up. My fingers are starting to hurt."

I pulled on my ties and felt the sharp bite as the twine dug into my skin. I was tempted to get to my feet and somehow try to get the door open. But that seemed utterly fruitless. Chances were both of our captors were outside the door and I wouldn't get farther than a few steps if I tried to make a run for it.

But at the same time, I hated the thought of sitting there waiting for them to do whatever they wanted to us. I was just about to suggest to Marjorie and Alex that we try the door, when it opened and both the guard woman and the skeleton man came back in.

He motioned at the couch and then sat down on the bed. The guard woman moved over to Alex. Without the slightest hesitation, she untied his bonds. Then she pulled Marjorie around and untied hers. Her grasp felt strong and tight as she turned me and untied my wrists. She tossed the twine into a corner and moved back over to the door where she stood with her back against it, staring across the room.

I rubbed my wrists and hands, trying to get the blood flowing again. We had just killed one of their people and now we were being untied. Why? This was getting stranger by the minute.

"I'm Patrick," the skeleton man said, giving us a half-smile. "Not my full or complete name, but enough for now. This is Shara." He pointed at the guard woman. She didn't move.

He was trying the "let's-all-be-friends" method, but I wasn't going to go along. I had a hundred questions and it was about time someone started answering them. If he wanted information from us, he was going to have to give a bunch in return.

"I hate games," I said. "So tell me straight off why you untied us."

Patrick smiled. "Because I don't plan on killing you, and it would be impossible to catch you again after the next cycle. So it seems to make more sense to untie you and see if we can talk. So answer a question for me. Why were you trying to free the Lomax?"

"To have her help us get back," Marjorie said.

Patrick leaned back on the bed and laughed. He was so thin it appeared his jaw would become detached from his skull at any moment. It was as if we were watching an animated skull from an old movie.

"Her help you?" he said after a moment. "I'm afraid that would not have been the case, even if it were possible."

"Why?" I asked.

"Because she is a Lomax," he said. "She is here to destroy this group in any way she can. I'm amazed she didn't kill you the first time you met, wherever that was."

Now I laughed a hard, purposeful laugh. "That's what I thought you were," I said. "Why should I believe you any more than her?" She hadn't actually said that, but telling him she had might put him off balance.

"She said that?" he asked. "And when did she tell you that?"

"Before we came through the mirror."

He jumped to his feet, his face tight and very serious. "How long before you came through?"

His sudden action caught me off guard. "Since she got here?" I asked. "Or since she told me?"

He looked over at Shara who also looked very worried. "She would have been able to signal soon after she discovered the mirror," Shara said to Patrick in answer to the unasked question.

"When did she discover the mirror device?" Patrick demanded. "She's been here for nine cycles. That's what we were going by. We assumed she came through immediately."

"I brought the mirror up out of the water twenty-four hours before that."

Patrick looked at Shara.

She shook her head. "They might already have it, depending on where the device was found in relation to their base."

Patrick looked back at me. "Where is the device located?"

"I assume you mean the mirror. It's about a day's travel into the Idaho primitive area. A very remote region."

Patrick nodded. "Then we've got at least this cycle."

"For what?" I didn't like the sound of what he was saying. Fred and Constance would be guarding that mirror. I sure didn't want them in the middle of any war.

"Time," Patrick said, "before the Lomax team Susan undoubtedly called to get to where you left the mirror. We can only hope our people will be able to trace us and arrive here before they get there. If not, we will have to make this fight alone."

"I have friends guarding that mirror. What will happen to them?"

Patrick's face twisted but held its cold look. "I doubt if they will be able to stop them. The Lomax are very efficient. They need that mirror to send a squad against us. Your friends will be fighting maybe six or seven like her."

"Fighting? How can I trust what you are saying any more than I should have trusted what Susan told me?"

Patrick shrugged. "Don't, then. I've untied you. You are free to go anytime you would like. But tell me, will your friends try to protect your mirror?"

I imagined Constance and Fred sitting in their lodge. That mirror was their only link with me. They would protect it with their lives. I would do the same if the situation was reversed. "Yes," I said.

"How many of them are there?"

"Three," I said.

Patrick shook his head slowly. "I'm sorry, but I doubt if they will have much luck against the Lomax. Lomax are a very cold and cruel people. They are called the Ice People for more reasons than their white hair."

"Then we've got to get back and warn them."

Patrick sighed. "I'm afraid that that's not going to be easy." He glanced up at Shara and then back at me.

"You mean you don't have a way back either?" Marjorie said.

Patrick shook his head.

"Did Susan?" I asked.

"The Lomax? No, she didn't either." Patrick stood, went to Shara, and whispered in her ear. She nodded and he turned and faced us. "I wasn't planning on showing you this, but it seems I may need your help in defending this ship."

He moved around the couch to a section of oak paneling on the bow wall. With a few light touches, the paneling slid silently back.

He motioned for us to come closer and Marjorie and I both moved over beside him.

In my life I had seen a lot of things that were so amazing or special that it, as the old saying goes, took my breath away. Usually, it occurred when I looked across a mountain range at sunset, or when I stood in front of a piece of fine art. I suppose it was a deep feeling of appreciation for something that goes beyond everyday beauty. As I stood in front of that open panel, I again felt that same deep, open-mouthed sense of wonder.

The area behind the panel was a deep black, with no visible corners or walls. It was as if I was looking into a huge, completely black room. Suspended waist high and what appeared to be only a few feet inside the blackness was a bluish tinted, crystal-clear replica of the *Titanic*.

I took a moment to simply stare at the fantastic beauty of the floating ship before I started to look at its details. It was at least ten feet long and three feet high, with the starboard side facing us. Every detail was there, yet completely see-through. I could look down through the boat deck into the first-class lounge. I could see the very booth Marjorie and I had sat in. I could see the shelves of books in the library and each step of the grand staircase.

That alone would have been enough, but hundreds of tiny globes of green light, single or in groups, dotted the insides of the ship. Some of the tiny balls floated slowly through the ship. Six green globes filled the small room beside the one bright white dot in the center of the ship. For a moment I stared at the tiny green globe that symbolized where I stood.

"The main time device that keeps us cycling?" I finally asked.

"Yes," Patrick said. "I'm afraid so."

"This is a time machine?" Marjorie asked.

Patrick nodded without looking away from the model ship.

"Amazing," Alex said from behind me. I glanced back at him. A little color seemed to have returned to his cheeks. A good sign. Marjorie reached out and squeezed his arm.

I turned back to gaping at the beautiful blue ship with its tiny globes. "I assume," I said after another minute of silence, "that you are from the future."

Patrick looked over at me. "Why would you say that?"

"Susan admitted she was," I said. "You being from the future, too, would seem to make as much sense as anything. Isn't this similar to your time devices?"

Patrick shook his head and looked back at the suspended ship. "Nothing at all, I'm afraid. This is as far ahead of us as one of your airlines would be to a covered wagon."

I kept staring at the suspended ship and the green globes. It looked so simple, yet so amazingly complex. "Is there any indication how this hooks up to the mirrors?"

"None that we have found," Patrick said.

"You mean there's no machinery?" Marjorie asked. "Just this?"

Again Patrick nodded.

"And therefore not much hope of finding a way to reverse the mirrors and send us back through. Right?"

Patrick shrugged. "There might have been, given enough time. Lawrence felt he was making headway. But we don't have the time."

He sighed and continued staring at the beautiful ship and the tiny floating green globes, all floating in the pure blackness.

"And now we don't have Lawrence."

CHAPTER SIXTEEN

First-Class Stateroom C-85
Fifth Cycle
April 14, 1912

AS I GOT older, I slowly came to the realization that there were no absolutes in the real world. I had been taught, way back, by television, by books, by my parents, that there were "good guys" and "bad guys" and that the good guys should always win. That nice, clean perception of the world dominated everything in my early years. Comics, movies, even the history books in school all screamed that one side was right and the other was wrong and all a person had to do was be on the right side and everything would be nifty keen.

Then I faced boot camp and the good guys made me carry a gun. The good guys dropped bombs on villages in 'Nam. And the good guys shot kids on college campuses. Suddenly, white hats and black hats didn't exist. They were all shaded in different tones of gray, the shade depending on which side you happened to be looking from. It was a terrible realization and one I fought against for many years. Mostly without success.

So who was on the right side this time? Who was the lightest shade of gray? Patrick or Susan? Both had said they wanted to protect the *Titanic* group from an enemy who wanted to destroy it. And for some reason, I had come to assume that the Lomax, whoever they were, were the ones the ship needed protecting against. I was beginning to doubt that the Lomax even existed. Maybe some great joker in the future had made up this terrible enemy for both sides to fight instead of fighting each other. I doubted it, but it made as much sense as anything else I had heard so far.

The logical side of my mind always wanted to weigh the facts, stick them in outline form, and then stand back to see what it showed. When that test failed, as it sometimes did, I always trusted my instincts. On both scales, Patrick was coming out ahead. And he was doing it by simple, small actions.

For example, the three of us were free. Marjorie had gone and changed into some clothes with only a promise that she wouldn't say anything to anyone about the ship in the wall. Shara had had no reason to call Susan a Lomax when she did unless that was what she truly believed Susan to be. Patrick had had no real reason to show us the blue crystal ship behind the panel. Yet he had. A few small actions that mounted up to trust. In this case, those actions were all I had to go on. It looked, for now, as if I was going to have to trust Patrick.

Besides that, if what he said was true, Fred and Constance would be in trouble. Trusting Patrick seemed to be the only way to help them. But not even Patrick thought helping them was possible.

As Shara let Marjorie back into the room, Patrick checked his watch. "Four hours until the end of this cycle. It's time we come up with a course of action."

I had been standing for most of the last hour in front of the scale model of the *Titanic*. Alex was back sitting on the couch and Patrick was sitting with his legs crossed on the bed.

Marjorie moved across the room and stood beside me. "It seems to me," I said, "that our choices are limited."

Patrick nodded slowly. "In many ways."

"You obviously have something in mind," Marjorie said.

I could feel Marjorie's arm brushing against mine. Having her standing there made me feel stronger. I liked that feeling.

"Yes, I do," Patrick said. "Defense. It's imperative to the survival of this group that we stop the coming attack."

"First off," I said, "why are you so sure there will be an attack? How and what are they going to attack? And how are you so sure of the timetable involved?" Those questions should keep him busy.

"Susan was the first Lomax to have found her way into this group. She came through unprepared and cycled very near Lawrence. She didn't expect us to be here, so we were able to capture her. However, I have no doubt that she sent for help before she came through, giving her people the exact location of your mirror."

"But why are you so sure they are coming?" I asked. "It seems to me that if they have time travel, they could send a group to a point right after she called them. Then they would be here and I wouldn't."

Patrick smiled. "It's too bad it doesn't work that way. We would already have our people in place and defending the ship. I suppose the Seeders, the inventors of that"—he pointed at the floating, clear ship behind me—"could have mastered such exacting time manipulation. But to both us and the Lomax, it's a totally new science. There are many, many limitations and complications. For example, to travel in time, you must not only move through time, but through a distance in space. And every mass has a general effect on the time and space around it."

"You mean a bed or a chair can affect time?" Marjorie asked. I could tell she was having trouble keeping from laughing. Alex had the same look of amusement on his face.

"In a slight way," Patrick said. "Everything is interrelated with everything around it. But it is the force of intelligence that has the greatest effect on the flow of time. That's one of the major limitations. That's why I am sure that the Lomax will not be able to send more than eight at us from your mirror. At least in the first wave."

"You've completely lost me," I said. "Are you trying to say that intellect has an effect on time? And on time travel?"

Patrick nodded. "All thought processes, whether from a house cat or from a scientist, affect the space and time around the entity. That factor alone creates incredible limitations. We can only arrive in your time at certain points and at certain times. And once a point is used, it cannot be reused.

"The Lomax have the same restrictions. If they had a team ready when she contacted them, and assuming the location of the mirror is as remote as you say it is, then your friends will be facing a very hard fight within the next few hours. Possibly longer if the Lomax were not ready or had already used their present window to the time. However, on this end we have to assume that they will arrive during the next cycle. We need to be prepared."

"What about help from your people?" I asked. "Haven't you been here longer?"

Patrick nodded. "I was here first. But it took a lot of our resources to get Lawrence and Shara through. I don't think we can realistically expect help this next cycle. And probably not for a cycle or two after that."

"And you're convinced they will attack the people on this ship?"

"Without a doubt," Patrick said.

"But why?" Marjorie said. "It makes no sense."

Patrick sighed. "Let me put it this way. The descendants of the people on this ship, and in a few other places like it, are the enemies of the Lomax. The Lomax figure if they can come back through time and kill the people in those groups, their enemies would be gone. There are time paradoxes involved that would take too long to explain, but in essence, that's how it would work."

"That's basically what Susan said. I suppose you'd do it too if you could?"

"Yes, I'm afraid so," Patrick said, looking straight at me without hesitation. "But so far our emphasis has been on defending our own as we find them."

Damned if I knew why, but I believed him. I still didn't trust him, but I believed him. My instincts told me the best thing

to do would be to step back and stay neutral. But with Fred and Constance right in the middle, it looked like I had to choose one side or the other. And if Patrick's side was against those who were going to attack the lodge, then Patrick's side I would join.

"If we assume what you say is true," Alex said, "then I assume we need to prepare for a fight. Do you want to draft other prisoners? Or what do you have in mind?"

"I hate the thought of doing that," Patrick said. "For obvious reasons. But I don't see much choice. Unlike Susan, the next wave of Lomax is going to come through your mirror armed and ready to fight. And they're going to cycle right with us."

"It's too bad we couldn't stop them before they come through." I looked back at the blue-tinted ship.

"That would be ideal," Patrick said, "but I'm afraid impossible."

I studied the model of the *Titanic* floating in the blackness behind me. There was something about those tiny green globes and the transparent model ship that was bothering me. Why would anyone build a time machine like that? It was so perfectly accurate, it was as if I were actually looking at the real *Titanic* from a distance. I felt the annoying feeling that I was missing something. That the answer was obvious and right in front of me if only I was smart enough to see it.

"Patrick," I said, "help me with something for a moment."

Marjorie lightly touched my arm as Patrick moved over and stood beside her looking into the blackness at the ship. Alex stood and joined us.

"You said Lawrence didn't find any other machinery except this model. Right?"

"We didn't tear out any walls, but he was completely convinced there wasn't any."

"Did he ever try touching the ship?"

"There's a field barrier just inside the panel. Reach forward and you can feel it."

I hesitantly reached toward the suspended ship until I felt a solid, invisible surface about six inches inside the panel. I ran my hand along it for a few inches and then pulled back. It felt like hard plastic, very smooth and slightly warm. Completely invisible.

"Did Lawrence have a theory why points marking the people are green and the one marking the location of the model is white?"

"None that he mentioned," Patrick said.

"What I don't understand," I said, "is why make a model of the ship? Hidden like this, it certainly wasn't for show."

"Maybe it's an actual picture," Marjorie said. "Like some sort of movie."

Suddenly the nagging feeling that I was missing something was gone. Marjorie was right. It was more than a three-dimensional picture. Somehow, it actually was the *Titanic* floating there in front of us.

"Patrick," I said, "did Lawrence mention that he thought this was a projection of the actual ship?"

"I think that was one of the angles he was working at. Why?"

"Let's assume that's exactly what it is. Why would someone build such a thing? To what purpose? From what's going on and what you tell me, it seems obvious that whoever set this all up were masters of the use of time. Why have something like this and no time-travel machinery? It doesn't make any sense."

"I agree," Patrick said. "It doesn't."

"It doesn't," I said, "unless you look at that white light as the hookup through time to a main power source."

"What difference would that make?" Alex asked.

"A great deal," I said. "If that is the connection to the main source, what would be the only thing that might come in handy on this side?"

"A control panel," Patrick said.

"Exactly," I said. "I would wager that those green globes represent some sort of time field around each of us. The same field that gives us such a shock when we touch a regular passenger or that makes the clothes and glasses we touch invisible. And that they are all green because everything is working fine."

"You mean," Marjorie said, "that each of those globes is a switch?"

"Possible," Patrick said. "It would be logical that the builders would set up a way to send undesirables back. They wouldn't want the actual devices on board for fear of discovery, but a control panel makes sense. It would be safer."

"Exactly," I said.

"But what good would that be if you can't reach it?" Marjorie asked.

"Did Lawrence say anything about the field barrier being a protective screen?"

"Just the opposite," Patrick said. "He thought the barrier was part of whatever held the model ship in place."

"So there should be something that is used to reach through the barrier. Obviously Lawrence didn't find anything like that."

"True," Patrick said. "But I don't think he was looking along those lines."

"Looking for what?" Marjorie asked.

I shrugged. "Damned if I know what it would be. But it's probably something so obvious we don't see it. Something used to activate that control panel."

"Excuse me," Alex said as both Patrick and I turned and started scanning the small room. "But I don't understand what you mean by control panel. I cannot see how it would be possible that this model ship could control anything."

I looked at Alex and suddenly had a very clear realization of how far the human race had advanced in the last eighty years. How could I explain a control panel to a man who had never seen an airplane, let alone a computer? Obviously he had heard stories about such things, but he had never had the chance to sit in an automobile or gaze in at the cockpit of an airplane.

"Have you been into this ship's wheelhouse?" Patrick asked.

"A few years back," Alex said.

"That's the room from which they steer the ship," Patrick said. "Correct?"

Alex nodded.

"But the entire ship isn't in that room," Marjorie said. "The wheels and the instruments in there are only the controls. That's what Doc is saying this model ship is. A control."

"But I don't understand how it could be," Alex said.

"I'm not so sure either," Patrick said. "But remember one thing about advancing technologies. The more complex the device, the simpler it looks."

Alex stared at the beautiful ship floating in the blackness. "So what are we looking for?"

"Something to press a few buttons with," I said.

"You know," Marjorie said. "If what you said is right, then wouldn't the builders put whatever they needed close by and in plain sight?"

"You might think so," Patrick said. "But where?"

"My father used to stick the house key inside the molding right by the doorbell," Marjorie said. "My mother always hated that." Marjorie stuck her head slightly inside the panel and then looked to her right. "How about this?"

With an audible click, she pulled a thin glass rod from inside the partition and held it up in the light of the room. It was four feet long, not more than a quarter inch in diameter, and tapered to a dull point on one end. It reminded me of the rods my mother used to have hanging from her drapes. "Always use the pull rods," she used to say. "Because your hands are dirty and it costs money to clean drapes."

Marjorie handed the rod to Patrick and then looked back inside the panel where she found it. "There are two more of them here," she said. "They all look the same."

"Leave them," Patrick said. "I can't believe Lawrence didn't find this."

"Too obvious," I said. "And like you said, he wasn't looking."

"So what's it for?" Alex asked.

"Maybe to press buttons," Patrick said. He turned and slowly stuck the rod at the model ship. The point of the stick reached the barrier and he hesitated for a moment. "Feels like I'm poking something very soft," he said. "I'm sure I can get it through."

"Don't until we figure out what we want to do," I said. "You might start something that can't be stopped and we want to at least have a plan ready."

He nodded and pulled the rod back. He leaned it in the corner of the room and then turned around. He was smiling. "It just might work."

I nodded. "If I touch it to my green ball in there."

"And you want to go?"

"I need to warn my friends. If that stick works, we might be able to stop your Lomax friends on the other side before they reach here. If nothing else, we can take the mirror and run like hell."

"I'm going with you," Marjorie said.

"I doubt if it will work that way," Patrick said. "Lawrence figured that each of us here is tied to the original devices that sent us. I'm afraid if we do get that to reverse somehow, then you would return to where you started."

"You mean the same time and everything?"

"I doubt that," Patrick said. "The cycles here are set up to parallel real time. You'd go back to whatever device sent you."

"My grandmother's hand mirror," Marjorie said. "I wonder where it's at now."

Patrick checked his watch. "We've got about three and a half hours left until the next cycle. We've got to be setting up some sort of defense."

"I agree," I said. "And I think I need to get back to my friends and set up something there. How far away can instruments track the mirror?"

Patrick shrugged. "If it's one of the early ones, maybe a few miles away. The newer ones you almost have to be holding. That's why we can't find them."

"If I'm in time, maybe we can get that mirror hidden."

"That would stop them as effectively as anything," Patrick said. "Give my people a chance to get here."

I picked up the thin glass rod. It felt unnaturally light in my hands. And like the barrier, it felt slightly warm.

"I'll be going along," Alex said. "If I understood you right, I can because I came through the same mirror."

"I'd rather have the help on this side," Patrick said.

"I'm sure Marjorie will be able to talk to whoever you might need. As you said, it would be advantageous to stop them before they get here."

"I agree," I said. "With Alex, there would be five of us on the other side. Almost a fair fight if your estimates are right and if it comes down to that. We should at least be able to slow them down."

Patrick shook his head, but didn't say anything more as I turned toward the model ship floating in the blackness. It was so incredibly beautiful, I wanted to stop and stare. But the large knot building in my stomach told me I'd better keep on if I was going to do anything at all. I'd been stupid enough to get here in the first place, at least I could be smart enough to try to get back.

I punched the pointed end of the rod slowly at the ship. It hit the barrier and I felt as if I were pushing it into a soft pillow. It took a little more pressure, but not much. Slowly, the forward resistance disappeared, but it still felt as if I had the rod stuck in a thick vat of pudding.

"I'm through the barrier," I said.

I eased the rod toward the ship. The closer it got, the longer and thinner the rod looked, as if I were holding on to a very long pole that got smaller off into the distance. I pulled it back a few inches and the rod shortened by fifty feet.

"Amazing," Patrick said. "It must be an actual dimensional projection of the entire ship."

"A what?" I asked.

"We are actually seeing the ship," Patrick said. "Or at least everything that is involved with the time field around us."

"So when I go poking at that, I'm going to also be poking at us?"

"In a sense, that's right."

"Does that change anything?"

Patrick shook his head. "It shouldn't. I think you're right in that it's an advanced control panel. You won't actually be touching any physical matter. Only the time fields around them."

"So if I touch the green globe that represents me, it might send me back?"

"Makes as much sense as anything else."

"What happens if it takes him out of the cycle?" Alex asked. "Turns him into a passenger?"

"I don't know," Patrick said. "It might, but I doubt that the builders of this would want to introduce people who don't belong on the *Titanic* into the flow of history. There would be far too many complications and possible repercussions."

"I don't like it," Marjorie said. "We don't know what might happen and it seems foolish to take such a chance."

I glanced at Marjorie. I could see and feel her concern. But to me it seemed worth the chance, just as making the dive and going through the mirror in the first place had been worth it. If Fred and Constance were truly in danger and this was the best chance of helping them, then I was going to take it.

I lightly touched her arm. I wanted to give her a big hug, but I didn't. Instead,

I turned back to face the model ship. "I think everyone should move over to the other side of the room in case my hand isn't too steady. I've got an awful small button to try to push."

"Damn it," Marjorie said. "I wish you wouldn't." She hesitated for a moment, then moved across the room to the far wall.

"Remember white hair," Patrick said as he followed Marjorie over to the other side of the room. "All the Lomax have white hair. They wear it proudly and never cover or dye it. They are uniformly strong and quick. Be very very careful."

I nodded. Alex moved over and stood beside me.

"You might want to get out of the way in case this blows up or something."

Alex shook his head. "I'm going back, also. After eighty years here, I really am not bothered by the risk."

"Good luck, folks," I said. I gave Marjorie a half-smile. I was going to miss her.

I eased the rod toward the ship. By the time I had two feet of the rod's four-foot length inside the barrier, it looked as if I were controlling a hundred-foot-long pole. Only I could still very clearly see the end of the rod, almost as if it were magnified.

I expected to feel resistance when I touched the side of the ship, but there was none.

Slowly, making very sure not to get the rod anywhere near the two other green balls beside mine and Alex's, I eased the rod through the side of C deck and toward the white light. I could clearly see the distinction between all of the globes. With two hands holding the stick as steady as I could, I eased the stick toward the glowing green globe that represented me.

As I touched it, I almost half expected to feel a real touch on my shoulder. Or maybe a shock. But there was no actual feeling. My green globe turned a bright, glowing red, like a warning light. I pulled the rod straight back out of the barrier, leaned it against the wall and waited, holding my breath. Any second I expected to have the blackness sweep over me and then find myself back in the lodge.

After a long few seconds, I exhaled loudly and looked first at Alex and then at the model ship floating in the blackness. Nothing had happened. It hadn't sent me back. It had simply turned my green globe to a red one.

"I was afraid that might happen," Patrick said.

So was I.

CHAPTER SEVENTEEN

Boat Deck
Fifth Cycle
April 15, 1912

"THREE MORE SONGS left," Marjorie said as the band started another ragtime tune.

"Lovely." I glanced up from the deck chairs I had been attempting to tie together with frozen hands and looked at the eight-piece band. The white life jackets over their formal dinner clothes gave them an almost comic look. I didn't think they were so funny. I hadn't thought so the first time I had been out here building a raft, and I didn't think so this time. They were ghosts a whole bunch more real than Gretchen and these ghosts frightened me something awful.

"I think this might actually work," Alex said, straightening up from where he had also been tying deck chairs into a raft. He blew on his hands. "At least it will give us a fighting chance."

"More than most of these poor souls got," I said, indicating all the passengers that were streaming past us toward the stern of the boat. The looks on their faces ranged from blank shock to total fear bordering on hysterics. I'd bet the look on my face was much closer to the fear side.

Alex sighed and studied the flow of doomed passengers. "After eighty years, watching this scene still bothers me. I always preferred to stay down below in my room." He took a long look at the passengers, slowly shook his head, and then went back to working on the raft.

One more look, a quick smile at Marjorie, and I did the same. The raft was our insurance policy. We'd had a long discussion about what we should do after my globe turned red and I hadn't gone anywhere. Patrick figured that I would cycle back to the lodge at the next cycle, or somewhere else. He figured the energy needed for transportation was only brought through from the source at cycle intervals. That was why, when I turned my globe red, I hadn't gone anywhere. His argument made a sort of logical sense, but I really didn't like the thought of gambling my life on it.

When I pushed him, he even admitted there was a very slight chance that I would stay right through the cycle and go down with the ship. I figured that would be a pretty good way for the inventors of all this to get rid of bad apples among the "prisoners."

But Patrick insisted it wouldn't work that way. The Seeders would never allow someone from the future any chance at all of getting into the current time stream around the *Titanic*. Logically, I would be sent back to my own current time.

I wished.

After considerably more argument, Alex had elected to also activate his globe. He figured he might as well tag along with me if that was how it was going to work. Since I was so good at it, I used the stick to turn his globe red. For a moment afterwards I felt as if I had killed him. Maybe I had.

After that, Patrick and Marjorie had gone up to the library to recruit a few defenders. Alex and I had gone down to E deck to talk to a few old friends of Alex's into also helping if there was a fight.

We found it hard to convince anyone to help, especially when both Alex and I were not really convinced whose side was the "right" side and whose side needed to be guarded against. We tossed the basic situation at them, plus some of our own doubts about Patrick, and somehow got a few to agree to meet up with him after the next cycle and do whatever they thought looked right.

Forty minutes after the ship hit the iceberg, Alex and I had worked our way back up the tilted grand staircase to the boat deck and started building the raft. We had nothing else to do and nothing to lose.

"How much time do we have on board after the cycle?" Alex asked. "I've always wondered what exactly happened, but past asking how many of these poor souls got killed, I never did."

"Not much, I'm afraid," I said, standing and trying to take some of the kinks out of my knees from kneeling for too long on the cold wooden deck. "The ship damn near does a headstand, then settles back to about forty-five degrees and slides

under the water. There are some reports that it broke in two at that moment. If we don't cycle, we need to be off the ship almost immediately."

"He's right," Marjorie said. "You'd have a better chance being in the water." She tried to give me a weak smile. I could tell she didn't like the idea of me going in the water. I didn't like it much either.

"Are we finished?" Alex asked.

I studied the raft. It looked solid enough. We had layered deck chairs like plywood, five deep. Each layer was securely overtied and then the next layer turned the other direction and tied. It was a hundred times better than my first attempt. "As good as we'll ever be."

"Which will it be?" Alex said. "Over the side or down the deck?"

"Down the deck," I said. "I don't think I could stand the shock of hitting the water. Let's see if we can float it off the deck as the water comes up."

"One song left," Marjorie said. "Remember that first funnel collapses. You don't want to be anywhere near it when it does."

I glanced up at the huge funnel that towered over us. She was right. We'd have to try to go sideways away from the ship. I moved around in front of the raft and tried to pick up the front end. It was heavy and I couldn't get it more than a few inches off the ground. But it would be easy for the three of us to drag it down the steeply sloped deck. The water wasn't yet up to the bow end of the boat deck, but it didn't have far to go.

We all got good holds and started pulling. In front of us, on top of the officers' quarters, a dozen men frantically worked at loosening the two remaining lifeboats. A few passengers stood on the boat deck, watching, or staring out at the lifeboats rowing away on the dark sea below. Almost all the passengers had gone toward the stern, climbing to the highest point left out of the water in hopes that the ship would stay afloat.

We dragged the raft down past the band and past the empty davits that stood mocking those still left on board. "Not too close to the rail," I said as we approached the bow end of the boat deck. "Don't want to get tangled up in it when the raft floats."

Alex nodded and we dropped the raft. The water swirled and splashed against the face of the deck. One swell washed up and drenched my feet and kicked the raft sideways toward Alex.

The sudden jarring sting of that intensely cold water brought the fear I'd been holding right to the surface. I didn't want to die. Not now. Not after finally starting to really feel alive again. Even with all my years of diving, I wouldn't last fifteen minutes in that cold water. If we didn't cycle, the raft had better work. I took a deep breath of the biting, cold air and forced myself to calm down.

Behind and above us, the band paused for a moment and then started into the hymn "Autumn." Another wave cut around us and sent cold jabs of pain up my legs and into my stomach.

Being careful not to slip on the slanted, wet deck, Marjorie moved over and gave me a hard, desperate hug, then one first and final kiss.

"I'll see you," I said as I hugged her back. "Don't think you can get rid of me this easily."

She smiled a half-smile at my stupid attempt at humor.

I kissed her a second time. One for me to remember. "Be careful," I said. Then I turned to Alex. "Ready?"

He nodded. "Why not?"

The next wave cut at our feet and kicked the raft sideways as the blackness of the cycle pulled me from the cold.

If I could have cheered, I would have. It looked as if we wouldn't be using the raft.

Good. Real good.

Now where were we going?

CHAPTER EIGHTEEN

The Lodge
June 30, 1990

ALEX AND I appeared, standing side by side, in front of the lodge fireplace. The mirror was on the mantel behind us. Constance was working in the kitchen with her back to us and I could smell venison steaks cooking from the direction of the outdoor grill. It was the best smell that had ever crossed my nose. We had made it. Patrick had been right. I wanted to jump up and down, dance and shout, but the pack held me tight to the floor.

"Better tell Fred to put on a couple more steaks," I said as I slipped the pack off and leaned it against the wall.

Constance jumped, sending the dish she was holding clattering across the counter. She jerked around. There was no way in the world I will ever forget the look of pure joy that filled her face as she saw us standing there.

"Doc!" she yelled. In the quickest move I had ever seen that big lady make, she was across the room and doing her best to break half my ribs with a hug. I hugged her right back. She felt damn good.

I'd been gone thirty hours and it seemed like a lifetime. Alex had been gone eighty-one years. I couldn't imagine what he was feeling right now.

The front screen door banged opened and Fred and Steven ran in. "Doc! Hot damn!" Fred shouted and started toward us. At that same moment Gretchen came through the log wall beside the fireplace.

Talk about a welcome back.

Constance pulled me out of the ghost's way and Fred moved over and slapped me on the back. In front of the fire Gretchen and Alex faced each other.

I glanced over at Steven. He was slumped in a chair, his eyes closed. I didn't want to think about what he was hearing in his head.

Alex looked completely stunned at seeing Gretchen. He started to take a step toward her, then stopped. The intense cold radiating from her wouldn't allow him to get any closer. I watched his eyes study her. I could feel the sadness and regret he felt. Eighty-one years was a long time, but it hadn't been long enough for him to forget.

Slowly, without ever breaking her intense expression, Gretchen faded and was gone.

I moved over beside Alex and touched his arm. He seemed in shock. Steven groaned and sat up. His face had gone white, but he was smiling.

"She's glad you have returned," he said.

Alex took a deep breath and straightened his shoulders. His hands shook as he fought for control. "I didn't mean to leave her."

"She knows," Steven said. "I could sense that she understood."

Alex sighed, moved over to the couch and dropped down on it. After a moment he asked, "How can I help her?"

"I think she needs you to return to the Inn," he said. "She waited for you there to return and she is still waiting."

Alex glanced over at me. "You said the town was gone. Flooded out. Is going back to the Inn possible?"

"If you mean go down to where she plays the piano, I suppose so." I turned to Fred. "Do we have enough tanks?"

He nodded.

"Then it's possible," I told Alex. Making a dive into that lake with a beginning diver would be hard, but we could do it.

"Will she wait a little longer?

Steven laughed. "She will wait as long as it takes."

"Thank you," Alex said.

I had a sudden idea and turned to Steven. "There may be some people coming to try to take Alex's mirror. If that happens, would Gretchen help us protect it?" I didn't know what she could do, but I figured it was worth the question.

Steven shrugged. "I doubt if she has any interaction at all with the living. She is tied to Alex and the mirror."

I shrugged. "You never know when that might come in handy."

"All right," Fred said. "What's this about someone coming to take the mirror? And where did you go? And who is this?"

I laughed. "It's a long story that for now we're going to have to keep short. And, yes, this is Alex. Even though you know that can't be possible."

I finished the introductions and we all moved over around the dining room table. Alex and I both ended up turning down Fred's offer to put steaks on the grill for us. My stomach was still full from the huge lunch Constance had forced down me before I left and Alex said he had eaten right before he was pulled through the mirror, so he wasn't hungry yet, either. He said he hadn't been hungry in eighty-one years and wasn't sure if he could even remember how to eat.

That statement set off a dozen questions from Constance, Fred, and Steven, so while they ate, I tried to give them a quick rundown of where I had gone and what had happened.

Fred wouldn't believe I had actually been on the *Titanic* and after three attempts, I gave up trying to explain to Constance how the six-hour cycles worked and why Alex was exactly the same age as the very hour he had left the mining town of Roosevelt in 1909.

Sitting there trying to explain what went on started me doubting the last thirty hours. Maybe I'd had a bad dream. Or too much to drink. I might have been able to convince myself it hadn't happened if not for the fact that Alex was sitting across from me and his grandmother's mirror was on the mantel. And I didn't want Marjorie to be a dream. She had been too solid. I wanted her to exist.

I ended my story with a fast explanation of how Patrick thought his enemies might be showing up here real soon to try to take the mirror.

"We have five new guests coming in right now," Fred said.

"How do you know that?"

"Mail drop this morning. There was a note in there that five people had asked directions into here in Yellow Pine. The note said they were almost at the summit when the mail was dropped."

"How long ago was that?"

"An hour," Constance said.

"So if someone is trying to get down that trail now," I said, "how long will it take them?"

"If they make it in the dark," Fred said, "I'd guess five hours at the quickest. Stupid thing to do."

"Well, if Patrick is right and they're going to try to take the mirror, we'd better be ready for them."

"If someone tries to take that mirror," Fred said, "we'll give them a fight."

The smell and the look of that blood-spattered hall in the *Titanic* came flooding back over me. I didn't want to have to stand and watch Fred's or Constance's face as the life drained from it.

I glanced over at Alex. He didn't like the sound of Fred's words either. "I hope we can find another way," I said.

"Suggestions?" Steven said. "If these people are as you say this Patrick described, then they will stop at nothing to get the mirror. Correct?"

"I really don't know," I said. "We could be defending the mirror from the wrong people. Patrick trusted us, but he really had no choice, except to kill us. On the other hand, Susan went along with the rules we put on her. She didn't try to take the mirror by force and I would wager she could have. We sure wouldn't have expected it."

"One thing is clear," Alex said. "If we do not stop whoever is coming down that trail from getting the mirror, there will be a battle fought on the *Titanic*. Some of my friends may be killed and I do not want that. There has been enough killing. I would prefer that we try to deal with it here."

"We could destroy the mirror," Steven said.

"No!" I said. Alex was also shaking his head. That mirror was my only way to Marjorie. "If nothing else, the three of you can take off and hide and Alex and I will go back to the ship to warn the others."

Both Fred and Constance were looking at me with looks that said, *You've got to be crazy*. I didn't blame them. With me saying I wanted to go back to the *Titanic*, it was amazing they weren't flat on the floor in fits of laughter.

"Could Susan have gotten word out to her people after she left here?" Steven asked.

"I don't think so. Patrick seemed to have her wrapped up right from the moment she got there. Plus he made it seem there was no way in and out of the ship except through the original devices like the mirror."

Steven nodded. "So they won't be expecting any resistance at this point."

"But they also won't come in unprepared," I said. "Susan told them who was here. We can count on that."

"It seems to me," Constance said, "that we don't really know who these people are and how they are going to act. They might come in as nice as can be and simply ask to use the mirror."

"They might," I said, "but I doubt it."

"But we have to find out for sure before we do anything," Steven said. "Right?"

"That's the problem." I said.

"That's simple enough," Constance said. "We'll let them come in and prove their intentions."

"You have a plan?" I asked.

Constance smiled her wide, infectious smile. "I have a plan."

***

Three hours later I found myself sitting on the same log Susan and I had sat on three nights before. Again tonight, the lake below me was a deep ink black, the air had a crisp, cold bite to it, and there were more stars in the sky than I could have imagined possible. But this time I was alone and scared. Not scared of the dark or the black lake, but instead of what was about to happen.

After two hours of working over Constance's idea of letting them come in and prove themselves, we had come

---

Some Classic Dean Wesley Smith Stories
Available at your favorite booksellers.

up with a plan of attack. Right now Constance was sitting at the dining room table, reading, and waiting for them to arrive. Alex was hiding upstairs. Fred and Steven were up the trail watching for whoever was coming. When they spotted our guests, Fred was to hotfoot it back to the lodge and warn everyone. I was to hide under the front deck and Fred would hide near the back door. Steven would follow them down the trail after they passed his location.

Constance was to see what they wanted and what their attitude was. If needed, on a signal from her, we were to all come in and surround them. Simple enough plan, if it worked. The simple plan for freeing Susan sure hadn't.

All of us had guns. Constance had a small pistol in the pocket of her apron. Alex had Fred's deer rifle, the same rifle that had killed Lawrence and Susan. Fred and Steven both had pistols. Constance's .22 saddle rifle leaned against the log beside me. I didn't like the thought of carrying it and Fred knew that. But in this case, with my best friends' lives at stake, it was better to be safe than sorry. Amazing how situations can change hard-held beliefs. I didn't plan on firing the rifle at anyone, but I actually felt slightly better having it beside me.

"Doc?"

The sound of Fred's loud whisper damn near sent me tumbling off the log and down the hill. My heart was pounding so hard, I swore they could hear it on the summit.

"Christ! You scared me to death." I grabbed the rifle and climbed the twenty steps back up to the side of the lodge where Fred stood.

"Sorry," he said. "I couldn't see you sitting down there. There's five of them

coming down the trail. One woman and four men. The woman looks to be in charge. They're all carrying guns. You ready?"

"No, but what the hell difference does that make?"

Fred squeezed my arm. "Be careful," he said.

"You too."

He scrambled back up the dirt path around the south side of the lodge while I ducked in under the front deck and lay alongside a small fishing boat he had stored there. From that vantage point, I could see the main trail leading right up to the front steps of the lodge.

I worked at taking slow, deep breaths to force myself to calm down. A long minute later I caught a glimpse of lights coming along the trail. The flashlight beams jerked through the trees as the people who carried them walked the rough trail. I could see five lights. Five of them. Five of us.

At the point where the trail forked, one branch going down to the lake and the other up to the lodge, they paused and clicked the lights off. I could tell they were all wearing similar uniform-like clothes, but other than that, they were nothing more than five dark shapes whose white hair seemed to glow in the black night, just as Susan's had done. They were her people. Again, Patrick had been right. At least about their hair.

"Around back," a woman's voice said. I could see her point in Fred's direction. She turned to another man. "Take a position in the front."

Two of the dark figures separated from the group. One climbed up the trail and around the lodge on the north side. I hoped Fred heard him coming. They had come prepared for a fight and were taking no chances.

The other climbed up and took a position behind a tree, thirty feet to the north of the front steps. I could see that he carried what looked to be an assault rifle in ready position.

The other three moved silently up the main trail to the front steps. They also carried assault rifles, but only one of the men had his in ready position. The woman and the other man carried their rifles on shoulder straps, slung around on their backs.

Once they reached the stairs, they gave up all pretense of being silent. They climbed the stairs and went across the front porch, their boots clomping against the wood, echoing even louder under the porch.

I crawled as silently as I could over near the stairs. If something happened, or Constance gave the signal, I wanted to be able to get inside as fast as possible.

Without knocking, the woman shoved open the front door with a loud bang and went in, followed immediately by the two men.

"Welcome," I heard Constance say through the open front door, "What can I do for you?"

"We've come for the mirror," the woman said. Her voice was low and sounded very cold.

"Mirror?" Constance said. "Oh, you mean the mirror on the fireplace. It's not my mirror to give away. It's hers, and I don't think she wants you to have it."

I could hear the tension and the almost-laughter in Constance's voice. Gretchen must have appeared again. She must have been standing in front of the mirror. I hoped she'd stay there for a moment.

I caught a glimpse of movement near the guard. Steven had moved up behind the man near the tree and as I watched, hit him hard across the back of the head with a baseball-bat-sized stick. The impact made a loud smacking sound and the man crumpled to the ground like a drunk falling off a bar stool. One down and four to go. I hoped Steven hadn't killed him.

Steven gave me the okay sign and started to disarm the man as the woman inside said "Please move aside."

"I don't think she's going to," Constance said.

I chuckled. It sounded as if Gretchen was staying longer than her normal visit.

"Move her aside," the woman ordered.

Steven finished tying the man's arms behind his back and started toward the steps. I crawled out from under the porch.

"I can't get near her," a man's voice said from inside. "She's too—"

The sound of a shot exploded from inside the lodge. Constance! God, they couldn't have shot Constance. They had no reason to. *Please don't let it be Constance.*

Steven beat me up the front steps and to the front door by a fraction of a second.

"Drop the guns!" I heard Alex shout from the top of the stairs.

There was another shot, followed instantly by the second, louder shot of the deer rifle.

"No more!" Steven shouted as he and I charged into the front room of the lodge at the exact same moment that Fred crashed open the back door.

One of the white-haired men lay sprawled on the floor, his head twisted sideways, a bloody hole in his chest. His rifle was half under the couch.

To my right, Constance crouched behind the kitchen counter, pistol in firing position, aimed at the woman.

The white-haired woman and the other man were in the process of swinging their guns up into firing position.

I shot by instinct, not raising the rifle above my chest. Steven, Fred, and Constance also fired. The explosion of sound in the enclosed lodge was tremendous. My ears rang and my eyes stung. The strong smell of gunpowder filled the air in a blue smoke.

Two of our four shots hit the woman in the chest, kicking her backward against the other soldier, knocking him off balance. In an instant, Steven and I both were on top of him, our combined weight and force driving him backward and to the floor. With Fred's help, we had him disarmed and his hands tied in only a few seconds.

Then I stood and turned around. Constance was kneeling beside the woman, checking her pulse. From the look of the two holes in her breast, she was dead. Even in death, her open, gray eyes held a cold, angry look.

"Everyone all right?" I asked.

Constance looked up at me and nodded. Her skin was flushed and she was breathing hard, but otherwise she looked fine.

"There's one of them tied up out back," Fred said. "He's going to have a headache for a while." Fred also looked fine and in control. Much more than I felt at that moment. Over the last day I had seen more death than I had ever wanted to see.

"Same with the one out front," Steven said. "I hit him pretty hard. We should check him out."

"Where's Alex?" I asked. Alex wasn't standing with us. And Gretchen was gone from in front of the fireplace.

I was the first one to the stairs. On the *Titanic* I had had trouble going down stairs fast, but I took those lodge stairs two at a time all the way to the top.

Alex was slumped against the wall near the bathroom door. Gretchen was standing beside him, not looking down at him, but instead at a space to his left, as if he were standing there.

I knelt beside Alex. Blood ran from a small round hole above his right eye in a stream down across his face and into his shirt. The back of his head was gone.

I glanced up at Gretchen. She smiled at me and then faded.

It seemed that Alex had finally joined her.

CHAPTER NINETEEN

Roosevelt Lake, Idaho
July 1, 1990

I DANGLED MY feet in the cold water and let the icy drops work their way into my wet suit. Behind me, Fred adjusted his regulator, gave it two hard breath tests, and then moved over and sat down. Between us on the sand was a cloth deer bag with Alex's body in it.

"Be careful," Constance said. Her voice was low and intense. Her grip was firm on my shoulder. She didn't like the fact that we were making another dive. I didn't like it much either. But all of us understood why we had to do it. We had to return Alex to the Inn.

"We'll be careful, don't worry," Fred said. "Follow us around the shoreline with the spare tank. We'll be back in a few minutes."

Steven patted the spare tank. "Got it right here," he said. "Good luck."

I checked the bag one more time to make sure it was tied securely shut, then pulled my mask down into place.

"Ready," I said.

"After you," Fred said.

I pushed off into the cold water and floated over on my back, using my flotation vest to keep me up while I cleared the fog from my mask one last time. The ice water dripped slowly down my spine. The regulator in my mouth tasted faintly of rubber.

As during the first dive, I felt an odd sense of being at home. I didn't like where we were making this dive, but I liked the feeling of diving.

Fred has his regulator in place and mask cleared. He gave me the thumbs-up sign as Steven slid Alex's body out into the water. I grabbed a hold of one side of the bag while Fred grabbed the other. Then I let the air slowly out of my vest and sank below the surface.

The sound of my own breathing filled the world around me and the feeling of freedom lifted my mood.

A few feet below the surface, we turned around and started kicking slowly for the bottom. I let my ears clear as I went and kept my gaze focused ahead and down. Fred stayed even with me and we pulled Alex's body slightly behind us. The bag seemed heavy in the water, almost as heavy as it had felt the night before.

We had started this dive at the same place as the first dive, only this time we were angling for the main section of the town instead of going straight down and working our way along the bottom.

The pleasant, weightless feeling of the slow descent relaxed me a little. I could feel some of the tension of the last few days floating toward the surface with my bubbles. But not anywhere near enough of it.

It had been a hard, sleepless night and morning since the fight. Two of Susan's

people were dead, and the other three were our prisoners. We had taken Alex's body, along with the other two bodies, and put them in deer bags in the fruit cellar to keep animals away from them.

We had stripped the three prisoners, tied them up in the barn, and then covered them with blankets for warmth. We hid their clothes and guns in case they somehow managed to get free. Then the rest of the night we spent cleaning up the blood. By the time Fred cooked breakfast at eight, you couldn't tell anything had happened.

Except I knew where Alex had died. I had been the one to clean up the remains of the back of his head and scrub the blood drop by drop from the carpet and off the log wall. The leaders, the politicians in Susan and Patrick's war, should be made to clean up after their own battles. After a few chunks of brain and a half dozen scraps of a friend's skull bone, the stupidity of killing for an unknown cause would soon become crystal clear.

But I cleaned it up instead. I had known Alex, if only for a short time. They hadn't.

At nine, Fred, Steven, and I had talked to the prisoners while trying to decide what we should do with them. The thought of being turned over to the state police seemed to absolutely terrify them. I figured it would. They were willing to agree to almost anything in exchange for our not doing that.

Actually, that was what we wanted them to say. Susan's people would be hardpressed to explain their background. But the last thing Constance and Fred wanted was having their lodge known as the place of the great shoot-out. Besides, how would we explain Alex? All the way around, it was better that last night's battle not go beyond the walls of Monumental Valley.

The prisoners agreed.

We made the three prisoners carry their two dead companions up the trail toward the Dewey Mine and then dig two graves above a stand of pine. We covered the graves with rocks and hid the remaining dirt. The graves would never be found.

Our problem then was what to do with the three prisoners. We finally decided that tomorrow we'd haul them to Boise and put them, without money or identification, on a nonstop flight to New York City. We figured that wouldn't hurt them, but it certainly would slow them down. We would take the mirror with us into Boise to let them think we were moving it to a safer hiding place. In exchange for our not turning them over to the police, the prisoners agreed to not cause trouble getting on the plane.

That plan would give me time to get some other clothes and supplies from home and get back to the *Titanic* to see Marjorie again, to tell her I was all right. Make sure she was. And be a part of this "new beginning" Patrick and Susan had mentioned. I didn't know exactly what that might mean, but thinking about it made me feel free and useful for the first time in years.

As far as Alex was concerned, we decided to first return him to the place where Gretchen played her song, then bury his body in the old Roosevelt cemetery. We all wished we could bury Gretchen beside him.

At forty feet we were swimming right over the old main street and could see the outlines of the old foundations. For some reason, I kept expecting to see Gretchen, walking along the old street. But she hadn't appeared anywhere since that last moment in the hall. She was nowhere in sight now. For some reason the bottom of the lake felt even colder and darker without her.

We swam straight to the place where we had seen her play. There were a few small holes in the silt where we had

Some Classic Dean Wesley Smith Stories
Available at your favorite booksellers.

pulled things up and I had found the mirror. Nothing else had changed.

We pushed Alex's body down into the silt in front of where Gretchen had played, then both Fred and I moved back, as if expecting something to happen.

The sound of my breathing seemed to get louder in my head. The water felt colder. The sun must have gone behind a cloud because it also seemed darker. We waited, but nothing happened.

I do know that I was expecting something. So was Fred.

After a moment I shrugged at Fred. He returned an arms-up question and then pointed at the surface. I nodded and we both swam and grabbed hold of Alex's body sack. So the idea to bring him back down here had been stupid. They had left together last night, off to live in the next world. We were wasting our time. I suppose, as the old saying goes, it was the thought that counted.

We turned and headed for the surface, pulling Alex's body between us.

We were almost twenty feet above the lake floor when the song started. It was full and rich and so loud that it pushed every other sense into the background.

Both Fred and I turned and looked back. The piano was again there. Gretchen was sitting at it playing Alex's favorite song.

For a moment, she played alone as she had done for years, staring into the mirror on the music stand in front of her. Then suddenly, the water all around her started to shimmer. The very foundation of the old building seemed to come alive.

The walls of the old Inn formed. Crystal walls. Ghost walls. Couples were dancing, the shelves were full of glasses and booze, men were standing at the bar. The music filled the room and the surrounding water with life.

I glanced quickly at Fred. He was seeing the same thing I was. I could tell.

I looked back at the scene and there, sitting at a table, the closest table to the piano, was Alex. He was leaning back in his chair, his legs crossed, sipping on a glass of brandy, and listening to the music.

For the longest time, his gaze never left Gretchen. His concentration never left the song. But finally he turned, looked up over his shoulder at us, and smiled.

With a slight wave of his hand, more of a thanks than a goodbye, he went back to watching Gretchen and sipping his drink.

Gretchen never took her gaze away from Alex.

I glanced over at Fred. He looked alien in his black wet suit and mask, bubbles floating from his regulator. We didn't belong here. I knew deep inside that this was the last time Gretchen would play her song for Alex. He had returned to the Inn for her. We needed to leave and let them continue on alone.

I nudged Fred and he looked over at me. I pointed up and he nodded. Even behind his mask, I could see that he was smiling.

So was I.

With one last look at the woman playing the piano and the man listening to her, we turned and started for the surface. Between us Alex's body felt very light.

We paused only once more to glance back at the music and the party. But we had climbed too far and could see nothing.

Fred pointed up and I nodded.

As we neared the surface, the last few chords of Gretchen's song faded into silence.

Coming Next Issue in *Smith's Monthly*

#1...October 2013

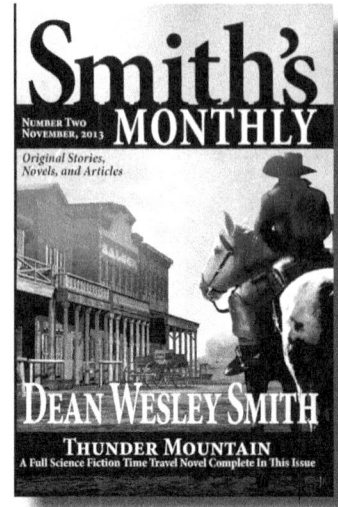

#2...November 2013

#3...December 2013

#4...January 2014

#5...February 2014

#6...March 2014

#7...April 2014

#8...May 2014

#9...June 2014

#10...July 2014

#11...August 2014

#12...September 2014

#13...October 2014

#14...November 2014

#15...December 2014

#16...January 2015

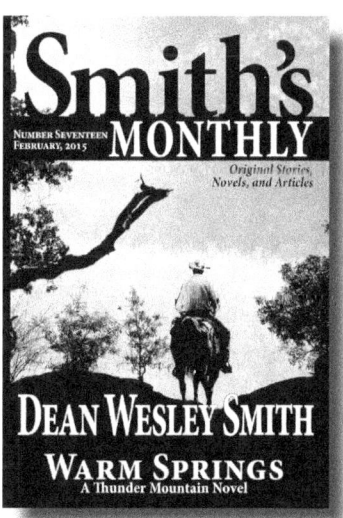

#17...February 2015

#18...March 2015

#19...April 2015

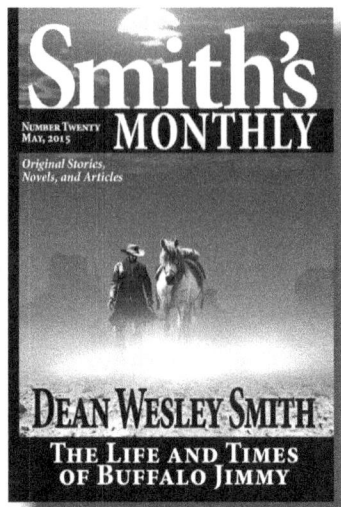

#20...May 2015

#21...June 2015

#22...July 2015

#23...August 2015

#24...September 2015

#25...October 2015

#26...November 2015

#27...December 2015

#28...January 2016

#29...February 2016

#30...March 2016

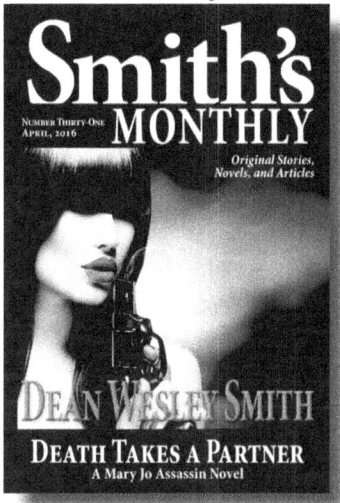

#31...April 2016

#32...May 2016

#33...June 2016

#34...July 2016

#35...August 2016

#36...September 2016

Thank You!!

I would like to thank the following wonderful people who support my blog and my work through Patreon. Your support is very important to me. Thanks!

Betsy Wilcox
Irette Y. Patterson
Kathryn Rooney
Wendy Lee Maddox
Jamie Curierre
Chris Cousino
Jane Lawson
Shantnu Tiwari
Miguel Angel Alonso Pulido
Nancy Hendrickson
Ryan M. Williams
Jacob Proffitt
Marian Goldeen
Gary Speer
Megan Bryce
Michelle Tatam
Ann Tucker
Kari Wolfe
Albert Lemke
Stacey Larson
Diane Darcy
Krystle Jones
Kari Gallagher
T. Thorn Coyle
Tasha Turner Lennhoff

Erick Lindman
Christopher Ridge
Terry Mixon
James Husun
Sherman Cox
Chong Go
Maria Grace
Grondpom
Fen
Robin Brande
J.R. Murdock
Kathleen McClure
Gunnar Gunderson
F.I. Goldhaber
Mary Jo Rabe
John Kilgallon
Dave Hendrickson
Jabberwocky
Eric Goebelbecker
Marsha Kessler
Scott Gordon
Martyn Folkes
John
Cj Lehi
Brenda Smith

www.ingramcontent.com/pod-product-compliance
Lightning Source LLC
Chambersburg PA
CBHW081150170626
46813CB00009B/3140